W9-AXT-341

Cover Design by Staccato Publishing
Edited by Heather Savage, Karen Reckard,
Brittany Dingman

Staccato Publishing Maple Grove, MN

First US Edition April 2014 ISBN: 978-1-940202-00-6

Downey Dedication: This book is dedicated to Jim & Nancy Downey, my in laws, they raised the man I love and did it right. They opened their home, family and hearts to me and taught me by amazing example what it means to be a parent. We miss you every single day.

Greene Dedication: For my husband, Don. What can I say? You've stood by me through thick and thin, thank goodness you love 'em thick.

Partners In Crime

A Novel By Downey Greene

CHAPTER ONE

Faye stormed into her dingy little basement apartment, slamming the door so hard the few pictures she had fell to the floor, their glass fronts cracking. Without missing a step, she began to throw anything and everything in her reach against the red brick wall. She didn't bother to watch as her possessions shattered everywhere, exploding into atoms and leaving a mess of broken dreams on her hardwood floor.

After what seemed like hours, Faye snapped her control back and looked around, surveying the destruction. Her breathing was labored, harsh, echoing loudly throughout the small, dark, dank place she called home.

Slowly shaking her head, she backed up against the nearest wall and slowly slid down. Pulling her knees up, she wrapped her arms around them, fisting her hands so tightly her fingernails drew blood in her palms. Resting her head on the tops of her knees, she began to murmur to herself and rock back and forth on her ass. Pain and anger radiated from her very core; her gut on fire, the need to lash out continued to burn her up from the inside out.

How could she have been so damn stupid, again? Michael, she thought angrily. He was not who she needed. He was not good for her.

She knew it. But yet, she let him in, again. Faye thanked her lucky stars she hadn't let him in all the way. She ran her hand through her hair, exhaling hard. She let him back in just enough for his latest betrayal to hurt like a bitch.

Palming the wall, she stood, slamming her ass and the back of her head against the wall in the process.

"Fuck!" She screamed until her throat burned. Faye closed her eyes, swallowed hard, and cursed one more time before pushing off the wall to head for a long hot shower.

The spray from the shower was tempered somewhere between lava and the surface of the sun, and as she ripped the clothes from her body, she let them fall wherever. She was no domestic goddess, by any means. Shit, she wasn't even in Queen Cleansalot's court. Under the scalding mist, she leaned her head back and soaked her hair, the sting on her skin was nothing compared to the sting to her soul. Michael, she thought again.

Vaguely fascinated, she watched as her bitter tears mixed with the scalding spray and were sucked down the drain. Irony could be a fucking bitch, she snorted and thought about the future that might have been, but instead followed the same path as her tears.

She'd wanted it to work, perhaps too much. Their relationship was forced; they had a long history, but deep down she knew. Didn't she? That was the core of the problem, she knew it in her gut but still, she'd tried. No matter how difficult things had been between them she would never betray Michael, not like that.

Faye leaned her forehead against the cool tile wall, sobbing harder. She wasn't sure which was worse, having her eyes open or closed. Open, she would see people's pity. Closed, well, she could only see Michael and Katrina, her so-called BFF. Yeah, she was some best friend.

White hot heat bubbled to the surface and Faye screamed one last time.

The bathroom was filled with steam as Faye stepped out of the shower, and foregoing a towel, she dripped dried and padded to her bedroom. Not giving a single rat's ass about her bedding, she plopped down on the edge of the bed and stared blankly into her closet.

It took several moments and a few dozen rapid eye blinks for Faye to register she'd not been staring blankly, but staring intently at her most recent purchase: a red leather micro miniskirt.

The damn thing was supposed to have been a surprise for Michael. It was so not her style, but yet again, she tried to make him happy and in the process was slowly becoming someone she didn't even know. Well, the surprise was on her, wasn't it?

Faye wrenched the garment off the hanger, thinking she really hoped Katrina was a good lay. Because he lost more in that moment, she snorted, in those 30 seconds than he could ever have imagined. The crimson material was so buttery soft, she found herself practically molesting the material. A wicked grin crawled across her face as she walked back through her small apartment, naked and barefoot, to her kitchen.

Shit, she'd almost forgotten about the mess she'd made. She shrugged and thought OFW. A couple of male coworkers taught her the abbreviation. They thought it would help her with her cussing problem. Though she really didn't think it was a problem at all, but if it made them feel better then fine. She knew what it meant long before their so called intervention: Oh Fucking Well.

What better way to work out her cussing issues and the need to banish her demons, she thought, as she surveyed her kitchen looking for..."Yes, there they are."

Faye grabbed the pair of kitchen scissors and stood with her bare ass against the counter, feet crossed at the ankles, as she started shredding the material to pieces and dropped each piece to the floor. She sighed heavily and tossed the scissors so they landed points down in a piece of the material, making it look as though the floor had been stabbed and bled out.

Wasn't there a song or something, Bleeding Love? Was that a good thing or what? She thought to herself as she padded back to her room. Music always held a special place within her and shit, why should this situation be any different? The perfect soundtrack to her shit storm of her love life.

So Faye, what now, girl?

She looked around her room and found herself standing before her closet door again, arms crossed under bare breasts, hip cocked.

"Hot damn," she said aloud and nodded, deciding then and there to go out and get good and drunk. And, she knew the perfect place.

Instead of continuing to stare into her closet, Faye turned on her heel and headed back to her bathroom. She towel dried her hair, ripping the terry cloth material from her head. The reflection from the bathroom revealed a wild tangle of blonde curls and sparkling blue eyes, like sapphires in the sun. Funnily enough, she felt much like her hair looked, wild, tangled, emotionally anyway, and a little reckless. Haphazardly, she applied a bit of makeup and then headed back to her closet for wardrobe selection. In the midst of her wanderings, it occurred to her she hadn't sat still since crash landing inside her apartment. Maybe the night out would do her some good, but all this back and forth was not doing her any favors. As a matter fact, she was getting a bit dizzy and queasy in the stomach. Without the benefit of a nice alcohol induced stupor, a queasy stomach was just...no fun.

After she was dressed in a favorite pair of jeans, red bustier, and the best pair of "fuck me" shoes in her meager collection, she stopped in front of her mirror and glanced at herself, "I am one hell of a hot mess."

Since she planned on stumbling home later, she grabbed only some cash and her house keys, and with one last glance at the disaster she caused, she shut the door and headed out.

***

Stammers, a local bar in her neighborhood, was nothing more than an abandoned track house with twelve tables and an ancient juke box situated in the far corner. Still, as familiar as the place was to her, Faye couldn't suppress her cop instincts as she entered and scanned the cozy interior. And she smiled at her favorite bartender, JoJo, as she slid onto a well worn leather covered stool and ordered a shot of Patron.

JoJo smiled back at Faye and quirked an eyebrow at her as she watched the woman slam the shot and slide the glass back across the bar. Both eyebrows went up and Faye nodded. The bartender shrugged and poured the shot, leaving the bottle on the bar. Whatever she was trying to erase, a shot or two wouldn't do it, but the entire damn bottle surely would. JoJo, an experienced bartender, knew that much and went on to tend to her other customers.

After the third shot Faye was feeling warm and friendly. She started playing with the rim of the shot glass and fingered the golden liquid, sucking the alcohol off her fingers. Head tipped back, tongue hanging out with her fingers suspended over her open mouth, the Patron droplet mere seconds from spilling itself onto her waiting tongue; something caught her peripheral vision and made her pause. Faye slid her eyes around but couldn't see anything. Damn it. The Patron splashed onto the bridge of her nose, almost sliding into her eye. She sat forward quickly, nearly knocking her head on the edge of the bar and slammed her palms on the edge of the bar, cussing. Looking around wasn't any better, she couldn't get her eyes to focus on any one thing in particular.

Damn. She knew she was being watched. Taking a few deep breaths, she took another scan of the bar. The place was fairly empty tonight and she was pushing intoxicated, but still, she should be able to figure out why the hairs on the back of her neck were standing on end. Just before she repositioned herself at the bar, she spotted him.

The source of her sudden inebriated paranoia was in the dark corner of the bar. Leaning against the wall staring at her, through her; his eyes seeming to see straight through to her very soul.

Faye shivered under his gaze, but looked him up and down. Even in her semi-intoxicated state, she memorized him, in all his sexy mysteriousness. She tucked his image away for later use. Smirking, she lifted the fourth shot to her lips, giving him a mocking salute with the glass.

He winked at her, a cigarette dangling from between full lips. Tall and angular but broad, he was built like a swimmer who lifted cars for a living. Faye swallowed a fifth shot as she registered the jeans that hung very precariously off his hips. The black t-shirt clung to him like a second skin, emphasizing his muscular build. He wasn't huge just, damn, just perfectly proportioned.

She looked into his eyes and froze for a moment, mesmerized. Caught in the web of his gaze, Faye had the sudden compulsion to wipe phantom drool from her chin. The appraisal of the dark man in the even darker corner continued, but Faye couldn't quite tear her gaze away from his eyes. It registered somewhere in her marinated thoughts that his hair was longer, ending with a wave that settled at the top of his shoulders.

But damn, those eyes. From her vantage point she couldn't tell their color, she only knew they were lighter. She thought maybe blue or possibly green. A full day's 5 o'clock shadow, complete with mustache and goatee as dark as his t-shirt and hair, stood out in stark contrast to his eyes. Those damn eyes drew her in and she couldn't let go. She didn't want to let go. The thought occurred to her, maybe, no, she was *sure* she could forget for a little while with those eyes.

Faye turned back to her shot and downed it. Winking at JoJo, she pushed the glass across the bar towards her. Hand up, Faye stopped her before she could question her. "Not tonight, JoJo. I'm on a fucking mission. Not driving. Staggering, possibly crawling home tonight."

JoJo shrugged and poured the next shot for her friend. The bottle steadily growing less full as the night wore on. Before JoJo finished pouring, a shadow fell spread out across the bar the bar in front of Faye, landing on her drink. For some reason, when she turned and found the dark and mysterious stranger standing beside her, she wasn't all that surprised.

"Numb yet?" Leaned back with his elbows on the bar, the cigarette blazing bright in the dim light from between fingers laced over his well toned torso. The male looked her up and down, licking his lips. With just that one sensual glance, he devoured her whole.

She froze in the midst of lifting the fifth, sixth, wait, seventh shot to her lips. Shit, she'd lost count. His words reminded her why she'd come in the first place. Before she downed the golden liquid, she looked his way, answering with a sneer. "There's not enough alcohol in this bar to accomplish that."

Another mock salute in his direction, and she slammed the shot. The alcohol burned on its way down her throat; Faye hummed against the sensation, feeling her body soak in the tequila.

"Sugar, you're going to be in a world of hurt tomorrow," he said quietly, shaking his head from side to side as he took a drag of his smoke.

Faye turned, anger emanating from her in waves, much like the fumes from the alcohol with which she was continuing to pollute her body. Through gritted teeth, she ground out the words, "Listen, I am *no one's* Sugar. Tonight, I am one bitter bitch. *Death* would feel better than *I do*, and, I hurt *now* so what the *hell* is the difference?"

He leaned in very close, whispering in her ear. "Oh Sugar, sometimes pain is a welcome pleasure."

Hoping to be inconspicuous, Faye dropped her left hand and gave herself a quick pat down, looking for her sidearm. Wouldn't he be damned surprised to find her gun shoving his family jewels up into his tonsils? Neurons fired sluggishly in her tequila sloshed brain as she finally remembered she'd left her weapon at home. Reaching into the pocket of her jeans and pulling out a wad of cash, not near as deadly but effective nonetheless, Faye tossed the bills with a generous tip to JoJo and whispered, "I can't even get drunk right." She pushed away from the bar looked up briefly at JoJo and ignored the male. "I'll see ya' around, Jo."

The heavy metal emergency exit door banged loudly against the wall as she stumbled into the alley. The tequila coursing through her veins numbed her pain just a little, but not enough. A weight sat heavily upon her shoulders, so she rested her forehead on the brick wall of the bar, hoping to transfer some of the burden, and all of her pain, into the bricks.

For fuck's sake, she couldn't get drunk, and couldn't be left alone. Ugh, might as well go home, she thought as she heard the door open again but didn't bother looking; she didn't fucking care who it was.

All of a sudden, Faye felt her hair being tugged back, just a little, and then a soft growl in her ear made her shudder. "Oh, Sugar, how bad do you want to forget?"

She groaned at his touch, arching her back. "Stop. Stop calling me Sugar. There's nothing remotely sweet about me."

Another low growl reverberated low in his throat as he licked up the side of her neck. "You taste fucking sweeter than heaven." Goosebumps rose up all over her body and she shivered from his words as much as his touch.

He spun her around and lifted both of her hands above her head, securing them in one of his. He nudged her legs apart with his knee.

A sudden and foreign feeling of shyness washed through her, and boy did that piss her off. A rush of heat colored her cheeks and made her salivary glands go on high alert, she swallowed hard and often, and she continued to look up at him, silently pondering her lack of flight or fight response. The need to feel something other than this aching pain that thrummed throughout her entire being consumed her. She needed to forget, forget why Michael hurt her, again, when he'd promised he wouldn't. And why one of her closest friends would betray her so deeply.

Shaking her head to push those thoughts aside, she again focused on the male body before her. Being this close to him, she realized his eyes were definitely green and his hair was lighter under the glare of the sole light source in the alley; a bare bulb hanging precariously over the rusted brown door to the bar. Her gaze shifted and focused on his left bicep. There, peeking out from under the sleeve of his t-shirt was what looked like a tribal tattoo. Faye made a decision to let everything go for now. Instead of being smart and manufacturing the flight response, she decided to focus on getting a better look at the rest of that tattoo. As she looked him deep in his gorgeous eyes, she whispered, "Please make me forget. I just need..."

The plea in her words stirred something inside him, a slow, lascivious grin slid across his face. The dark stranger pressed pressed his index finger to her lips, effectively shushing her. At that action her temper tried to flare, but the beauty of the tequila haze made that particular action impossible. Instead, she opened her mouth and sucked in his finger not so gently, biting it.

"Ah, fuck!" he hissed, ripping his finger from 'ıer mouth. With gentle but firm pressure, he wrapped his hand around her throat and held her with a lusty glare "That wasn't very nice."

Quivering under his gaze, Faye tried to close her legs but his knee, having maneuvered between them, blocked her efforts. Damn, she tried frowning at him but shit, that smile was, she groaned, panty melting. Oh hell, she wasn't wearing panties.

Faye continued to struggle to get some relief from the ache between her legs. The seam of her jeans rubbed against the cleft of her sex. Even if she could squeeze her legs together it still wouldn't be enough.

As if he knew what she was thinking, he pushed his hips against hers to still her squirming and warned her with a low growl, "Sugar, stop moving. Now."

She froze and locked eyes with him, once again groaning at his words and gaze. He whispered in her ear, "What's your name?"

"No!" She barked. "No names."

He chuckled. "So, that's the game? Okay Sugar, let's see if we can't make you forget, eh?" He ground his hips into hers again, nipping at her collarbone before he pulled away with both her wrists still in his one-handed grip, and dragged her to an unlit corner of the alley. If anyone came by or out the door they wouldn't see them. Hear them probably, but not see them. For the second time, he pushed her up against the brick wall and raised her hands above her head, giving them a firm push and telling her without words to keep them there.

For some reason, she knew if she called halt, he'd immediately release her, she didn't know why or how she knew that, but that knowledge was as all she needed. As she nodded her ascent, she bit her lip.

Given the green light, he began the arduous task of unbuttoning the bustier. The last fastening undone, he groaned as her breasts spilled out. Her nipples hardened instantly, not just from the cool night air caressing her naked flesh. The garment, tossed to the ground and quickly forgotten, he began to flick and pinch her hardened little peaks. "Let's see how sweet you taste here." He leaned in and devoured her left breast, circling his tongue around the small areola and then flicked his tongue over the distended nub. He scraped his teeth over the sensitized flesh, hearing her hiss as she thrust her breast further into his mouth. Caressing her other breast first, as he continued his torment of the first, he gave that nipple an attention grabbing pinch. "Be a good girl and stay still."

Faye's loud groans echoed off the alley walls. She whispered through gritted teeth, "Damn it, I'm trying." Her body was on fire. His tongue felt like fire and ice at the same time, building her up to an inferno, yet quenching that fire with his talented mouth. She moaned again, needing more of his touch.

As if he read her mind, he unsnapped her jeans and kneeled down in front of her. Hooking his thumbs in the waistband of the body hugging denim, he shimmied them down and growled a long hard, "Fuuuuccccckkkkk. God damn, Sugar." He sat back on his heels caressing her naked thighs, looking up at her. "Look at you." Leaving her jeans around her knees for the briefest of moments, he slipped two of his fingers through her slick, wet folds, slowly sliding the digits out and into his mouth, sucking on them loudly.

Her eyes flew to his. She moaned and tried to spread her legs wider.

"Oh, aren't you a sweet thing." Winking at her and fake frowning, he chastised her. "Damn, you seem to have forgotten your panties. I was so looking forward to ripping them off that fine ass. Ah well, there's always next time." He lifted one of her feet out of her heels and slid her jeans the rest of the way off. Repeating the process with her other leg, he replaced both feet back into her impossibly high heels.

Now gloriously naked in sky high crimson stilettos, her breasts covered by her hair. As the male continued to kneel before her, Faye imagined this must be what a goddess feels like being worshipped.

Gazing up at her with an expression of pure lust and desire, he leaned forward and nudged her legs wider, positioning his face in between her thighs. He took a deep inhale of her scent before sliding his tongue ever so slowly through her slit, and over her most sensitive button.

She screamed as her hands flew to his hair, gripping it tightly, as she thrust her hips forward.

He chuckled at her, tsk'ing. "Sugar, where do your hands belong?"

Cursing, Faye reluctantly slid her hands out of his hair, giving his head a hard tug as she released his dark tresses.

"You so need to be taught a lesson," he growled into the apex of her sex.

Grudgingly, she raised her hands above her head again, but glared down at him, "Just fuck me. I've had enough life lessons for one day, thankyouverymuch."

"Agreed, Sugar," he chuckled at her complaint. "Tonight I'll take away your pain. But, rest assured, someday soon I'll spank that sassy ass of yours."

Outwardly, she scoffed at him. Inwardly, she trembled at the thought of his large hand coming down over her ass to teach her a lesson. But, he had no idea who she was and what she'd been through. Faye shrugged to herself. It didn't matter, they'd never see each other again after tonight.

His tongue went back to devouring her. He crooked his head back and speared his tongue inside her. Feeling her walls starting to convulse on his tongue, he moaned, sending a vibration through her entire body. The muscles in her legs quivered and his hands traveled up her flat stomach, feeling those muscles bunch as well. He was in a mental war with himself now. Knowing she was close, did he want her orgasm on his face and down his throat, or all over his cock? He growled in answer to himself. Why not both?

Faye tried not to move, but it was impossible with what his masterful tongue was doing to her. Panting and whimpering, she stood on tiptoe, allowing him access to all her most private flesh. She moaned as he pulled away from her and looked down at him, pleading silently, and was rewarded with his face disappearing between her legs again. And, oh God, yes. She was so close to the edge, she wanted to fall over and never return.

He ground his face in harder against her sex, feeling her breathing pick up. She was on tiptoes, even in those fucking sexy-ass shoes. He pulled his face back to look up at hers.

Yeah, so fucking close. He dove back for his prize and scraped his teeth along the hardened nub peeking out of its hood, sucking it hard between his lips, and she screamed as her body flew apart in ecstasy.

"Mmmmm...aaaaahhhhhhhh!" She screamed her pleasure to the empty alley and into the inky black night.

While she was still in the last waves of her orgasm, he removed his face from her sex, stood in front of her and made a show of licking his lips. Locking his gaze to her still hungry eyes, he unbuttoned his jeans, yanking them down roughly. He palmed his cock, still licking her essence off his lips and smiled. "You close to forgetting yet?"

She groaned and nodded, hissing out, "Yesssss."

Not bothering to disrobe completely, he smirked as he pushed his jeans past his hips. Their bodies now pressed flush against each other, he could feel her diamond hard nipples poking into his chest, even through his t-shirt. "Oh Sugar, I know what you were thinking." His breath caressed Faye's ear and cheek. "I. Will. Be. Seeing. You. Again." He licked the shell of her ear. "And you will tell me your name before this is done." Pulling back, he bit her bottom lip, sliding his tongue into her mouth.

Her essence still coated his tongue and she moaned at their mingled tastes. He continued to devour her mouth like he was starved, starved for her. Finally, he released her mouth and gripped her waist. With one hand, he reached in his back pocket and withdrew a square foil wrapped condom. The wrapper was easily removed with a little force from his teeth and a dramatic flourish. And with the precision of years of back alley fuckings, he rolled the rubber on, single handed. Fully dressed to get down and boogy, finally, he lifted her effortlessly to slam his cock inside her throbbing, soaked core in one swift mind-blowing motion. "*Now,* you can put your hands down," he growled into her ear and gave her lobe a sharp nip.

She wrapped her arms around his neck, gripped him tightly and ground her core against his pounding cock and thrusting hips. Faye wanted him harder, deeper, faster. She thrust her head back, lost in the feel of him inside her, when suddenly she froze, scoring his back with her nails in a panic. "Stop! F-forgot...c-condom."

His chuckled response vibrated through her chest, his body was that fused to hers. "Pay attention, Sugar, it's already on."

"ThankGod," she sighed loudly.

Her body was vibrating from his renewed and relentless onslaught. She was so close again, already. He was driving her closer and closer to the precipice with every thrust. His hands squeezing her ass, she had her long legs wrapped tightly around him and her ankles locked at the small of his back.

He slid his hand between their sweat slick bodies and began to rub and roll her sensitized nub between his finger and thumb.

Faye's body bucked against his hand, moaning.

He nipped her collarbone and growled. "No, not yet. I gave you a freebie, this one's mine. Only when I say."

Faye wasn't a pouter by nature, but she felt her bottom lip protrude and her shoulders sag. In between his pounding thrusts and finger scraping of her distended nub, she was certifiably pouty. She realized that the heady mix of this mysterious male and the tequila had her mind blissfully blank, except for the pure pleasure she was reaching for and that which he withheld from her. Her body started an uncontrolled vibrating and spasming; she couldn't hold off much longer. Was he crazy? Did he mean what he said? When will he say?

He saw the pout hit her entire body and he couldn't help the slight chuckle. She wasn't ready. He gave her the freebie earlier, she needed it. But this one, this one he needed. There...fuck yeah. There it was, that delicious blush. Her body convulsing and paralyzing, she listened. She was doing her best to hold it off. Leaning forward, he growled in her ear, "Come now."

It was as if he had complete control over her body. She screamed again. Spasms of pure ecstasy thrummed through her body. The walls of her core convulsed rhythmically around his cock, and with one final thrust and a growled, "Fuck, yeah," he followed her into the throes of bliss.

Wrapping his heavily muscled arms around her waist, he let her sag against him, each panting into the others shoulder. He stroked her sweat soaked hair, planting chaste kisses to her neck and cheek. "Tell me your name, Sugar."

Laying her cheek on his shoulder she swallowed hard. "My name is...Faye...Faye Kane."

He squeezed her briefly and chuckled. "Ah, my very own Sugar Kane. I told you, you were sweet."

Faye couldn't help the sluggish smile that crept across her face; he definitely didn't lie. She'd forgotten it all. For one sweet moment, he made her see and touch the stars.

With great reluctance, he pulled himself from her warmth and settled her gently on wobbly legs. Removing the condom, he secured his jeans.

Faye stood in the alley naked as the day she was born, dazed as she watched him stride over to the dumpster and discard the well used condom. As he sauntered back towards her with the most beautiful smile, she knew there would be no morning after regrets.

As he approached her he peeled off his shirt, smirking as he saw her eyes go wide. "Arms up," he ordered for the umpteenth time, waggling the tee in front of her. "You've trusted me this far, Sugar. What more could I do to you? Never mind, don't answer that."

Faye raised her arms and he slipped the shirt over her head. The damn thing came to mid-thigh on her. Faye couldn't help her next action; she gathered the front of the shirt and lifted it to her nose, inhaling deeply, moaning at his scent of dark spiced cologne and male musk. As she did, she glanced up at him, finally getting the full effect of that tattoo. Even in the shadowed alley the design leapt out at her. The tribal art was simple yet beautiful. Starting on his left pec, it travelled up his shoulder and ended just above the elbow. She was sure it wrapped around to his back as well.

As he gathered her clothes from the ground he turned, giving her a clear view of his back. Just as she suspected, the tattoo did in fact wrap around his shoulder blade and continued down the back of his arm.

When he stood, he took her hand and dragged her towards his truck, parked almost directly across the alley. He dug his hand in the deepest recesses of his jeans pocket to fish for his keys. Jangling them at her in triumph, he proceeded to open the passenger's side door for her. "Come on, Sugar Kane, let me take you home. We are so not done yet, I owe you a spanking."

Yelping as he gave her ass a good swat, she climbed in to the cockpit of his late model SUV. Settling against the black vinyl, she laid her head back, eyes closed.

He nudged her thigh and smiled, waving her clothes at her as she turned her head and slowly opened her eyes. Grabbing the bundle from him, she let him shut the door after telling her to buckle up.

Faye leaned back and shut her eyes a second time, sighing and thinking what a completely fucking crazy ass night. She toed off her heels and tossed the clothes onto the floor next to them. Pulling her knees up to her chest, wrapping her arms around them, she was lost in her own thoughts until his question pulled her back.

"Faye, where do you live?"

Laughing out loud, she remembered the shambles she'd left her apartment in. "Oh, just around the corner a wee bit. But...uh...my place is a wreck."

He shrugged as he turned the key and revved the motor. "You got a bed?"

Blinking at him, "Yes."

"We're golden."

Faye's apartment was only around the corner, but as she sat in the truck, a virtual stranger's truck, staring out the passenger's side window, panic started to consume her. What in the hell was she doing? Fucking someone in an alley was fun and yes, dangerous, and destructive, but taking off with a stranger in his vehicle, was suicidal.

Faye, wake the hell up! Leaning forward, she slid her legs back down and shook off the orgasm euphoria. She grabbed for the door handle. "Stop, let me out. Let me out!"

He whipped his head to the side. "What is it? Wait. Let me pull... Damn!" Slamming his hands on the steering wheel, he watched helplessly as Faye jumped from the still moving truck.

Faye, barefoot and half naked, took off running away from the male, and his truck, as fast as she could go. Traffic and cloud cover were her friends as she fled.

She slammed into her apartment yet again, breathing hard as she bolted the door locked and slid the chain into place. She gave her door a good hard kick, yowling as the toenail on her big toe peeled back. Limping to her bedroom, she bypassed the debris and threw herself back on the bed, digging the heels of her palms into her eyes.

Nope, no morning-after-the-one-night-stand regrets for her, oh no. Same-night-stand psychosis and all out lunacy were the specials on the menu and she had some from columns A and B.

"Can you say glutton?" she whispered to her empty bedroom.

CHAPTER TWO

"Shit." He couldn't believe his luck or lack thereof. She'd just up and leapt out of his truck. Who the fuck does that? He looked at the seat beside him as if he was trying to will her form back in its place. A flash of color caught the corner of his eye and he looked down at the floor, and smirked. Her clothes. She'd forgotten to grab her clothes.
He laughed as he put his truck in gear and drove off thinking, what would Freud have to say about that?

It hadn't taken more than fifteen minutes to get to his apartment, yet he was still consumed with thoughts of his Sugar Kane and what would have possessed her to jump out of a moving vehicle like that.

Unlocking his door, his mind was still on Faye and their tryst. He tossed his keys on the battered end table intending to head to the kitchen to grab a beer out of the fridge. A light switching on in the living room grabbed his attention first. Slowly, he turned his head and addressed the man sitting comfortably in the brown recliner. "Millie, you're late. I waited man, what the fuck happened to you?"

The man called Millie stood and lit a brown cigarillo, blowing out a plume of blue-gray acrid smoke and addressed the other male. "Griff, good to see you," looking over his shirtless form with obvious disdain. "Perhaps you want to go find a shirt?"

Shrugging as if to say fuck you, he kept his tone neutral. "No man, I'm good."

He ignored Griff's attitude. "I'm surprised you're alone, after all, that little lady sounded like she was having quite a time. Thought maybe she'd be trailing after you like a little puppy dog or at the least, you'd have a leash on her."

Millie'd been circling Griff, scanning the small apartment as he did. He finally stopped in front of the other male, spreading his arms wide. "Here? Why here, Griff? Don't I pay you enough?"

Griff hung his head. Scrubbing his hand over his beard, he turned his palm to rub his cheek, then the back of his neck. "You still having me tailed, Millie? After all this time? You chose the meeting place man, not me." Griff stood stock still, keeping a watchful eye on the other man. Just because Millie was alone didn't make him any less of a threat. If anything, an alone Millie was an even more lethal Millie. "I couldn't help it, man, I waited for you for hours and I got bored. That chick," he shrugged, "nothing special. I've had better. If I knew you were into watching man, I'd have set it up different. Wanna beer?"

Millie nodded and took a drag off his cigarillo. "What a good host you are, Griff. Beer sounds great. The tail's been removed, you know that. I couldn't meet you, something came up, so I had Harrington drive to the bar. When I got out, I could hear her screaming from out front. Damn, I thought you were killing her." Millie hung his head smirking. "Speaking of killing..."

Griff walked the few steps to his kitchenette and grabbed out two Guinness Stout bottles, popping the caps and letting them fall wherever. He mouthed cuss words to his fridge and shadowboxed the wall with the two open beers in his fists. Beer slopped over his knuckles and he swore out loud, "Fuck."

"You okay, kid?" Millie raised his voice.

"Yeah." Griff reappeared, handing a bottle to the other man. "So that's what this new meet and greet was about? Offing someone? Christ Millie, you had me nearly pissing my pants in there. Fuck." Griff rubbed his chest, his heart hammering. "Sit, spill. Damn."

Millie laughed and took his seat again in the recliner, resting his ankle on the opposite knee. "Tell me about the girl from the alley. Who was she?"

Griff looked up from his spot on the threadbare couch, the bottle of Guinness frozen in midair on its way to his mouth. "Nothing to tell, man. She was just some barfly. She polished my knob, I made her scream, we went our separate ways. You want her number, man?" Griff sat back with a sarcastic smirk.

Millie shook his head. "No, Griff, I don't want the slut's number. Just wondering why she took off out of your truck running for her life? You didn't roofie her, did you?" Millie narrowed his gaze at the other male, studying his expression.

Trying to figure out where he was going with this line of questioning, Griff leaned forward, positioning the beer bottle in between his hands. Smirking he kept his tone neutral. "Never had to before, why would I start now? What's this leading up to, Millie? You know I don't like this shady business bullshit." Griff stood and stalked over to the other man, pointing his finger in Millie's face. "What the fuck, man? You just got done saying you removed the tail. You got something to ask, fucking ask."

"Ha! That's why I like you, Griff. Straight shooter, my kind of fucker." Millie stood and took half a step towards Griff, letting the man's finger hit him in the chest. Millie's voice grew dark and deadly. "Tone is everything, boy. I removed the tail. I thought Harrington and I could catch up with you if need be. So yeah, I had him follow behind you, not tailing you. We drove by your ride when she hopped out. I'm surprised you didn't see the Rolls. Listen, kid, I just needed to know if you did anything untoward to that girl. I can't have my employees getting unwanted attention from the local boys in blue. If you get my meaning."

Leaving his finger poked firmly in Millie's chest, Griff replied just as darkly, "Sense *my* tone, Martino. Your scare tactics do nothing for me. You either trust me or you don't. I fucked that girl into near unconsciousness. She was a willing participant. And since when are you so fucking worried about the blue line? You got half the precinct in your back pocket. A snap of your fingers and anything that happens to your employees will be wiped out of existence. Why are you giving me shit, man?"

Millie started pacing the room again. It wasn't typical of him to be the first to back down from a confrontation, but standing still for too long made him more jumpy. He put the cigarillo between his lips and walked around the small living area that doubled as Griff's bedroom. "Seriously Griff, why do you still hang here? I pay you good. Damn good. And you're still slumming it. Why?" He waved both his hands as if to erase the question. "Never mind, not my business. Live in the gutter if that's what you want." Sighing heavily, he got down to business. "Griff, we got an infestation."

Griff watched as Millie walked away. He stared at the man's back and shoulders, noting the differences and similarities between the two of them as he had numerous times in the last eighteen months. Griff was a full head taller than Millie. But Millie was bulkier; not fat, just bulky. Griff always thought Millie looked uncomfortable in every stitch of clothing he'd ever worn because of his size. In fact, Griff had a good chuckle every now and again, thinking the man's skin didn't fit him any more comfortably than his overpriced suits did.

"Shit, Millie. Are you sure? You've been paranoid in the past and look where that landed ya'. What's the intel and from who?"

"Whom. I'm pretty sure that's the proper grammar. No reason to sound uneducated, right? Intel, uh, let's just say the Blue Bird of Justice sang a song of six pence in my ear.

Maybe a touch more expensive than six pence, but the song was quite compelling." Millie turned and laughed, "Had a good beat and you could dance to it. You ready to cut in, Griff?"

Griff raked his hands through his unruly hair, making it even more unruly. "Of course. I'm ready for the six feet under watusi, you know that. I just need to know who my unwitting partner is."

Using his index and middle fingers Millie reached inside his suit coat and pulled out a photograph, flinging it across the room at Griff. The picture hit him in the chest and fluttered to land face down on the floor. Arching a brow at Millie, Griff bent down and picked it up. His face remained expressionless as he looked into familiar sapphire blue eyes. Griff nodded, raising only his eyes to Millie. "Same compensation?"

"Double compensation. High priority. Make sure it looks, uh, good, right?"

"Right."

Millie set his beer bottle down, walked over to Griff and clasped him on the shoulder. "Trust is easily broken and rarely repaired. See ya' at the club."

Griff realized he hadn't moved from his spot in the middle of the living room for what seemed like hours. He heard the click of the front door and released a breath he hadn't known he was holding. With slow and deliberate movements, he lowered himself into the recliner, recently vacated by Millie. He tipped his head back and stared at the water stained ceiling until they were nothing but brown blurs.

"Fuckin' Millie. Son-of-a-bitch." He raked his fingers through his hair again.

He couldn't believe he'd walked into his own apartment and hadn't noticed Millie sitting in his living room. That could have been a deadly mistake.

Griff had still been savoring the bouquet of that sweet little piece all over his face and fingers, and just like some teenage cherry, heavy petting for the first time, was lost in his own fucking world. Damn. Get your head screwed on right, Griff, shit. Shit.

Millie was the newest resident to the small area in Philly known as The Block, and Griff was Millie's newest employee. He'd come across the man's radar about two years ago.

Griff grew up on the streets of Philadelphia; a latch-key kid, mostly on his own. Left to his own devices for everything but a roof, he became a petty criminal and grifter, hence the name Griff. He'd spent his fair share of time in juvie, only to be released the last time to find his parents had moved and didn't think to leave their only son a forwarding address. At sixteen, he was alone in the world and made his way just fine. Even better, in fact, without the encumbrances of even their limited adult supervision.

In the last two years, Millie'd had Griff followed, beaten, tested in a myriad of other ways, and Griff was still standing. Millie was right about one thing, trust was easily broken. But he'd proved time and again that he could be trusted. As a matter of fact, he'd impressed the man to such an extent, now Griff was as near to his right hand as Millie's own fingers.

Griff looked at the picture again. "Shit." He crumpled it and threw it to the floor. Another fucking test, but why?

Slapping his hands on his thighs, Griff stood heavily, moving stiffly to the bathroom. Maybe a shower would help clear his head.

The bathroom was nothing more than a closet with a shower stall, toilet, and sink installed haphazardly by a not very qualified plumber and or carpenter. Griff had done some repairs on the fixtures himself and adjusted the hot water tank so he actually *had* hot water to cleanse his body and mind.

He'd found the mirror at a thrift shop and hung it above the sink so he could see to shave and brush his teeth. Being able to see one's reflection while applying a sharpened blade to flesh certainly cut down on the nicks.

Griff went to strip off his shirt when he realized, again, he was shirtless. What the fu-ah, Sugar. He laughed, shaking his head as the memory of her taking off out of his truck in nothing but his t-shirt made him chuckle, still a little confused.

He shrugged and felt a tightness in his shoulders. Frowning, he turned and looked in the mirror. His reflection gave him an evil glare and he nodded, growling, "Good girl," as he saw the claw marks on his non-tatted shoulder. The hot spray of the shower stung the marks on his shoulders as he stepped into the stall. Griff hissed, but tilted his head back and let the water wash away the stress of Millie's visit. Fucking Millie.

Twenty minutes later, Griff stepped from the stall, toweled himself off, and drew on a pair of sweat pants sans briefs. He walked out of his apartment barefoot and jogged to his truck. As he'd stood under the spray of the shower he'd remembered that with her bolting so randomly and without much planning, she'd left her clothes behind. If Millie was going to test him, now would be the time to start studying the subject in question.

He ripped the passenger side door open and the scent of female musk hit him so hard his cock kicked in his pants. Griff steadied himself by resting his hand on the side of the truck, hanging his head and groaning. Once the initial wave of scent had ebbed, he reached inside the cab and grabbed her discarded clothes off the floor, nearly dropping her sexy as sin shoes in the street. Dick that he was, he grabbed the pants first and held them to his nose, inhaling deeply. Shit.

That may not have been the best plan. His sweats were now tented out before him so far he cast a ridiculous shadow beneath the street lamp.

As he bent down to grab the bustier and shoes, he felt a cold hand and fingernails trail down his naked back. "Wanna date, shugah?"

For a brief moment, Griff froze. Could it be? He slowly turned his head. No, of course it wasn't *his* sugar. Straightening, he gave the hooker a slow smile. "Not tonight, Lana. Didn't take my little blue pill."

Lana, Queen of Whore Hill, as she was known, licked pink gummy lips. She was missing one of her front teeth and the other was severely chipped. Fluffing her bright pink cotton candy hair, she cocked her hip and eyed his obvious erection. "Mmmm, shugah, let momma take care of that for you. No charge. Little blue pill or not, that ain't gonna feel too good come mornin'."

Griff stood and laughed at her, pulled the elastic waist band out, looked down and raised his eyebrows. "Huh, thought that was a vitamin. Gonna have to do something about that, after all. Be good, your highness, givin' hand outs isn't going to sit too well with Poppa Jig." He gave her chin an affectionate chuck with his index finger. "You need help with him, anytime, you know where I am."

A flicker of moistness flashed in her chocolate brown eyes, she blinked once and it was gone. Lana gave him a rueful smile, "I'm good, shugah. Gotta smoke?"

He barked out a laugh, "Just where do you think I'm hiding a pack of smokes, Lana?" He jogged off with Faye's belongings clutched to his bare chest. Turning to yell back to her, "You know where I am."

She nodded at his retreating back then turned towards a slow moving car. The car stopped and the passenger side window rolled down smoothly. Lana leaned in. "Wanna date, shugah?"

Back inside his apartment Griff went through Faye's clothes. He chuckled as he pulled her keys out of the front pocket of her pants and read the smart ass message. It was round, about the size of a fifty cent piece with a yellow tag on it that said:

CAUTION: I Like To Get Drunk and Hump Things.

"Ironic," he laughed. He pulled out $27 and change, that was it. No ID, no car keys, no wallet. What did that mean? Think, Griff. He started pacing, looking at the small pile of meaningless possessions. Cabs were too expensive these days, what with the rising price in fuel. So, she walked to the bar. She walked?

He picked up the mile-high fuck me shoes. "In these?" She did like to live dangerously, apparently. Walking in these things he thought, as he wiggled the shoes, means she lives fairly close to the bar.

What did she say? She said...she said...she said she lived around the corner a wee bit.

"Shit." She took off before they'd made it to the first stop light and ran. Which direction? He closed his eyes and pictured the scene again. The look of panic on her face, the way she grabbed for the door handle like he was going to rape and kill her, she ran...ahead, straight ahead. Griff nodded to himself. "Now we're getting somewhere."

As he paced, his bare foot kicked something and he looked down. Furrowing his brow, he crouched down and picked up the wadded ball. What was it? Unfurling the stiff paper, ah the picture. He swiped his hand over his mouth and grabbed the back of his neck, staring at the image. His thumb traced the female's face then he placed the picture on the small pile of personal possessions. He palmed his thighs as he stood. "I guess it's time for an official meet and greet, Faye Kane."

CHAPTER THREE

BANG! BANG! BANG!

Sprawled face down on the bed, Faye lifted her head slightly in the direction of the noise, her hair was like a blonde spider web across her eyes. Using her right hand, she swiped the web out of her face and listened intently to the incessant banging at her front door. She tried to shake the fuzzy fog clouding her brain and, catching a glimpse at the clock in the process, she groaned aloud.

Two o'clock in the afternoon! She'd slept like the dead, and who the *hell* was trying to get into her apartment?

Faye stilled, listening as the person seemed to be searching for the key she normally had hidden in the ornamental rocks and porcelain junk on her stoop. Glancing at her night table, she focused on the object the intruder was looking for.

Sitting up abruptly, she pulled up the shoulder of the over-large t-shirt in which she passed out and looked down at herself, freezing when memories of the previous night came roaring back.

For a moment, she let it all cascade over her like a warm, incredibly erotic, blanket. First, the anger, the betrayal, her utter meltdown, and then the events that came after.

She refused to give in to the urge to regret what came after. Her habit of pushing everything down hadn't worked last night. It was so unlike her to utterly explode the way she did. So unlike her to do what she did with a perfect stranger. Smirking, she remembered one of Michael's biggest complaints. He always said she was too buttoned up, unemotional. Well, wouldn't he be so damn proud of her now? Raking her hand through her hair, she let a small smile escape at the memory; it was absolutely awesome. Throwing herself back on the bed, she squealed like a school girl with a crush. Look at that, there's something to be said for temper tantrums and anonymous sex! Thanks for that life lesson, Michael.

Before she had a chance to further bask in her memories, she was jarred back to cold reality by a voice she never wanted to hear again in this life or any other. "Come on, Faye. Please open the damn door."

Snapping her head up, she felt the anger bubbling to the surface all over again.

How dare Kat come here.

Flopping back down, she pulled her pillow over her head. She didn't want to see her former best friend. Not now, not ever. She was more betrayed by Kat's actions than Michael's. She'd thought Kat a sister of her heart; sisters did not betray each other.

The banging and jiggling continued for what seemed forever. Finally, with a kick and a curse, Kat seemed to get the hint and everything suddenly became quiet.

Removing the pillow and tossing it across the room, Faye heard the pinging of her cell phone somewhere in the distance. She tried to remember where she left the damn thing. Last night was such a kaleidoscope of memories, but she specifically remembered not bringing her phone to the bar.

Sliding out of bed, she headed to the living room, stopping abruptly as the reminder of her meltdown stared back at her. Stepping over the debris, she headed to the kitchen and started a pot of coffee.

Her small apartment was not much to look at normally, but now it looked as if a bomb exploded. Smirking, she thought, yeah, a sugar bomb. While she was lost, contemplating his nickname for her, her landline started screaming for attention. “Hello.”

“God damn it, Kane, why the hell don’t you answer your cell phone?”

Wincing, she glanced out the kitchen door at the mess. “Uh...Sorry sir, I can’t seem to locate it.”

“Well, find it. And get your ass to my office. ASAP.”

“On a Saturday, Cap?”

“Yes. Now!”

Coffee in hand, she maneuvered her way back to her bedroom wondering what was going on. It wasn’t uncommon for her to work weekends, but her boss never called a meeting on the weekend. Not unless something bad was going down.

She guzzled the coffee and took a quick shower, carefully taking his shirt and hanging it on the back of the bathroom door. No time to go down memory lane now, but oh she would later. In her head, she started planning a threesome. Some bubble bath, her bathtub, and her self would all take a stroll down memory lane later that night. Not bothering with makeup, she threw her hair in a ponytail and went in search of her regular wardrobe; a comfortable pair of jeans, button down shirt and boots. She was no fashion diva, but she did know shoes.

Faye froze as she was digging at the bottom of her closet, falling back on her ass as she remembered she’d left her favorite jeans, along with the rest of her clothes, in *his* truck.

Damn.

That was why she'd needed the spare key from under the ceramic frog. Her keys, her cash, and her clothes...all left in his truck.

Slipping on her favorite boots, she pushed the worry from her mind. There was nothing she could do about it right this minute.

Taking her car keys off the hook by the door, she silently thanked God she didn't bring them last night. One last backward glance at the horror of her apartment and she closed the door, heading to her car. As she approached her baby, she smiled wide. Her apartment might not be much to look at, but her car, her car was her pride and joy.

Fondly, she took a moment to remember how she'd saved and squirreled money away for the longest time. She'd kept a picture hanging by her bed of exactly the car she wanted long before she'd learned how to drive. Her brothers teased her mercilessly. They never cared what kind of car they drove as long as they had one. Being the youngest of three, and the only girl, made her feel like she was always picked on. Her brothers thought her position meant she was the princess, always getting her way. In the case of the car, she grinned wickedly, she might have to agree with them. When her dad's buddy mentioned there was a 1967 Cobalt Blue Mustang Convertible in mint condition for sale, she was pumped. Then, when she called on it, the seller informed her the car was sold.

Faye moped for weeks. Her oldest brother, Sam, was sympathetic. Her other brother not so much, that wasn't surprising considering he was devil's spawn and ironically named, of all things, Christian.

The morning of her high school graduation, she woke to her dream car parked in her parents' driveway. They may have teased her about getting her way, but her dad told her later they both helped him wash and gas up the car for her big surprise. It had been her baby ever since.

She loved the area where she lived. She loved, even more, that she was able to serve the very community that helped raise her. Cruising through her neighborhood towards work, she tried to imagine why her boss called a meeting.

As she came up on what her colleagues called, "Whore Hill," she looked around. All was quiet this late Saturday afternoon.

To those residents who lived in the small community just outside Philadelphia, it was simply called, "The Block." But, to the good old U.S. Postal Service, Pine Hill, Pennsylvania was where you mailed your Christmas cards.

Parking and heading inside the office building Faye stopped at her desk, frowning and rolling her eyes when she spotted the swear jar.

The guys at the station told her she had a mouth to rival any truck driver. Typically, she shrugged them off and blamed it on the fact that she grew up with brothers. Never mind *she* probably taught *them*.

She used words at college that made the jocks blush. When she reached the academy, the guys razzed her something fierce. By the time she hit vice, her trash mouth reputation preceded her. The department created the swear jar as soon as Faye was transferred. Her mouth had bought many a donut and several rounds at the local pub.

Looking around, it was clear the place was fairly quiet for a Saturday morning. The good citizens must be on their best behavior, she thought. Tossing her keys on her desk, she knocked off her nameplate. Bending over, she picked it up and grinned.

Detective Faye M. Kane.

Faye never got tired of hearing that or seeing it in print. The nameplate was a gift from her oldest brother. Sam worked in the same precinct, but he was on the fifth floor in Robbery/Homicide. She thought when she was promoted she would see him more often, sadly that was not the case. Their schedules never seemed to mesh. The only time they got together was the occasional Sunday dinner at home when neither could put off their mom any longer, or their incredible need for Rita's Water Ice, a local chain stand that sold a hybrid of Italian ices and slushies known as water ice.

She, Sam, and Christian always loved going to Rita's. Besides the delicious water ice, it was bonding time for them. Since Christian was in the military, the three of them hadn't been there together in forever. Faye knew Sam suggested they go now just so they could talk and touch base, each checking to see if the other had heard from their absent brother.

"Kane, are you going to stand there grinning at yourself or get your ass in here sometime today?" Startled, Faye dropped the plate on her desk and headed into the captain's office.

"Shut the door."

She shut the door and wondered why in the hell he was so damned cranky. But that was also his nature, all bark and on some days, one hell of a bite. He was no taller than Faye, although his girth was twice hers with a gut that naturally filled out the Toys for Tots Santa suit. The hair that crowned his balding head was once brown, but was now peppered with white, skipping gray completely. Though for all of his bluster, Captain Howard Jensen was always fair and just with his squad, but his bite today seemed extra sharp and Faye wasn't sure why. She smirked to herself as she wondered if maybe he'd found the old picture of Ed Asner as

Lou Grant pinned to the dartboard in the break room. Rough days and ass chewing always called for a bit of shoot the boss-or boss's look alike-in the face. They'd just closed a huge case earlier in the week and nothing had come up that she knew of since. The entire department was still basking in the triumph of closing the case that had taken the better part of two years to put together.

Sitting down across from him she waited, impatient yet quiet, until he slid a file across the desk to her. She picked it up and glanced at the name on the tab and her eyes went wide.

She looked up at him, cocking her eyebrow. "Martino 'Millie' Maliano? Seriously, Cap? You really think it wise to start a file on this snake? Where are the rest of the guys? What the fu...fadoodle is going on?"

The captain just shook his head and stared at her.

"Yeah, yeah, I know, but at least I stopped myself. I'm getting better." She stood up and stalked out of his office, pulled a fiver out of her jeans pocket and tossed it into the jar. Returning to his office, she flopped into the chair.

"A five?"

"Hell yeah, seems to me it's going to be that kind of meeting."

He hid a grin and motioned with his head for her to take a good long look at the manila folder that held some very interesting facts about Mr. Maliano.

She hunched forward and began to pore over the file. Page after page she turned to more inflammatory information on a man who claimed to be helping their community. Faye had known from the moment he moved to Pine Hill that he was no good but no one could, or would, see past his money and power to question the character beneath the facade.

Anger and contempt rolled around in her gut. She felt somewhat vindicated that her boss had taken the time to listen to her these past months. The fact that he started this file proved that, like her, he believed this man to be a criminal and a toxic existence to their little corner of the world.

She'd started to believe all her pestering was getting her nowhere. Moonlighting these past few months, she'd been trying to find something, anything to make her captain believe what she knew in her gut to be true. As a matter of fact, she'd spent so many off hours lurking about, the captain had to start a special file just for the complaints he'd received on *her*. Last she heard, it was at least an inch thick.

Continuing to scour the file, she froze when she came across a particular picture. She picked it up and stared at it, there was something there, niggling at the back of her mind. Who was the man with Millie?

He looked so familiar. She couldn't place where but she knew this man. The picture was fuzzy, his profile blurry, but damn if she didn't know him from somewhere.

Sliding the picture across the desk to Captain Jensen, she tapped the man's face. "I know him from somewhere, Cap. I can't put my finger on it, but it'll come to me."

He looked up at her. "Okay, then that's where we start. Him. See what you can dig up. Quietly, Kane. We don't need to get on Maliano's radar, not yet."

"What about the guys?"

He shook his head vehemently. "No, not yet. We need to keep this between us for now. This can't get into the wind yet, there'll be hell to pay if it gets out too soon. Maliano has too many influential friends; we'd be dead in the water if he even got a whiff of what we already have."

She stood suddenly and went to her desk, unlocking the bottom drawer. Squatting, she dug inside and found what she wanted. Straightening, Faye clutched something to her chest and headed back to the office to hand him another file. He took it from her with a questioning look on his face.

"Okay, so Cap...I know you've been deterring me from investigating Maliano, but I had to follow my gut. Sir."

He pointed to the chair for her to sit down again. "I expected nothing less from you, Kane. That's why I called you here today. Listening is not your strong suit."

Faye let out a long breath. "Sir..."

Cap held up his hand. "Kane, let's move on. We have a situation. We need to quietly gather as much info as we can and meet again. Soon. Agreed?"

She nodded and stood. "I have some ideas. You can keep that file, sir. I have more copies." He lifted his eyebrow at her.

"I don't have a good feeling about this guy. I'm covering all my bases," she smirked, "and my ass."

Her captain chuckled. "Alright, Kane, keep me posted."

Turning, she headed out of his office with an idea on how to proceed. Lost in her own thoughts, she nearly missed him calling her back.

"Kane. Kane!"

She stopped just outside his doorway and faced him. "Sir?"

The look on his face was sad; all at once he looked like a man who had something to lose. "Faye, please be careful."

She nodded, furrowing her brow, and watched him as he went back inside his office and closed the door. Absently, she grabbed the keys off her desk and headed to her locker. The sudden change in the captain's demeanor had her concerned, but her plan for the evening was overtaking those concerns. Finally, she remembered the combination to her locker and ripped the door open. Faye grabbed the makeup bag stashed inside, stalked to the counter and began applying the products, grimacing at her reflection. She hated all this girly shit.

Once she was made up, she pulled her hair out of the ponytail, shaking it out. She didn't even bother to pull a comb through it, she just let the tangles fall where they may. Looking at herself intently, she undid a couple of buttons on her shirt, gave the girls a little fluff then surveyed her work. It is what it is, she thought, as she smirked at her reflection.

Packing up her stuff she headed out, suddenly realizing she might not have relocked the drawer at her desk. Sighing, she stalked back into the squad room, which had started to fill up with the shift change officers and detectives, as well as their most recent detainees.

Everything seemed to be in order, including the locked bottom drawer. The other shit littering the top of her desk could wait until Monday.

On her way out she heard catcalls and whistles. Not even bothering to turn around, she raised her right arm and flipped her coworkers the bird. The cackling continued and she couldn't decide which were worse, her fellow cops or the damn people they had in custody.

Faye grimaced as she heard someone yell, "That finger's worth ten bucks, Kane.

***

Dusk was falling around her as she pulled up in front of Silk. The club had the façade of being on the up and up, but she knew in her gut that the place was not what it appeared. Just like the man who owned it was not who he pretended to be.

Faye took a quick peek at herself in her review mirror, shrugging. Hopping out of the car, she did the jog and walk thing the rest of the way to the club. She'd been there many times before, always searching for something to prove her instincts right.

There was no bouncer yet at the door, apparently it was still a little too early for the professional partiers to be out. Faye sashayed to the bar, putting more shake to her ass than was necessary and sliding onto the seat as the bartender gave her the once over.

He appeared to like what he saw because he lingered a little too long on her ample cleavage. Mentally, she gave herself a high five.

When his eyes met hers he winked and she gave him the full wattage smile. “Hey there, what can I get for you?”

Pausing, she tapped her chin thoughtfully before shrugging. “Why don't you surprise me?” Thank God this bartender was new. She'd never seen him before, which meant he hadn't pegged her for a cop, yet.

Playing up on the newbie status, she deliberately leaned forward to watch him make her surprise libation. Using her elbows, she squeezed her cleavage together. He grinned and stared like a teenager, nearly spilling her drink.

As the male reached across the bar to deliver her drink, another male arm came out of nowhere and made a grab for it. “Franky, shut your mouth. You need a tic-tac, one, and two, you’re drawing flies, man.”

She froze, her eyes going wide as she continued to stare straight ahead. Fu...dge! Faye shivered as she recognized that voice. What the eff was he doing here. Here! She gave herself a mental slap and took a deep breath.

Before she could calmly turn around and properly address the Twilight Zone style sitch, he whispered in her ear. When she felt his breath on her neck she nearly groaned out loud.

“Well well, look what the wind blew my way, again. That wasn’t very polite, or safe, jumping out of my truck like that, Sugar.”

She tried to twist around but he wouldn’t let her.

Her eyes darted all around, catching the chuckle and shake of the bartender’s head as he walked to the other end of the bar. Stiffening her back at the sound of his nickname for her, she gripped the bar and swung herself around, hard. He lost his balance just a bit, and as a result, she was able to turn all the way and face him dead on.

She kicked her chin out at him. “How many times do I have to tell you? Don’t call me that!”

Regaining his footing, he grabbed her hand in an iron grip and dragged her off the stool. Undeterred, he pulled her towards the back of the club, past tables and booths and the VIP area, and growled, “At least one more, *Sugar*.”

She realized as she was being dragged through the club that the walls were vibrating to the sound of Rihanna’s S&M. She couldn’t help the blush that travelled over her as the song brought back unbidden images from the previous night’s romp in the alley.

He banged through a door and locked it, backing her up against a red velvet covered wall and caging her body with his arms.

Faye's body pulsed to the beat of the song, her breathing labored. She lifted her eyes to his and he pointed at her, grinding out between clenched teeth, "Not. A. Fucking. Word. Sugar."

A smile pulled at her lips. Funny, the first thing that came to her mind was, he was going to have to put money in her swear jar. She was, after all, on the job. Not that he knew that.

A look came over his gorgeous chiseled features, a sinister, smoldering look. Grabbing the back of her hair, he gripped tightly. He pulled her closer and said, "You owe me an apology, Sugar."

Hearing him deliberately continue to call her that damn name, combined with the arrogance of wanting an apology, she rolled her eyes. Giving herself a mental slap, she quickly forced her exasperation down and glued on a big stupid ass grin. She didn't want her inner struggle written all over her face. Staring up into his eyes, feigning innocence, she lifted her eyebrow at him. "Do I?"

He considered himself a pretty tolerant guy, but between those expressive eyes and that sassy mouth, he wanted to take her over his knee. Not to mention that defiant kick of her chin she liked to use, for what, he had yet to figure out. No one had ever gotten so under his skin, especially in such a short span of time. She ignited a fire in his gut that not only threatened to burn him, it was going to consume everyone even remotely close to them when it turned into a blaze. Struggling for control, he returned her smile and winked. In one swift motion, he hooked the back of her knee with his left leg. Lowering her down to her knees, while still firmly gripping her hair.

The sudden change of elevation and position shift made her stomach dip. Or was it the spontaneity of the moment? Faye had always been buttoned up; by the book, scheduled to within the millisecond of the day. She didn't like surprises, and was known on more than one occasion to draw her weapon over off book moments. So, being here in this moment with the mysterious male, had her heart racing in panic and maybe a little excitement, if she had to be honest with herself.

Taking a deep steadying breath, Faye thought, why the hell not? Maintaining eye contact, she began to unbuckle his belt and expertly freed his hard length from its denim confines. As soon as she saw the rigid flesh, she licked her lips in anticipation of tasting him, all thoughts of anything else gone.

He groaned and gripped her hair tighter, pulling her towards his throbbing erection.

She adjusted her position, spreading her knees to make herself more comfortable. Vaguely, she noticed that the song changed. The mood shifted, her body was tingling as the song, Skin by Rihanna washed over her. This song, like the male before her, was pure sex.

Feeling completely wicked, she grabbed his cock, wrapped her hand around his girth, and tugged him closer. Looking up at him through hooded lids, she slid him into her mouth, feeling him stiffen and barely heard his whispered groan, "Sugar."

Hearing the raw guttural lust elicited in his groan, her nickname made an almost literal down shift in her brain. Faye had never felt so wanton and empowered. This nameless male had made her feel this way and more, in less than twenty-four hours than she ever had in her entire life.

She continued to work his cock with her mouth. Taking him to the back of her throat and sliding her tongue over the thick vein, finding his most sensitive spot, she felt his thigh muscles bunch while his hand fisted into her hair tighter. The slight tingles of pain in her scalp let her know he was pleased with her ministrations, and didn't that make her heart slam inside her chest. She brought him to the edge of pleasure and then backed off only to build him up again and again, just as he had done to her the night before.

He had her head angled so she could gaze up into his eyes. Those eyes. From the very first they had her sucked in. She felt him arch and knew he couldn't hold back much longer. Faye worked him faster and took his cock deeper. With one last thrust of his hips and swipe of her tongue, she watched as he threw his head back and growled, "Fuck, Sugar."

She worked her throat, swallowing every drop, until he yanked her head back, growling. "Enough."

Faye sagged, dropping her ass back on her heels. Her head fell forward as he loosened his grip on her hair only slightly. Errant strands hung askew, obscuring her view. She could still taste him on her tongue and was trying to steady her breathing when he yanked her to her feet.

He pushed her up against the wall again, his body flush against hers. Brushing her blonde locks from her face, he leaned in to whisper in her ear. "Damn Sugar, I like the way you apologize." He chuckled. "You have no idea what you do to me."

Imagine that. That little endearment didn't irk her as much anymore. She had some idea of what she did to him, the evidence was pressed into her. She ground her hips against him, moaning.

He reached for her shirt and attempted to unbutton the garment. But, muttering a curse, he ripped it open, sending buttons flying and pinging off the walls. Palming her breasts, he let out another stream of cuss words as his phone chirped loudly. He stepped back from her as he searched his pocket for the source of interruption. Looking at the caller ID, then her, he ordered, “Don’t. Move. I need to take this. We aren’t done.”

As he stepped out of the room, she caught his profile and gasped. A light bulb went off in her brain almost singeing her retinas. She quickly, and discreetly, surveyed where they were. Eyes wide, she didn’t believe it.

They were in the women’s bathroom. She exhaled hard and quickly threw her hair up in a ponytail, using the scrunchy she’d been wearing as a bracelet. Trying to remain calm, she pulled herself together, took a few deep breaths, and tied the ends of her ruined shirt together.

Listening at the door, she didn’t hear him on the other side. Faye pulled the door open slowly and looked around. She saw that he’d moved to a quieter corner and was talking animatedly. Just then he turned away, yelling into the phone,

“Don’t Griff me, fucker. Make it happen.”

And that was when she made a break for it; swiftly walking through the club, pushing her way around the crowd that had formed while she’d been otherwise occupied. She noticed the bartender staring at her with a questioning look. She ignored him and barreled past the bouncer, out into the bustling street.

Never stopping or looking behind her, Faye pulled her keys from her pocket, ripped her car door open and threw herself inside. She didn’t even take the time to put on her seat belt. Hauling ass out of the parking lot, she saw him fly out of the club, screaming for her to stop. Which she didn’t. Not until she’d squealed to a stop in front of her apartment building.

She finally allowed herself a deep cleansing breath as she cut the engine.

What had she done? Who was he?

Leaning forward, she rested her head on the steering wheel. Closing her eyes, she flashed to his profile as he left the bathroom, then to the picture in her captain's file. He was the blurry figure in the picture standing by Maliano. She had never been so sure of anything in her life.

Gathering her thoughts, she heaved herself out of the car and trudged into her apartment. Oblivious to its new and apparently constant state of chaos, she went directly to the bathroom, dropped her clothes and climbed in the shower. She hoped to stop the numb feeling that was creeping through her body with copious amounts of hot water.

When she stepped out of the shower, she dried herself so much her skin was pink and raw. Grabbing his t-shirt, she put it on, breathing in his scent; reminding her of their most recent run in. His scent triggered her body's instinctive yearning for him while her mind screamed at her that he was not who or what he seemed.

Climbing into her bed she closed her eyes, trying to block the past twenty-four hours out and let sleep envelope her.

CHAPTER FOUR

"What?"

Faye sat up in bed, woken from the sleep of the dead. She looked around her darkened bedroom, she swore she'd heard something.

Damn. If Kat had snuck in to try and talk to her, she'd knock the shit out of her.

Faye bit her lip. She thought, no she knew she heard something. Reaching over to her nightstand, she slammed her hand around, looking for the switch on her lamp.

"Leave it off, Sugar," the male's voice nothing but a deep growl in the dark.

Faye gasped and scrambled back against the headboard. Shit, her gun was in the kitchen on the counter. She brushed trembling hands through her sleep mussed hair. "I...I know who you are and who you work for. If...If y-you knew who I was, you wouldn't be here right now. S-so, you'd better just go, if you know what's good for you." She hated that her voice trembled and she really hated that her body reacted to the thought of him in her room.

Movement inside her room, the sound of heavy footsteps moving across the plush carpet, and a soft chuckling had her eyes flashing, searching the darkened space for the mysterious male.

"Good to know, Sugar, but you see, I've never known what's good for me. You know who I am, hmmm? You sure about that?"

She nodded into the darkness. "I dug up your rap sheet, *Griff*!" She spat his name, satisfied that for once she had one up on him. "Griff, aka Ian McManus, like that's a real name. I'd believe it more if I found your 'real' name was John Smith. When did you get the nickname? Couldn't find when or how you got it and to be honest, I don't really care. What I do care about is your current employer, Martino "Millie" Maliano? Slick Millie? Philanthropist and all around savior of the neighborhood, right? WRONG! I've got more dirt on Millie than could fill the Grand Canyon. My problem though, Griff," again she spat his name, "it's all circumstantial." She knew she was rambling. Yet she was hoping to throw the mysterious male off course, get him off kilter so she could get to her gun, still all the way in the kitchen. "Shit," she muttered as she scrubbed a hand over her face.

There was nothing but silence and darkness in her room. As a matter of fact, all she could hear was her own breathing. Was she talking out loud to herself? She must have been dreaming and...and...and what? Awakened in the middle of the dream and arguing with a figment...The bed dipped and the scent of dark spiced cologne and male musk invaded her senses. Her heart started to race and she tried melting into the headboard, but strong arms gripped her upper arms and pulled her up on her knees.

"There's that sassy mouth again. Since I've all ready fucked it, I think I'll make good on my promise." In one swift motion, Griff moved and pulled Faye over his lap. Yanking her panties down, he landed three sharp swats to her ass.

Faye squealed in surprise and anger as she was spanked. Spanked? She wasn't a child and who the hell was he to spank her? "Fuck you!" Scrambling away from his body, tears pricking at the corners of her eyes, somewhere it registered that the hands hadn't tried to hold her in place or force her to do anything else.

"That's right, Sugar. Fuck me. That's exactly how I've felt ever since I laid eyes on you the other night. Completely and utterly fucked."

Faye felt more movement on her bed. Still in the dark, she pouted. What the hell was that about? Two times this male had made her pout and it pissed her off.

She realized he had moved up the bed and straddled her curled up figure, placing a knee on either side of her legs. Brushing his knuckles across her cheeks, he thumbed her jaw line, tipping her head up to feather soft kisses against her lips. "Red means stop. Understand?"

Against her better judgment, Faye nodded and whispered, "Yes."

Griff whispered in her ear, "Sir. Yes, Sir."

She nodded again. "Yes, Sir." Her body heated at the implied command and she hated herself even more.

"Good girl. Now, arms up." His hands moved down to her waist, felt for the hem of the shirt she was wearing, and slid the garment off tossing it into the darkness.

She felt him move again and sighed as his chest pressed into her face. Her tongue snaked out of her mouth and swept a hot trail over his flesh. She was rewarded with a deep, rumbling growl, barely noticing the feel of the silk rope being twined between her wrists and attached securely to the headboard.

Griff groaned at the feel of her tongue on his chest and had to control the urge to shove his tumescent cock inside her talented mouth again. He sat back on his heels, picturing in his mind's eye what she must look like trussed up just for his pleasure as her bedroom was black as pitch and his imagination was the only place to see her trussed up...for now.

Large calloused hands started roaming her body. Faye arched into his touch, panting, nearly begging for more.

“Shh, relax. I’ll take care of you. Red means stop. Say it.”

She sighed heavily. “R-red means stop.”

Griff pulled back and slapped her pussy. “What?”

Faye’s body shuddered at the change of tone in his voice, she groaned at the stinging slap to her throbbing folds. “Red...means...s-stop, S-Sir.”

“Good girl.” He rewarded her by caressing her swollen lips and pearlized nub. Faye thrust her hips up to encourage his touch but he pulled his hand away. “Please.”

Griff pressed his hand into her hips, pushing her back down on the bed, “Quiet. I’ll take care of you...in my own time.”

Faye gasped again. In his own time? Not fair! He’d barely done anything to her and her flesh was already burning her alive. She needed more of him and his dangerous touch, “Pl...Please, Sir?”

Before she could say more, he took her mouth in a crushing kiss. Griff forced her mouth open and plunged his tongue inside, moaning at her unique taste. His hands travelled over her body, seeking her nipples, circling her areolas. Faye thrust her chest out and Griff chuckled as he took the erect little nub between his forefinger and thumb and pinched and twisted.

Faye screamed at the foreign sensation. She wanted to be pissed and pull away from the pain, but the zing that flooded her system turned quickly to pleasure and she felt her eyes roll in her head.

"That's it. Feel it, all of it." Griff released the stiffened peak and moved his hand down to the apex of her sex. He teased her swollen, wet folds. Pressing his thumb into her entrance, he removed it then brushed the thick digit across her pearled little bundle of nerves.

Faye's head thrashed from side to side, her chest heaved with each labored breath. Never in all her sexual experiences had anyone made her feel like this. Sex was always fun and sweaty, but nothing like this.

Suddenly his touch was gone and she whimpered at the loss. "No, come back. Please!"

"Shh, I'm right here." He caressed her cheek as he stepped out of his sweats and fumbled with a foil wrapped condom. He kept his hand on her to reassure her he'd not left her as he donned the rubber. Two handed, rolling on a condom was tricky enough, but one handed was damned near impossible, but for the second time, he came out the clear winner in the One Handed Prophylactic Relay. Finally, getting the damn rubber on, he knelt on the bed. "Miss me?"

She cringed when she heard her pouting response. "Yes."

Griff barked out a laugh as he wrapped his arms around her thighs, yanked roughly, and impaled her wet heat on his thick shaft.

Faye's back arched at the sudden stretch and burning pleasure from his erotic invasion and maddening pace. A flush of embarrassment raced through her as she realized the racket her headboard was making against the wall. Her neighbors were sure to hear the banging and her screams. Griff lifted her legs, gripped each ankle and held them out wide as he slammed his hips against her sex.

"Ummmmm...G-Griff, please... Please. I'm going to..."

"No! Not yet." As he continued to thrust he gritted out, "That's mine." Griff released Faye's right ankle, dropping it to the bed. Moving her left ankle to his left hand, he changed her position, and his thrusting depth.

Faye found herself half on her side, quivering, sweating, whimpering from her compounding need to have a cataclysmic release that was likely to light up the neighborhood.

"Focus." Griff brought his hand down on her ass again, the smack echoing off the walls.

His stern tone, coupled with the smack, helped her regain some small semblance of composure. Disgusted with herself, but unable to control the plea in her voice, she begged, "Ahh, please, Sir."

Her inner walls started clamping down around his cock, making it harder for him to plunder her sex. "Yes, Sugar, now. Come now." Fuck, her walls clamped his dick in a vice, trapping him inside as her body flew apart in ecstasy. Griff let his head fall back on his shoulders as the familiar tingling sensation raced across his lower back, up the shaft of his cock, and out the head. He filled the condom as he growled his bliss to the darkness.

Panting, Griff leaned over and untied her wrists. He painted her face with kisses. "Sugar, you're amazing." Leaving her long enough to discard the well used condom, he returned to pick her noodle-limp body off the bed and carry her to the bathroom. She threw her arms around his neck, sighing.

Griff adjusted her body as he turned the shower on, stepping in gingerly and letting the spray hit her back. She sighed again as he ran his fingers through her hair, getting it wet. Putting on a condom one handed was a shit ton easier than showering while holding a sated and limp female, Griff though, this shit should be an Olympic event.

He didn't want to lose his footing for fear of hurting her, but knew that setting her down wasn't an option, at least not one he wanted to consider.

Once satisfied the sweat was rinsed from her, he stepped them both out of the shower, wrapping a towel around her body. On the way out of the shower he saw his t-shirt lying on the floor in a heap. He chuckled, laying her on the bed then grabbed the shirt off the floor to slip it over her head. Before leaving, he placed a soft kiss to her forehead. "I'll see ya' around."

***

"What?"

Faye sat up in bed, awakened from the sleep of the dead. She looked around her darkened bedroom. She swore she heard something.

Damn, if Kat had snuck in to try and talk to her, she'd knock the shit out of her.

Faye bit her lip. She thought, no she knew, she heard something. Reaching over to her nightstand, she slammed her hand around looking for the switch on her lamp.

Her hand hovered over the light switch, waiting for... why did this feel like some weird deja vous? Faye continued to hover her hand over the switch and waited for a voice in the dark to tell her to leave it off.

Shit, Faye, get your shit in a pile. It was just a dream, a highly erotic and very real dream, she chastised herself.

Faye switched the light on and blinked at her room, her eyes immediately training on a chair that was pulled to the side of her bed. She gasped, her hand flying to her mouth as she saw her clothes: her favorite jeans and red bustier, folded neatly, topped with her sky high red heels.

"Oh hell no!" Faye kicked the covers off, bounded off the bed, and felt the tightness in her groin. "Oh god." She looked at her wrists and saw a light pink area where they'd been bound, just like in her dream.

"Yup, it was a dream, Faye. Just a damn dream." She moved through her apartment, stepping over the mess. The mess... she spun around in circles looking around at the *not* mess. What the fuck? Her apartment had been cleaned?

"Shit shit shit." She pounded to her front door, ripped the thing open and looked outside, not sure what she was expecting to find.

Yeah Faye, your midnight marauder is going to be standing outside your door with flowers and chocolates and an, "Oops, my bad," expression.

"Shit." She slammed the door, turning the deadbolt and sliding the chain into place.

Slowly, she walked to her kitchen to make a pot of coffee only to find a full pot, ready to go. A note leaned against the Mr. Coffee machine. Faye cussed again and picked up the folded piece of paper, reading aloud to the empty and now clean apartment.

Sugar,

Nice place you have here. A mini-hurricane seemed to have landed in your living room and left a disaster area in its wake. I had a devil of a time finding a broom and dustpan, but as you can tell, I worked it out.

Your keys are hanging in the cabinet above the sink. You should really consider changing your hide-a-key spots too. There was some chick here with long dark hair looking for your spare key. I think I did a pretty good job at scaring her off. Don't worry, I used my own special brand of charm to get inside – your apartment. The other was just a bonus.

I've wagged my tongue long enough. I hear you stirring, which is my signal to get the hell out.

-G-

P.S. By the way, in the middle of that shit storm I found your cell phone. Charge it and keep it on you. You're welcome. I had your clothes dry cleaned. You owe me $33.72, I'll collect another time. You know you love it when you owe me. I know I do.

"Sonofabitch!" Faye crumpled the note and threw it across the room, seething.

***

Griff laughed as he entered the darkened club. The place was empty and practically desolate at this time of day, but that didn't dampen his mood. Three encounters with that woman in almost as many days and he couldn't wipe the smug look from his face.

"Someone's full of himself today," Millie's voice floated up from behind the bar.

"Millie, Jesus H. man. You and this sneaky shit, what the fuck? And," Griff scowled, "what the hell are you doing behind the bar?"

Millie smiled. It was something like a great white smiling at you before he bit your leg off. "Inventory. I think Dino's skimming, little bastard. I brought him up from nothing.

Stealing from family, regardless of blood ties, should never be tolerated. Walk with me." Millie emerged from behind the bar and headed towards the back of the club.

Griff hung his head and smirked as he passed the women's lavatory, images from the other night with Faye flashing through his mind.

Millie pushed inside the room, not bothering to hold the door open for Griff, who slammed his hand against the wood paneled door to keep it from banging him in the face. Griff didn't bother looking around, having been inside this place more times than he cared to recall. He merely settled into an overlarge wingback chair, resting his ankle on the opposite knee.

Being done in plush maroons and deep browns gave Millie's office a very warm feel to it, but Griff had to stifle a shiver anyway. "What's up, boss man?"

Millie palmed his desk as he sat in his Italian leather executive chair, keeping mud brown eyes on Griff's ever present smirk. "You look like the cat that ate the canary, Griff. Who you knockin' around with?"

"We're close, Millie, but not that close, my brotha'." Griff snorted out a laugh. "You wanna tell me why the second meet and greet? I mean, at least this time I didn't need a change of shorts. But ya' gotta stop with the sneak and peeks." Griff laughed again.

Millie nodded and steepled his fingers so the twin index fingers tapped his chin. "I gotta proposal for you, Griff."

Griff held up his hands in a defensive posture. "Whoa, Millie, man I'm really not into dudes."

Millie slammed his hands on his desk. "Shut the fuck up for two seconds, Griff." Once Millie was satisfied he had

Griff's full attention, he nodded and continued. "Thank fuck. Sometimes your smart assitude is enough to give me the scratch. Shit. Let's get right down to business. First, how's the contract?"

Griff smiled and licked his lips, "Sweet as candy, man. But seriously," Griff cleared his throat and straightened up at Millie's scowl, "I've got her under surveillance. Gotta get her routine down and then I can make a plausible exit strategy for her."

Millie nodded in approval. "Good. Keep me informed. Second, you got time to keep tabs on Dino and his sticky fingers?"

Griff nodded. "Yeah man. I mean, you sure?"

"Too many shots given out and not enough cash in the till. I'm sure. Keep your eyes peeled in case it's not him. I want to know regardless. Third, my proposal," the leather on Millie's chair creaked as he slowly sat back and regarded Griff. "I'm having a bit of a soiree at my house this weekend. I want you to come. I need a bodyguard of sorts. Of course you'll have to clean up a bit. I mean shit, Griff, do you own anything besides jeans, black t-shirts, and motorcycle boots?" Millie laughed, sounding like a donkey choking and sneezing at the same time.

"Hey, I like my wardrobe. My shirt and boots always match. And bodyguard? Damn, Millie, I'm not going to sing that stupid song to you." They both laughed.

Millie pulled a large, fat envelope overflowing with cash from his desk drawer and tossed it in Griff's lap. "Payment in advance for the gig. Get a suit, preferably a tux. And if there's enough left over, a decent apartment. Shit."

Griff stood, stuffing the envelope in his back pocket. "Fuck you, Millie. What time?"

“Six, on the damn dot. And keep your dick in your pants. You’re there for me.”

“You really know how to spoil a guy’s fun, man.”

Millie watched as Griff left his office. He sat back in his chair again, narrowing his eyes as his door clicked shut. Picking up the handset of his phone, he dialed. “Yeah. Just left. Watch his ass.”

CHAPTER FIVE

She was still grinding her teeth and festering as she reached to pour herself a cup of coffee when banging on the door pulled her out of her unwanted reverie. Storming to the front door, Faye ripped it open and yelled, "Damn Griff, enough is enough. What the fu..." The curse froze in her throat as Kat breezed in, carrying coffee from their favorite place, Back to the Grind. Kat was babbling. Faye was dumbfounded as the dull, incessant chattering droned in her ear like a buzzing bee needing to be swatted.

Faye stepped outside and peeked her head out the door and around the corner, half expecting to see Griff standing with a smoke and that irritating smile. Faye pulled her head back inside and stared, mouth agape, not believing Kat had the nerve to come back.

She could still hear her former friend's diarrhea of the mouth and not once had she heard the word 'sorry,' only justification after justification. Quietly, Faye closed the door and calmly made her way to the kitchen, all the while, watching Kat, who'd just finished her rambling.

Kat slammed her hands down so they slapped on her jean clad thighs with a hopeful, "Ya' know?"

Leaning back against the counter, Faye smiled at her. Oh boy *did she* know. Taking a calm, steadying breath, she turned and reached for the breadbox. "Would you like some cinnamon toast?" Reaching into the breadbox, she fiddled with the wrappers, and just as Kat smiled and said, "sure," Faye turned back, her gun aimed directly at Kat's smiling face. "Looks like I'm all out of cinnamon bread, and damns to give."

Kat's eyes widened and her smile died a quick death. She began to step back and reiterate all the same bullshit she'd spouted upon entering Faye's apartment.

Grinning like an evil fool, Faye hit the safety and used her eyes to motion to the front door.

Kat went to grab for the coffee she'd brought, but Faye cocked the hammer and shook her head. "Oh ho. Not. A. Chance. Leave the coffee, Kat, it's the least you can do. You can have my damn sorry ass ex-boyfriend, but the coffee, hell-to-the-no."

Kat threw her hands in the air and headed for the front door, muttering, "Fine, once a bitch, always alone."

Faye slammed the door on Kat's ass and barked out a harsh laugh. Stalking back to the kitchen, she reached for the coffee she'd commandeered. As she sipped the piping hot, extra dark roast, she closed her eyes. "Yeah, yeah, but at least I have the coffee."

***

Why was it so hard to let people in? Perhaps she had a serious character flaw, Faye thought.

She sat on her bed, sipping coffee and chewing thoughtfully on a piece of cinnamon toast. Faye laughed as she looked at the toast and shrugged her shoulders as she spoke to her food. "What's a bit more betrayal between former best friends?"

She'd turned the stereo on to try to drown out the events of the last couple of days that continued to churn inside her head. Faye squeezed her eyes shut, but no matter how she tried, she couldn't shut off her long term or short term memory. Which was the lesser of two evils? She snorted out a laugh as she wondered if it was too late to start smoking pot.

"Great," she sighed as she realized her long term memory had won this battle. Faye'd spent her whole life keeping others at arms length.

Kat not only slipped through her forcefield, she'd knocked the whole damn thing down, like a wrecking ball destroying a condemned building.

Flashes of the first time she met Kat at the coffee shop, Back to the Grind, flooded Faye's memory, not in any linear sequence but tumbled around like clothes in a dryer. Not only was Kat a frequent customer but she worked there as well. Faye, a college student in perpetual white t-shirts and gray sweats or, if she was feeling dressy, faded jeans. She would never forget Kat's persistence to get her to loosen up. Faye wanted, no needed, to finish college and follow her dream of becoming a cop. She'd made a deal with her parents that if she excelled at school, they would not stand in her way of becoming a police officer.

Smiling, she remembered her parents thinking that once she went to school she would forget their bargain. Faye never wavered, though. She'd been worse than a dog with a bone. She knew exactly what she wanted and she wasn't giving it up for anyone or any amount of the frat parties she'd purposely avoided, along with the other college ritual, promiscuous sex. Who needed sex when she could have a gun?

Faye'd made it a habit of going to the local coffee place almost every day between classes; she'd down a bucket o'coffee and study while perched at a window table.
By the beginning of the second week, Kat knew Faye's order by heart and constantly teased her about going crazy and ordering something different. Faye wiped an errant tear from

her cheek as she remembered the day their friendship was sealed.

Faye had gotten up for her third or fourth refill of coffee. She was such a frequent customer she never bothered to wait for a waitress, namely Kat, to come and refill her cup. But, Faye had been distracted and tired as hell at having pulled another all night studying session. She'd accidentally bumped into a gentleman with a very large, hot coffee. Screaming, she cussed a blue streak as the man's coffee spilled down her front.

Faye'd never seen anyone react so damn quickly. Kat grabbed her and pulled her into the staff locker room. She stripped Faye's coffee soaked shirt off and pushed her under the shower, cranking the cold water.

Faye bitched through chattering teeth about not having any clothes to put on, then shook her head and gave Kat a horror struck expression at the outfit she was waggling in her new friend's face. The lime green capris with daisies embroidered on the cuffs were bad enough on their own, but the brown and gold paisley shirt Faye was sure had visited Studio 54 a couple dozen times, was her limit.

Faye never cared about making a fashion statement but shit, she wrinkled her nose at the clothes and Kat, well Kat roared with laughter as tears streamed her face.

Kat was used to wearing clothes that screamed, "Hey world look at me." Not so much, Faye.

Gathering some much needed will power, Faye forced the memories below the surface and refused to give them floaties any time soon. She hoped, rolling her eyes at herself, that they'd drown.

Draining the last of the coffee, Faye yawned. She'd spent a good bit of the night, before the salacious tryst, tossing and turning trying to come up with a feasible excuse to engage Millie at Silk. The man knew she was vice, there was no way to get around that little fact.

"Sooooo," she said aloud, clapping her hands together. She had to work with what she had. Bounding off the bed, she opened her closet door and dug out her "hoochie" clothes. Working vice, she'd had to wear many interesting outfits. Faye turned to toss a couple of possibilities on her bed when her eyes caught the folded jeans, bustier, and shoes Griff had returned to her. She swallowed hard and pushed back the number of illicit encounters she'd had with the virtual stranger, Ian "Griff" McManus. Like that was actually his real name.

Her body responded to the mere thought of him in ways that pissed her off and she groaned aloud. How the hell was she going to pretend she didn't know him if she couldn't even think about him?

As she was comparing the advantages and disadvantages of two other provocative outfits, another thought struck her that made her stomach do somersaults: How would he react when he realized what she was doing? And did she really care? With great effort, Faye forced her attention back to the task at hand; a couple of good bangings did not a relationship make.

***

Rain and wind danced around her as she made her way into Silk. The moment she stepped into the club the music struck her like a punch to the face. Taking a deep breath, Faye scanned the room and shook out her hair. Immediately, her gaze landed on him. She willed her body not to react and sauntered to the bar to order a drink, a dirty martini with two olives and an onion.

She slipped off her black raincoat and hung it over the back of the barstool, stiffening as she felt a shadow fall across her shoulders. Faye decided to forgo the "hoochie" clothes in favor of a little black dress. But for the shoes she went to the max; pink, sparkly, and sky high.

Smoothing her palms down the sides of the short dress, she turned and, with a slight smile, looked up at the shadow. It was time for her to turn up the charm and turn down the cop. Never breaking eye contact, she grabbed the drink the bartender put in front of her and smiled again as the stranger tossed a twenty dollar bill on the bar. Raising an eyebrow, she took a long sip as she continued to watch the stranger from over the top of her glass.

Inclining her head, she held up the glass. "Thank you."

She had a feeling he was sent to scope her out. She knew she was being watched closely, from two different areas of the club. The stranger asked her to dance, but she sweetly and respectfully declined. He bowed, smiled, and told her to enjoy her drink.

Taking another sip as the stranger sauntered off to a darkened corner of the club, Faye grabbed her drink and jacket. She wound her way through the sea of undulating bodies to a semi-quiet corner booth, sliding into the seat with her back against the wall. From this vantage point she could see the entire bar and most of the dance floor.

Before she knew it, she'd finished her drink and sat bobbing her head and drumming the table in time to the heady beat of the sexy music. No typical club or house music for Silk, oh no, the music the DJ played or was ordered to play, Faye thought, was all sensual guitar licks and heavy bass beats.

"The better to thrust, my pretty." Faye threw her head back and laughed at herself.

A deep male voice shook her from her laughter and demanded a dance. She leveled a gaze at him and mentally cursed her body for reacting, instantly, to that voice.

Rather than trying to shout her response of, "Not in this life, pal," she simply shook her head. Trying to ignore the strong, warm male hand pulling her roughly from the booth, turned into a miserable failure as he frog marched her to the dance floor. Once there, he spun her away and pulled her back at the last second with more grace than she could have thought possible. Their bodies pressed flush against each other. She could feel the anger radiating off him in waves as well as his arousal, grinding against her thigh.

Griff moved his hand to the back of her neck, applying a not so gentle squeeze. Bringing his mouth to her ear, he bit the lobe hard enough to make her yelp. "Got your attention now? What in the hell are you doing here, Sugar?" he growled. "Or should I just call you, *Officer* Kane?"

Faye reached around and threaded her fingers through his hair. Using it as leverage to pull him even closer against her, she whispered back, "Oh, *Ian*," her tone dripped with acid, "is that a problem for you? Don't you want to see my big gun?"

He stiffened and ground his arousal harder against her, then growled and pushed her away roughly. Grabbing himself he shot back, "One big weapon is all this relationship can handle, *Faye*."

Momentarily shocked by his crude response, she blinked and quickly squashed down the feelings his behavior evoked, refusing to let him see just how his actions affected her. As she stumbled back, Faye was caught by unfamiliar arms. She looked behind her and her mouth dropped open as she stared directly into the muddy brown eyes and shark toothed smile of Martino "Millie" Maliano.

Without thinking, she reached under her skirt and whipped out her Glock, aiming it at Griff. She grinned and stalked back to him with purpose, gun never wavering. But before she could reach him, she was grabbed around the waist and lifted off the ground.

"Okay, okay, settle down there, feisty." Millie whispered and chuckled at the same time.

Faye realized everyone had stopped dancing and was staring at what was unfolding on the dance floor.

"Put the gun away, Detective Kane, you're causing a scene. We both know your captain wouldn't be nearly as impressed with your behavior as I am."

At the mention of her boss, Faye came to her senses. But, before she could let it go, she shimmied out of Millie's grasp and sashayed over to Griff. Batting her eyelashes, she pushed the gun into Griff's hard-on. Licking her lips, she stood on tip-toes, necessary even in the sky high heels. Faye pressed her lips against his. "It's *Detective*. Get it right."

Before she turned to leave she slid the gun up and down his shaft, anger sizzling off her as she let her eyes bore into him. She whispered so no one else could hear. "By the way, there's fucking," she lifted her weapon from his groin with a hard shove, deliberately making a show of her gun, "But *this* is the only relationship that's real."

Stepping back and smiling, she kept her gaze on Griff's green eyes. Making a show of sliding the hem of her dress up her silky thighs, she slipped her gun back in the holster and readjusted her dress, flipping her hair as she turned. Faye put an extra swing in her hips as she walked away from the dance floor.

Breathing out a heavy sigh of irritation, she flopped back into the booth at her "quiet" table. Heart pounding in her chest, she grabbed the fresh drink she hadn't ordered and guzzled the whole thing. Some of it spilled out the corner of her mouth.

She was still being watched, but before she could decide what to do next she felt someone slide in beside her.

Glancing to her right, she saw Millie holding a third drink out to her. Taking it from him, slopping a few drops down the front of her dress in the process, she guzzled that one too. Shoving the empty glass back at him, she gave him a dismissive glance. "Are you handling waitress duty tonight, because I could use another."

Millie snapped his fingers and a waitress appeared, taking the empty glasses and disappearing. He began to grab Faye's jacket and she cocked her eyebrow at him. "Am I leaving already?"

"Why Detective, what kind of host do you take me for?" He slipped his arm around her as he guided her to the back of the club.

As they approached the VIP area, she spotted Griff staring at her from a darkened corner of the lounge. She ignored him. Faye couldn't help but do a double take as the extraordinarily large man guarding the VIP velvet rope moved aside to allow them entrance. She wasn't sure if she was staring because he was almost literally the size of a brick wall or because of how the strobing lights of the club shone off his gorgeous mocha skin; which just so happened to make him look like a Nubian god guarding the realm. He caught her staring and gave her a wink as she was ushered by.

Millie handed Faye's stuff to the waitress who was delivering their drinks. Guiding Faye to a booth in the corner, he set her drink down on the table and grabbed her bicep forcibly. "Well, Detective Kane, unlike Griff, I remember your proper title." He squeezed her around the neck.

She neither blinked nor moved. She glanced around and saw Griff about to pounce, his jaw scissoring, his posture that of a lion ready for the kill. Faye mentally willed him to stay put. Fed up with all this male posturing and dominance, she rolled her eyes. Rough stuff in the bedroom, fine, whatever, but in public...E-fucking-nough!

Millie shook her by the throat to get her attention. "So Detective Kane, tell me, what's a nice little vice cop doing in my club packing heat, and waving said heat at my favorite employee?"

As much as she knew she should play dumb blonde, she couldn't. It wasn't her style, and if she was going to play this out she needed to be herself, to a degree.

Having made her decision, in a quick series of movements she turned the tables on Millie. Faye took a step back and turned, causing Millie's hand to release its grip on her throat. Quickly, she grabbed Millie's hand, twisted it, stepped behind him, forcing the extremity up between his shoulder blades. With her other hand, she reached around and grabbed his balls, giving them a twist for good measure.

Smiling into his back, Faye whispered in his ear. "Let's get this straight, Millie. I didn't like your employee manhandling me, and I certainly won't take it from you, either. I don't give a damn how powerful you think you are." On the last word, Faye gave his cajones a good twist for emphasis. Looking around as his men descended upon them, Millie barked out a laugh. Lazily raising his hand and swatting them away.

Faye released his arm and nuts, surreptitiously wiping her nut grasping hand on her dress. Ball handling was one thing, but he'd sported wood as soon as she vice-gripped his jewels. Faye had to stifle a gag and a shudder. Walking around his body to face him, she looked him square in the eye. "Do you have a problem with me being here?" She tilted her head, cocked a hip, and batted eyelashes. "I figured I would see what all the fuss was about at the infamous Silk, but if you're too threatened by little ole me," she batted her lashes again, "I can go drink and shake my ass elsewhere."

He barked out another laugh and pulled her close to him so she could feel his arousal; she swallowed back the bile for a second time. Faye really hoped she could sell this. She reminded herself she had no damn choice. It was time to bring this cockroach down and the department had given her no other option.

Smirking, she wiggled against him. "Something funny, Millie?"

"You are one brazen bitch and, against my better judgment, I like you."

She reined in every ounce of control she had. "Why Millie, aren't you the sweet talker? Can I have my other drink now? I seem to have worked up quite a thirst."

He scooted her inside his special booth and slipped in next to her. The other booths in the lounge were open on either side, but Millie's booth only had one entrance/exit. He always made sure he was seated in that position, especially when he had a lady friend to entertain.

Faye suppressed the urge to break his hand as he rested it on her bare thigh. Instead, she reached for her drink and took a good healthy sip with a fleeting thought that she needed to pace herself. Unfortunately, she'd lost count of how many martinis she'd had. She looked at the drink and wrinkled her brows, thinking. Number three or four? She couldn't be sure. She shook her head, there was no way she could drive home; she foresaw a taxi in her immediate future.

Faye leaned back and sank into the plush seat. Millie was distracted, talking to one of his men who had approached. She couldn't quite make out their murmuring, but he was steadily growing more and more pissed; his grip on her thigh tightened.

Before she could peel him off, he slammed his hand on the table and motioned to Griff, who immediately strode towards them. Millie stood, leaning on the table. "Griff take her dancing, now."

"Boss?"

"I need to make a quick call. Entertain my new lady friend until I get back."

Faye didn't like where things were heading and tried to scoot passed Millie's bulk. "Sorry boys, I don't need any more manhandling. Thanks anyway." She sighed heavily, waiting for Millie to get out of her way.

Both men turned to regard her, Millie smirked. "Detective, humor me. I'm not much of a dancer, let me admire you while I deal with a problem." He lifted a brow, waiting for her answer while Griff held out his hand to her. Millie nodded and walked out of the VIP area, a dark expression coloring his features.

For a split second she contemplated spitting on them both. *What in the hell was she thinking? She was playing with fire and she wasn't going to get burned. Nope, not Detective Faye Kane. She was most definitely going to get scorched.* Taking a deep breath, she placed her hand in Griff's and allowed him to lead her onto the floor.

As they walked away Millie yelled, "Hey, Griff, keep your fucking hands to yourself. She's not one of your back alley sluts. Capisce?"

Griff raised his hand and waved him off.

Faye stumbled at Millie's last statement and Griff's arm shot out to steady her. She shrugged him off, though she gave his hand a firm squeeze before she pulled from his grip. Even though it was Millie's comment that made her trip, it was Griff who made her feel completely off kilter. One minute he was a total ass, the next he was taking care of her. The anger she'd felt earlier waned. Tipsy and confused, Faye wished desperately things were different.

She wove her way to the dance floor and turned to face Griff. He spun them around so his back was to Millie. Faye closed her eyes and let the music wash over her. Gyrating her hips, she lifted her hands to her hair, seductively sliding her fingers through her tresses.

Moving her body, Faye felt Griff pull her closer so he could whisper in her ear. "You're killing me, Sugar. I want..."

Slowly, she slid around behind him, swaying and grinding her body against his, remembering how well they fit together. She yearned for it to be simpler, for it to be as simple as a man and a woman and what they felt for one another. But, it wasn't simple. She let her hands roam his body, he moved to the beat with her, and she whispered. "Please, you need to stay out of this. I'm not sure how in the hell he knows about your back alley escapades, but he obviously doesn't know that it was me in that alley. It needs to stay that way. Let it alone, Griff. I promise I'll try to keep you out of it."

Griff spun and pulled her flush against him, grinding and moving to the music as if they were one. He danced like he made love; with an intensity that took her breath away. She lifted her hands in the air and threaded them through his hair, almost moaning out loud from the look in his eyes.

What was it about this man? Was he the unknown factor screwing up her perspective on this case? She'd never let a man interfere with her job before, why now?

He stared at her for a moment before he shook his head, just a little. "You have no idea the shit storm you've stumbled upon. You need to walk away from this, Detective, before you get hurt."

Dread wove its way through her and she dropped her head to his chest, fighting the urge to scream. She whispered to him, an ache in her chest she'd never felt. Not even Michael's betrayal made her ache like this. Angry, yes, betrayed, HELL YES. But, this ache was new and terrifying. She hated the confusion and indecision it made her feel. They continued to dance, not realizing the music had stopped. Their brains may not have realized it, but their bodies did. They were made for each other.

"It's too late. Much, much too late, Ian." Before he could comment they were pulled apart, both dazed for the briefest of seconds.

Griff growled, "What the fuck?" He reached out for Faye's warm lithe body, but Millie swatted at him.

"I said to keep your hands to yourself, kid. The song's over, wake up. Now, go help Johnny with an unfortunate issue that's come up."

Griff glanced at Faye one last time, turmoil glowed in his beautiful eyes and it made her remember the first time she saw them staring at her from across the bar. Turning, he stalked away and she resisted the urge to follow him. She had a job to do and she damn well would do it. At any cost.

Millie grabbed for her. "That was quite a dance, Detective. Something going on with the two of you?"

Faye found her inner actress and slipped into his arms, wrapping herself around him like a snake. Breathlessly, she whispered in his ear, "You said you wanted a show, Millie. I aim to please." She nodded in Griff's direction and wrinkled her brow. "And him? Please, he's nothing."

Millie leaned in and kissed her. Faye locked her knees together to keep either or both of them from following a destructive path to his balls.

She wiggled free and smiled up at him. "How about another drink?"

He kept his arm around her as he led her off the dance floor towards the VIP lounge. Sliding his hand down, he palmed her ass as they walked. The man's arrogance would surely be his demise. After all her digging and pestering, he actually thought she wanted him.

A small smile crept across her lips. Well, it was all in her favor. She would use it and all his other conceited traits to bring him down, and she would bring him down. Hard. And anyone else that got in her way.

A scuffle at the rear of the club drew her attention. It was difficult to see between the strobing lights and the typical dim lighting inside the club. But she swore the focus of the scuffle looked like her captain being roughed up and escorted to the back by the bouncer who'd reminded her of a brick wall and a scowling Griff. Faye narrowed her eyes, trying to focus. Then the song ended and the lights went out, coming back on with the next song. When they did, the trio was gone. Her captain? Faye shook her head, nah, not him. Not here. Not possible.

She was contemplating bolting towards the exit when Griff reappeared, striding towards them and scowling at her when he saw where Millie's hand was resting. "Boss, we have a problem that needs your...uh...special attention."

Millie pulled her closer. “You can’t handle it yourself, kid?”

Griff stared Millie down. “No, boss, it needs your immediate attention.”

Millie turned to Faye and yanked her to him, kissing her thoroughly. Releasing her, he palmed her cheek. “Sorry, Detective, it appears there’s no play time for me this evening.”

She licked her lips. “Damn shame, Millie, I was so looking forward to a play date.” She shrugged. “Ah well, your loss.” She winked at him and walked away, deliberately not making eye contact with Griff.

Before she could make her escape she was grabbed. “I’ll be in touch, Detective. I’m having a get together at my estate and I’d love for you to be my guest.”

Faye mentally jumped and fist pumped, a slow wicked grin spreading across her face. “That sounds lovely, Millie. I look forward to hearing from you. And by the way, I do have a name. Detective is a little formal for us, isn’t it?” She blew him a kiss, then turned and went in search of the waitress who’d taken off with her jacket.

After her belongings had been returned to her, Faye headed to the ladies room. She was exiting the stall when she spotted Griff, arms folded as he leaned against the obviously locked door.

Glancing around, she realized they were alone and she remembered the last time they’d been alone in this room. Sighing, it seemed tonight was a night for memories, she thought.

“What’s the matter, Detective?” he growled.

Ignoring him, she walked to the sink to wash her hands. Her sole focus became drying her hands until she was suddenly all too aware of the enticing male and the rapidly shrinking lavatory. Faye stiffened as he approached her from behind and wrapped his arms around her waist. She stared at their reflection.

His gaze burned her to her very soul. Spinning her around, he kissed her, pouring all his anger, frustration and something she refused to label into that kiss.

She kissed him back, wrapping her arms around him and holding on for dear life.

But, before the kiss could escalate, she pushed herself away from his warmth and safety. *Safety?* Inwardly she scoffed. Pseudo-safety maybe. Pull yourself together, Kane.

He opened his mouth to speak his anger along with all the other damn inconvenient emotions building within him. But she shook her head and put her finger to his lips to shush the unspoken words she feared.

Faye kissed his cheek, walked around him and grabbed her things off the counter. Unlocking the door, she clutched her belongings as if they were a shield as she hastily made her way through the throng of people. Without a backward glance she continued walking until the cool evening air shook her from her reverie.

Confusion rolled over her, she was only mildly aware of how she'd wound up outside. The sudden change in temperature and noise had her blinking rapidly as she swept her thoughts into a neat little pile. She stared at the large black luxury car parked obnoxiously on the sidewalk on the other side of the velvet ropes. And, standing by the expensive obstruction, was Millie who produced a red rose from behind his back and handed it to her. Smiling, she thanked him, super sweetly, and slipped right back into the dangerous role she was playing.

He opened the door for her but she began to protest, saying she would call a cab. "Don't be silly, give me your keys and one of my men will drop off your car."

She mentally ran through the inventory of her car, wondering if there was anything in it that could potentially cause a problem. Considering Millie all ready knew she was a vice cop, she was safe.

Faye fished for her keys and grudgingly placed them in Millie's outstretched hand. "Thanks Millie, I appreciate your thoughtfulness."

His shark-toothed grin oozed slick charm and made her want to vomit all over his expensive Italian leather shoes. "See, Faye, I'm not the bad guy you think I am." He barked orders to the driver. As she slid into the leather seat and shut her eyes, the several drinks in too short a time plus the cool night air had her head swimming.

The limo started to pull away and then stopped abruptly, nearly unseating Faye from the buttery soft leather seat.

"Hey." She yelled to no one in particular.

The door opened and Griff leaned inside, pointing one finger at her, his other hand on the roof of the car. He growled. "Sugar, he's playin' with you now. But shit's about to get critical and he's going to get bored of your little game. Real. Fucking. Quick. He'll make you worse than dead, and personally I ain't that much into necrophilia."

Griff straightened and pounded the roof of the car, shutting the door on her glazed expression. He slammed his hands on his hips, cussing at the night sky, and really wishing he had someone to hit.

He stalked back inside the club just in time to see Dino making change for no one in particular and slipping the change into his pocket. A predatory smile crawled across Griff's face as he approached the bartender.

Dino turned and laid a lady killer smile on Griff. "Hey man, you scared..." WHOOMP!

Griff walked right up to the kid and used his muscled forearm and elbow to permanently kill his thousand watt smile. The kid hit the floor like a wet sack of shit. Blood spilled from Dino's mouth and nose as Griff placed a heavy boot in between the kid's shoulder blades, pinning him. He squatted down, reached his hand out and grabbed a fist full of the kid's hair. Yanking his head back, he pointed a finger in his face. "I see you with your fingers in the cookie jar again and I'm taking two of them, just because I fucking can." Griff released Dino's head by throwing it forward against the floor. It made a satisfying thunk as Griff walked away from the semi-conscious figure.

He stopped at the end of the bar and turned back to the kid. "Your shift's over for the night." Griff laughed as Dino crab walked away. He snapped his fingers to Carl, a barback with shaggy blonde hair and eyes that didn't miss a trick. "You're on and, I'm *watching* you."

Carl nodded and swallowed nervously as he eyed Griff. The man grabbed a bottle of Jameson, a tall glass and stalked to his usual table in the back of the club where no lights shone, but the whole club could be seen. Carl knew from experience the guy would place his heavy boots on the table, right foot crossed over left. But the drinking thing, that was new.

Carl went to work cleaning up blood and glass. "Man-oh-man. Between the two of 'em, Millie and Griff. Griff's not the one to be pissin' off, man. He's one scary fuck." Carl sang to himself as he continued to clean.

CHAPTER SIX

Griff untangled his ankles and let them drop heavily to the floor. He stood, palming the half drunk bottle of Jameson by the neck, and dragged it off the table.

Typically half a bottle of Jameson had no effect on Griff, but being this was the second bottle he was working on, the effects were going to be extra special. He snorted at his own joke; nobody understood him.

Staggering unsteadily to the back of the club to Millie's office, he banged his way inside. "Gimme 'er keys."

The room's occupants, who seemed to be in the middle of a quiet, yet heated argument, looked at the intruder simultaneously. Three pairs of eyes took in the disheveled, weaving form Griff presented. Only Millie reacted. Standing to his full height, he straightened his suit coat.

"You're drunk? Great. Get the fuck home and sleep it off." Millie depressed a button on his phone and spoke to the room, "My office. Two seconds."

Griff swung his head around and glared at the man in the chair. His eyes flickered to the door as Carl came bounding in out of breath. "Yeah boss?"

Millie tossed Faye's car keys at the kid and pointed at Griff. "Take him home first and then take Ms. Kane's car back. Have Dino follow you."

Carl shook his head and swallowed hard, no one contradicted Millie's orders but he didn't know about Dino. "Dino's out for the rest of the night. He had an," he raked his hand through his hair and glanced at Griff for assistance that came in the form of a shrug and a smirk, "accident."

"Accident? What the...Griff? Wanna tell me what misfortune Dino found?"

Lifting his two hands and twisting them, Jameson bottle still in one of them, Griff grinned maliciously. "Two hits, me hitting him. Twice. Ha."

Millie scrubbed his hand down his face, sighing and growling, "Fine. Fine. Carl, have Sherman follow you. Come straight back to my office and we'll discuss Dino's shift change."

Carl nodded and held the door open for Griff.

Griff snorted at the three suits in the room and, as he passed the man in the chair, he bent down and sneered directly into his face, "Your ass is mine." He pushed himself up and gave a salute to Millie. He then dropped his hand on the man's shoulder and with a bit of force, knocked the chair over with the man in it.

Millie yelled to Carl, "Get him the fuck out. Now!"

Carl jumped and reached his hand out to grab at Griff.

Though drunk, Griff was still able to level a gaze at the younger male that made him think twice about even breathing in his direction.

Carl dropped his hand awkwardly and cleared his throat. "Ah Griff, m-maybe we should go?"

Griff brushed by him and staggered through the bar to the parking lot. He made his way straight to Faye's car, Carl jogging after him.

"How'd you know this was the right one, man?"

Griff smirked. “Just call me Oz, the great and powerful. Don’t look too close behind that curtain though, kid, you might not like what you find.”

Confused at his cryptic response, Carl closed his gaping mouth, slid behind the wheel and pulled the classic Mustang out into traffic.

The whole ride to his apartment was filled with silence. Carl started to annoy him with all his ‘oooh’s’ and ‘aaah’s’ over what a sweet ride the ’67 Mustang was and how he wondered if the chick who owned it wanted to sell it and blah, blah, blah.

By the time Carl pulled into the driveway, Griff was ready for the silence of his apartment. He was so ready, in fact, that he didn’t even wait for him to slow down or come to a complete stop. He opened the door and jumped out as Carl was circling the apartment complex parking lot. “Thanks for the ride, lady.” Griff laughed, not many people would understand the reference and he doubted Carl would either.

Griff stumbled into his apartment, swaying as he entered his tiny living room. Tossing his keys, he didn’t even bother to look where they landed. He started to raise the bottle to his lips when he looked at his hand, empty. He spun. “What the...?” He slapped his forehead. He’d left the damn bottle in her car. Just his luck. She wouldn’t even appreciate his little gift.

Chuckling to himself, he staggered into his kitchen and ripped open the cabinets. There had to be... ah, there, behind a box of macaroni and cheese, in residence prior to his moving in; a dusty bottle of Jameson. “Score.”

He dragged the bottle down, knocking over the macaroni. He was momentarily transfixed as he watched the dried pasta spill, cascading down like a waterfall, “Cool.”

Popping the top on the ancient bottle, Griff took a long swig, staggered back into his living room, and paced the length. He couldn't for the life of him fathom what the hell had happened in the last few days. Things were on track, his life sane for the most part, and he had a clear objective. At least, until she showed up in that fucking bar, with that look in her eyes. And that body. Fuuuck, that body. Thank you, he had. A few times. And he was sure he would again several more times.

Another long draught of the liquid that no longer burned, and Griff raked a hand through his hair. More thoughts of her body wrapped around his, her phantom taste on his tongue, vivid memories of her sighs and screams flooded his consciousness. He paced faster.

The vibrating sound of his cell phone put a quick pause on his ruminations. Scowling at the number, Griff hit the answer button. "What? Yeah...Yeah. Did I not just say 'Yeah' twice? What the fuck? Meet? When? No, I said *no*. Probably because I'm hammered, that's why. Tomorrow?" Griff scrubbed a hand down his face. "If I have to, then yeah, but you're buying breakfast; the greasier the better." He hit the end button, staring at his phone before he threw it at the wall.

Griff continued to pace his living room, this time kicking over the shitty coffee table, he threw the lamp in the same direction as his cell, growling with the follow through. All of this was done with an eerie sense of calm. No screaming for the king of control, just deliberate destruction.

Griff yanked his hand back as a shard of glass from the lamp ricocheted off the wall and impaled itself in his forearm. "Fucker." Blood blossomed from the gash so rapidly, he ripped his shirt off and covered the wound to stem the flow. He stalked to his bathroom, turned the cold water spigot to on, and waited for the brown liquid to turn clear before he could rinse his arm. Tossing the ruined shirt and the glass shard in the trash, he chastised himself, "Fuck, Griff, get a grip." Leaning on the sink, he continued to speak to his reflection. "Griff, Griff, Griff, Griff." He smiled grimly. "Time for you to get your head out of your ass, my man. That god damn blonde tornado's fucking your head up."

Standing slowly, he tilted his head to the side, regarding his reflection with a cold sneer. His eyes slid to the tattoo on his left shoulder and bicep. The tribal art mixed with the barbed wired was his own design. Only he knew what the swirls and dips conveyed; he was the only one who needed that info, that shit was personal. He blinked away the memories trying to push through his drunken haze. With a shake of his head, he pushed them back. Calmly, almost methodically, he hauled his fist back and punched the mirror, staring at his now broken, cracked reflection. "Remember who you are." Not caring for what stared back at him, he pulled the ruined mirror off the wall and heaved it over his head out the door, watching it bounce off the hallway wall, the glass from the mirror shattering even more and sending deadly pieces of shrapnel everywhere.

Griff walked out of his bathroom, noting how the shards of glass made a satisfying crunching sound under his boots as he stalked back into his living room, hand leaving a blood trail. During his quietly destructive storm, he'd forgotten all about the injury to his arm, barely registering the dull throb. When he entered his living room, he swiped a hand down his face, taking in the drab little living space.

With a feral growl, Griff started dismantling the place. Anything hanging on the walls, sitting on the floor, or remotely resembling furniture ended in a heap in the middle of the room, looking a bit Pollockesque with the blood smears on everything.

Griff knocked his bottle of Jameson off the end table; it started bleeding its contents on the floor where the couch once sat. He made it just in time to give the poor thing mouth to mouth. As he tipped his head back he lost his balance and fell over, the bottle skidding across the room and coming to rest in an area unseen in his current state of semi-consciousness.

"Fuck it," he muttered and closed his eyes. His last thought before he passed out, "Wouldn't Dilly get a kick out of this mess; even the king of control had a breaking point."

***

Faye practically skipped into the office humming, "Walking on Sunshine," she laughed at herself. She really hated that song. She should have been hungover, but when she got up this morning she felt refreshed and well rested. The bullpen was nearly empty, save for Lister and Barnett who were locking and loading just as she was entering. "Anything fun?"

Lister shook his head on the way out. "Not sharing. This one's ours, Kane. By the way..."

Before he could finish, the captain poked his head out of his office. "Kane, glad you could join us today. My office. Now."

Faye blanched at the captain's gruffness. As she walked passed her desk, she dropped a twenty inside the swear jar. She just had a feeling. "Gonna need to stop at the ATM at this rate," she muttered as she stepped into Cap's office. She straightened her shoulders, steeled her backbone, and started to say something smart, until she saw the other man in the room.

Michael Dieter, Director of Internal Affairs stood and held his hand out to Faye. "Detective Kane, a pleasure as always. Nice to see you've dressed up today."

Faye felt her cheeks flush at his comment, ignored his outstretched hand and whipped her head around to Captain Jensen. "What the hell is he doing here?"

"Ladylike as always, I see." Another biting retort from Michael had her clenching her fists at her sides.

"Kane, Dieter, enough. I know you two had a bit of a falling out but this isn't personal, it's business." The captain waved his hand in Michael's direction, "Proceed."

Michael sat back down with a self satisfied smile and motioned for Faye to do the same. Lacing his hands together, he steepled his index fingers and rubbed his chin against them before speaking. "Word on the street, Detective Kane, is that you're getting quite cozy with the Maliano family. Do you have anything to say?"

Faye leaned toward Michael and hissed, "Who's the cocksucking snitch?"

Michael smiled congenially. "That's not your concern. And, am I to take that as confirmation of your involvement with one or more members of the Maliano family, Detective Kane?"

Faye slammed herself against the back of the chair, "Captain?" But the captain merely shook his head and Faye dropped her hands into her lap, sighing. "I've been running an investigation on my own time. Everyone knows Maliano's dirty, Mike, we just need proof and I can get it. He likes me, damn it." She stood quickly, kicking the chair in the tiny office, the back of it stuck in the drywall.

"Detective, I'll ask you one time to control yourself," Captain Jensen bellowed.

Michael raised his hand at the captain, shaking his head. "Captain Jensen, I can handle this. I've been front row, center to these little temper tantrums on numerous occasions. She'll calm herself, we just have to wait her out."

"Fuck you." She spat at Michael. Temper tantrums my ass, she thought, as she glared at him. Not once had she lost her temper with him. If anything, she tamped down her emotions for his benefit. Everything was always for his benefit.

"Effective immediately, Detective Kane, you are on unpaid leave pending further investigation into your involvement with the Maliano family. Please turn in your service revolver and badge." Michael stood and gave her a superior smile.

Faye put her hand on the butt of her gun, images of drawing and blowing Michael's brains out danced like sugar plums in her head. Instead, she slammed the gun on the captain's desk, took her shield from around her neck, and placed it next to her gun. Furious, she looked at the captain. "This is bullshit, we both know that."

***

Faye kicked in the door to the common use locker room and did some pacing and attempted some deep breathing exercises. But, as she was already near hyperventilating, the deep breathing only served to make her dizzy. Ready to burst, she went to her locker and grabbed the handle. Barely audible, she heard the pneumatic door whisper closed on a soft snick and froze.

"Same old Faye. Dirty mouth, hot temper, hard edges." She whipped around to glare at Michael.

"You won. You've wanted me out of the game for awhile, you come to gloat?"

He shook his head, wiping the corners of his mouth with finger and thumb. "Just doing my job, baby doll."

“Don’t. You lost the right to call me that the second the head of your dick entered my best friend.”

“Mouth or cu...” His words were cut off as he ducked to avoid a flying projectile whizzing by his ear or risk having a goose egg sprout on his forehead.

Faye was breathing heavily, a look of loathing on her face. “And you call my mouth dirty? Damn it, Michael, that was my favorite perfume, too.” She walked up to him, crossed her arms over her chest and tilted her head. “Why, Michael? Tell me why her? Why Kat?”

“That’s a lot of why’s bab...uh...Faye. Because she let me? Sounds lame, but you two were, are polar opposites. You’re tough, hard edges; always in control, always buttoned up, until you blow your top, like today for example. And damn, you have a body to end all bodies, not that you even realize it. Smoking hot, hotter than Kat’s even. But you never let anyone see that part of you. Again, until today. What’s with the get up?”

Faye looked down at herself. She hadn’t deviated much from her typical style. Still jeans, but skinny jeans that hugged every curve, knee high black boots with enough of a heel to make her ass stick out. The shirt she chose was a simple black button up, though this one was tailored at the waist and the last button at the top was low enough to reveal a hint of cleavage and a skosh of the swell of breast, thanks to the gravity defying lingerie underneath.

She shrugged. “I don’t see anything different. What are you talking about?”

Michael shook his head. “Kat is Steampunk meets Bohemian on the outside and feminine and sexy inside and out. That’s why. She exudes femininity and you, well, you exude shell casings.

She blanched and, to cover it up, slapped him across the face. “We’re done here.”

Michael smiled, rubbed the side of his face and nodded as he pulled out his cell phone. “Yeah, done.”

***

The captain had just hung up his phone as Michael exited the locker room, cell phone in hand. Captain Jensen narrowed his eyes, watching as Michael pushed his way outside into the bright sunlight. “Wonder what he’s up to,” he muttered to himself.

Before the captain could ponder that for too long, his phone rang and all thoughts of Michael and Faye were forgotten.

***

Millie sat at his desk, nodding into the phone. “Thanks for the update. There’ll be a bonus in this week’s take. Good man.” He placed the handset on the cradle with a slow grin.

***

No tears for Faye as she pulled into her spot at her apartment. She was thankful to whoever drove her car the previous night, they hadn’t changed her seat, mirror, or radio stations. She was a bit annoyed at the half drunk bottle of Jameson rolling around, though.

Damn Griff.

No tears as she entered her apartment either; carrying her small box of possessions from the precinct, including her swear jar. Exasperation quickly pushed aside all other thoughts or feelings. “How’d I know you’d be here?”

Griff sat in an overstuffed chair, ankle crossed over knee, bandaged hand and arm resting on his boot. "You must have ESPN2 or is it The Ocho?"

Faye worked the key out of her door, blowing out a breath as she kicked it closed behind her. "You could've at least made coffee. What happened to your hand?"

Griff looked at his bandages. "Cut it shaving. Sorry baby, I didn't expect you home so early. I was busy with the kids and housework while you were at work. How was your day, honey? Care for a martini?"

"Shut up. Really not in the mood for you or your sarcasm, just go." She set the box on the kitchen counter facing the living room, leaned on the counter and hung her head, suddenly very tired.

Large warm hands settled on her shoulders and rough whiskered lips kissed a spot behind her ear. "Hey seriously, why are you home so early?"

She snorted. "Suspended until further notice, because of you and your boss. Thanks."

"Shit, Sugar, I'm...that sucks."

"Yeah, doesn't it though. Oh, and..." For some reason she almost let it all out, that Michael was the one who suspended her. And what was that crack? Not feminine? Did that mean she wasn't a woman to him? She continued to let her head hang and shook it slowly. "Didn't I ask you to leave?"

"What were you going to say, Sugar?"

"Nothing. Now go." She pointed towards the front door but Griff grabbed her arm and spun her around to face him.

He lifted her chin and gave her a look she was learning to recognize. "Last chance. What were you going to say?"

"Last what? Griff come on, just leave. I want to be alone." She couldn't deal with him today. As disgusted as she should have been that he was in her apartment, especially after the way they'd parted company last night, she couldn't pull up the level of ire his breaking and entering into a cop...into her apartment should warrant. Clearly no amount of attraction was going to bridge the gap between their enormous moral differences. Badge or no badge, she had a job to do. He was in her way. She would have to go around him. Or through him. Why did the idea of that rub her wrong? How in the hell had a one night stand gotten so out of control so damn quickly?

Griff leaned down and kissed the tip of her nose. "I was so hoping you'd say that." Laughing, he grabbed one of her wrists.

Snick. Snick.

"Griff!"

He grabbed her by the hips and backed her up against the counter in front of the coffee pot. Taking the chain holding the bracelets together, he pulled her arms above her head, and hooked it on the cupboard door handle. He stepped back and nodded. "Perfect. What were you going to say?"

"You're an asshole. Let me go!"

He raised his eyebrows. "I'll let you go, if you tell me your nipples are hard because you're cold and *not* because you want my teeth clamped down on them. Hmm, speaking of clamps, got any clothes pins?" He laughed at her slight intake of breath, then continued. "I'll let you go," Griff slid his hand between her legs, driving the seam of her jeans against her core, "if you tell me the reason the crotch of your pants is soaked because you sat in something instead of all that sweet juice leaking out, begging for me to lap it up. I'll let you go, if you tell me that the thought of being strapped down and completely at my mercy while I fuck you nine ways from Sunday, bringing you to the edge of coming over and over, not granting you permission until I know that the force of your orgasm will leave you unconscious." Griff stopped and took a breath. He hung his head and gave it a shake. The imagery made him lose focus. Slowly, he raised his head and looked at her, what she saw there had her trying to take a step back. Griff took her chin in his hand. "I won't hurt you, Sugar, but I will make you see stars. Tell me I'm wrong, and I'll let you go."

Faye swallowed hard, suddenly all the moisture in her mouth was gone and she couldn't seem to quit blinking. Her head spun from the possibilities. Wasn't she already at his mercy? She shook her head slowly, chewing her bottom lip thoughtfully, then whispered, "Griff...let me go."

Griff dropped to his knees in front of her, gripped her thighs, and put his face in the apex of her jean covered sex. "Your pants are soaked and you smell...amazingly edible. How about my teeth clamped down on your clit? Would that make you talk, or scream?" He stood slowly and caressed her ass, moving his hands up to her chest and thumbed her breasts through the combined fabric of her bra and shirt. "Nipples hard as diamonds. Your skin is warm and flushed. Have I said, I love being right? Because I do. This outfit is so sexy. I hope you have more shirts like this, I'm afraid this one is ruined." Grabbing each side of her shirt, he ripped it open, buttons pinging everywhere in the kitchen and living room. He groaned at the white and pink lacy bra barely containing her large breasts. Griff dipped his head and bit the small rosy protrusion through the material. "Sugar, my dick just jumped to attention. This is gorgeous and sexy as hell."

Faye sighed and yelped as his teeth bit down on her nipple. She was having a hard time reconciling his words with what

Michael had just said to her; 'not feminine, you exude shell casings.'

"Griff," she whispered painfully, "you don't have to say that. I know I'm not...sexy."

Abruptly, he stood to his full height and took a step back. "Who told you that?"

"It doesn't matter. You don't have to pretend anymore. I'm in with Millie, I'm going to the party. You've done your job. Well. Trust me, we're good. Now, let me go." Her tone was almost a plea, almost.

He took half a step back and crossed his arms over his chest, staring at her, trying to discern if she was fishing for a compliment or if she was serious. Shit, she was serious; someone had really done a number on her head.

Turning away from her, he grabbed the kitchen shears from the butcher block. Spinning the tool on his fingers, he approached her. He placed the point of the scissors at her throat and pressed in just slightly. "Trust me."

Faye nodded quickly, even though every instinct inside her should have told her to scream and kick and try to get away from the psycho wielding scissors. Instead, her instincts were screaming for more, more, more.

The scissors glided down her sternum, opening them slightly, and fitting them beneath the little bow on the front of her bra.

Snip.

The flimsy material flew apart and Faye's breasts spilled out, bouncing slightly from being released so abruptly. The scissors went to work again, with Griff's assistance. This time, on the black silk shirt. "I like silk on you. Don't worry,

I'll replace everything I ruin." The blades of the shears made quick work of the shirt, sliding easily through each sleeve and down to the neck.

Griff knelt before her and removed each of her boots, then slid the shears beneath the tight denim hem and cut slowly, carefully, up her shapely leg. Kissing the outward swell of her hip, then giving her freed ass cheek a light smack, he dragged the shears across her waist and to the other side of her ruined jeans. With much less work than exerted on the first side, the denim fell away easily.

She was completely naked, vulnerable, and at his mercy in her kitchen. He nodded. "Yeah, I like that shit." Griff tilted his head, looking at her, then shook his finger. "Nah, something's missing." He turned on his heel and left her alone as he went on the hunt. It wasn't long before she heard his victorious cry of "Success" and his footfalls grew louder as he returned to the kitchen, grinning lasciviously.

Faye laughed and shook her head as he held up the pink stilettos she'd worn the previous evening.

Griff knelt before her again, gingerly placing each foot in the shoes. Straightening, he took a step back and nodded. "Perfect."

Faye smiled broadly. "I'd say." Aided by the extra inches of height, with a wiggle and a scoot she was able to lift the chain off the cupboard handle. "I'm free."

"Damn," Griff laughed at his miscalculation. Still chuckling, he turned away from her again and headed for the living room as she yelled, "A key would be nice. Griff?"

He stood in the middle of the living room as she approached, hands hanging awkwardly in front of her. That was, until she waved her hands in front of his face. "Earth to Griff. You've had your fun, now let me go."

"Oh, I haven't even started having fun yet." He grabbed the chain and pulled her to the wall, attaching the cuffs to the planter hook about three inches from dead center between the couch and television. Just out of reach even for her long legs.

She growled and stomped her foot. "Griff."

He put his hands on his hips and hung his head. "You ready to tell me what you were going to say a few minutes ago?"

"It was nothing; certainly nothing for you to concern yourself with. Now please, let me go."

"You've said that a few times, but what I haven't heard is your safe word. Remember it? Say it any time, and we're done here." His voice dropped lower, there was that look again. "Do you want to say it?"

Faye's eyes grew wide in panic, and for some reason, she couldn't begin to fathom she shook her head no.

Griff nodded and went back to the kitchen, rummaging noisily in her utility drawer. Returning, slapping the flat of a wooden spoon into the palm of his hand. "From this point forward, speak only when spoken to. You will refer to me as Sir and your safe word is...say it for me, Sugar."

Faye swallowed hard and whispered, "R-red."

Griff walked around her, tucking the handle of the spoon beneath his arm, and, reaching in his back pocket, he pulled out a pair of black leather driving gloves. As soon as he pulled each of them on and balled his hands into fists, getting the feel of the material, he moved to her side and...

Smack. Smack. Smack.

Faye yelped at the three rapid smacks to her ass, then let the sharp sting wash through her system, settling into a slow burn further south.

Griff gripped her hair and yanked her head back. "What were you going to say, Sugar?"

She shook her head, fighting back the urge to speak and the prick of tears threatening to spill.

Smack. Smack. Smack.

Faye continued to shake her head, even as the burn on her ass caused a flooding from her loins and her nipples to stand to such stiff peaks they were painful.

Griff shook his head and moved around to her front. Her head was hanging, chest heaving, and a fine sheen of sweat had formed all over her body. Griff lifted her chin with one hand as he slid the spoon through her wet folds with the other.

Faye barely registered his leather clad hand as he caressed her face. Her legs nearly buckled and a quiet groan escaped at the feel of the spoon on her swollen and sensitive flesh. Her eyes flew open as the now former kitchen utensil was removed, and she watched Griff lick the spoon.

He laughed at the shocked expression on her face, then quite swiftly, and without malice, he landed a hard smack to her folds.

Faye's head fell back as she screamed, the intensity of the feeling of the wooden spoon slapping against her core and feminine lips had her knees buckling and she heard herself beg, "More. Please."

Griff smirked and nodded, whispering in her ear, "Your wish..."

Smack. Smack. Smack.

Faye was biting her bottom lip so hard she thought for sure her teeth would slice right through it. One more hard smack and she knew she'd be flying off into the orgasmic stratosphere, and she tensed for it. Ready for her knees to give and her sight to go black. She waited, and waited. Lifting her head, Faye looked right into Griff's green eyes, alight with passion and something else.

Griff merely smirked and shook his head. "No coming. Not until I say." He crossed his arms, the flat of the spoon poking above his bicep, her eyes watching it as he paced. He saw, and smiled wide as he pulled the spoon free. "You want this?" He watched her eyes go wide and she nodded quickly. "You really want this? Tell me what you were going to say." Her head worked from side to side and Griff's eyes narrowed. "You *don't* want this?" Slipping the flat of the spoon through her folds, he heard her gasp and gave her pussy another flick with the spoon; not hard, but enough to get her attention. Another little slap and her knees gave out and her breathing picked up. One last smack had her begging for more, again. "Tell me what you were going to say, or I stop."

He saw panic flare in her eyes. "No. No you can't."

He smiled. "I can, Sugar, and I just might say your safe word for you...Red."

"No! Un-red! Don't! I'm not feminine! He said...he said, I'm not feminine." She trailed off at the end as tears slid out the corner of her eyes.

Griff focused entirely on her and slowly lowered his arms to his sides. "What?" She shook her head and sobbed.

"Please don't make me say it again."

Griff cupped her face and searched her eyes. "Hey, it's okay. I'm still here. Tell me what happened."

Through sobs and hiccoughs, Faye recounted her exchange with Michael from earlier in the day.

"Sonofabitch. I'm going to ..." He didn't finish his thought out loud. He needed to finish *her* though. It was more important than ever. "Okay, Sugar, okay. Sh-sh-sh. I'm here...I'm right here." Grabbing the spoon out of his back pocket, he began running it over her folds and swollen little nub.

The feel of the rough wooden instrument against her silky flesh had her senses on overload. Her legs trembled and she jerked on the cuffs. "S-sir, p-please...I need to...mmmmm..."

Griff stroked her back and squeezed her ass cheeks. "Sh-sh-sh...I know what you need."

Smack. Smack. Smack.

On the last smack, Griff commanded, "Come now, Sugar."

It was a good thing Griff had tightened his hold on her as Faye's body flew apart. She fell into him as she threw her head back and her knees buckled. Her loud keening wail filled the apartment, the fleeting thought of her neighbors hearing ran through her consciousness, but was soon swept away by the tidal wave of pleasure that threatened to drown her.

But Griff was the only one to see her tears and hear her sobs. With one hand he reached up and untangled the chain from the plant hook, picking Faye up by the crook of her knees. Her head flopped on his shoulder, eyes half-closed. Griff sat on the couch with her on his lap, reaching behind him and grabbed the afghan to cover her naked, trembling body. He would be sure to have a private conversation with

Michael Dieter, and soon. Not feminine. Who the fuck was he to destroy this woman's self image? Cocksucker.

***

Across the street from Faye's apartment, a nondescript man sat in a nondescript car talking into a prepaid cell phone. "Sure is. Been here for a few hours now. And from them sounds been coming from in there, man he be doin' somfin' right, if ya' know what I mean, man. Yes, suh. Yes, suh. Thank ya, suh." After the man hung up he made a squelching noise with his lips. He really hated that fake ass dialect. Ready to wipe away the aftertaste lingering from the offensive verbiage, he lit a smoke and settled in for a long day of snooping.

***

As Griff sat holding Faye in his arms he leaned his head back, thinking this was a much better way to spend the day than how the morning originally started.

Griff had woken up with a pulsing ringing in his head and a sandpaper tongue. As he lifted his head he realized the pulsing and ringing weren't coming from his head, but from somewhere else in the living room.

Shit.

Opening his eyes, he took in the disaster area that had staked its claim on his apartment, the result of his drunken decorating from the night before.

The pulsing and ringing continued, annoying him as he stood awkwardly and staggered around the room. Griff noted the noise grew louder as he approached a cell phone sized hole in the drywall. Shrugging, he reached his hand into the hole and dug around until his hand touched a hard object, a hard vibrating object.

Pulling his arm out, he looked at the phone, miraculously still in one piece. Griff pulled a face. "Good phone." Then scowled as he looked at the number. Too early to be dealing with Millie and his paranoia, Griff thought. Besides, he had a much needed free breakfast waiting for him at The Junction Diner. He made the obvious choice.

After a quick shower and a change of clothes, Griff only felt mildly hungover but knew after a large plate of Hangover Helper from The Junction, he'd feel like a new man.

The tinkling of the tiny bell on the door of the diner had the half dozen customers stopping mid-bite and looking to see who would be joining their morning coffee clutch. The patrons, in unison it seemed to Griff, wrinkled their noses at the sight of him and turned back to their coffees and plates of eggs and toast.

Griff saw Dilly before he even stepped inside the restaurant. Shit, anyone with 20/1000 vision could see Dilly; the man stood out. Even Griff, who was very secure in his sexuality, could admit the guy was good looking.

Dilly, Jon Dillinger, no relation, smiled at Griff over the rim of his coffee cup. "Bout time, man." Dilly flashed him a perfect smile, his long, black hair hanging over one shoulder. Dilly was more than half Native American, though if you asked him, his mother, or father, none would or could agree on the exact percentage.

Griff grumbled something back that Dilly supposed was a good morning with a few expletives thrown in, and he threw his head back and roared out a laugh. Shaking his head, Dilly grinned as Griff ordered the Hangover Helper from the pretty little waitress, Vanessa, according to her name tag.

Vanessa hustled over with a pot of coffee and turned Griff's cup over for him, but he grabbed the pot from her. Looking at the pot now in his hand, he actually contemplated drinking directly from it. "How bout' you just get me a straw or, even better, an IV?

Vanessa blushed and bit her lip. "Ummm. sir...M-Mister? That's not allowed. The owner will get really mad."

Flipping his hand to dismiss her and the owner's would-be anger, he stubbornly shifted his grip. "This stays here." He poured the coffee into his cup, sloshing it everywhere, then guzzled it down, not coming up for air until the cup was empty. Griff raised his eyebrows at her as he was pouring another cup, downing that one too, and ignoring the 2nd degree burns to his mouth from the scalding liquid. He started coughing and wiped his mouth with the sleeve of his shirt.

"Baby girl, I'll pay for the carafe. You don't want me to not have this much coffee. Trust me."

After she wrote down both their orders, Vanessa sighed nervously and walked away, wringing her hands. Dilly roared with laughter at the girl's agitation caused by his obviously hung over friend, "Jameson got you down again, man?" He took a long sip of coffee from his own cup. "Okay, so you know you're playin' with fire, right? I mean, vice and Millie? And which are you, the bucket of water to douse the flames or the accelerant?"

Vanessa returned with a giant platter of something vaguely resembling food and set it in front of Griff, then set down Dilly's much smaller plate of poached eggs, whole wheat toast, and turkey bacon. Dilly wrinkled his nose as Griff stirred his Hangover Helper into one unrecognizable plate of slop.

"Man, that looks like an autopsy gone wrong."

"Shut up." Griff was in the middle of shaking half the bottle of hot sauce over his plate of Hangover Helper and stared at Dilly. Slowly, he set the bottle on the table, folded his hands together, and hung his head. "I got it handled. The party's a go and some pretty heavy hitters are on the guest list. The game's afoot, as Sherlock would say, so get your panties out of a twist."

"Don't wear 'em," Dilly laughed.

Griff grimaced. "Thanks for the visual. You know, I've been thinking," Griff forked some of the autopsied breakfast and halted, utensil poised, "You should be the one working for Millie."

Dilly tipped his head and knitted his brow. "How's that?"

Griff smiled slowly in triumph and started singing, "Dilly and Millie sitting in a tree..."

Dilly roared with laughter. "You're an asshole."

Both males finished their breakfasts in silence with lingering stares from waitresses and male and female patrons alike and about a thousand refills of coffee apiece. Griff was on his third carafe of coffee, all the empties lined up on the table. He assumed the poor waitress was afraid to take them. Who could blame her?

Dilly downed the last sip of coffee, slid out of the booth and threw some bills on the table. Griff looked up just as the sunlight hit the other man's eyes, the brown color turning to a mirage of reds and golds. Dilly leaned over the table on his fists. "You're playing with fire, Griff. Know when to dial 911, got it?"

Griff nodded. "Got it." Griff turned in his seat as he watched his friend leave the diner and burst out laughing as Dilly bumped into Vanessa on purpose. As she was leaned over a table writing an order, he rubbed his substantial male anatomy across her ass.

***

Back to the present, on the couch, still holding Faye, Griff sighed and kissed her temple, his brain screaming 9-1-1.

CHAPTER SEVEN

Faye slowly came awake. Dusk was falling all around her living room, and a slow smile settled across her face as she realized she was still cradled in Griff's lap. She wondered how in the hell she could smile when most of the events of the day had gone to shit, quickly.

Listening to Griff's even breathing, his heart beating like a song against her cheek, she replayed her clash with Michael. Disappointment filled her mind that her captain did not or would not back her up. But even through the haze of anger and frustration, she found a ray of sunshine.

Michael was wrong and Griff proved that to her today, and every time they'd been together.

Somehow Griff knew exactly what she needed even if she didn't have a clue. Every encounter she'd had with this male had taught her a little more about herself. Letting him take control, even sexually was hard for her, but in so doing she'd discovered another part of herself and she felt free, at peace. Faye would never look at her cuffs the same again. She'd always joked about playing with them like that but it was just that, a joke. The mere thought of what they'd done with them made her shiver.

Before Griff, she never would have figured she could play that rough, or would want to play like that and enjoy it. She blushed and had a mild case of self-consciousness as she remembered the tears, sobs, and begging. Yet Griff seemed to understand and made no judgment against her. Looking up at him she smiled. Who'd have thought? She traced a finger down his arms and around the seam of the gloves he still wore. Where in the hell did these come from? She made a mental note to ask him.

As her eyes slid from the gloves to his face and then to the red marks on her wrists, caused by the cuffs, her thoughts suddenly turned to the moment when she had to hand in her gun and badge; it made her heart ache. Trying not to dwell on the fact that she was suspended and the task that still lay ahead of her, she wiggled free from Griff's embrace, careful not to wake him.

Thinking as she padded naked to the bathroom, suspended or not, she was attending that party and she would do whatever it took to bring Millie down. His organization would not survive when she was through with him.

She looked in the mirror and saw her eyes were still puffy from the meltdown. Shaking her head, she splashed water on her face and took a deeper look in the mirror. Her hair was wild and her eyes, though swollen, still looked wanton. She tried to primp herself a little but her curls had no intentions of being tamed.

After her failed attempts at primping, she decided she'd try her hand at her bedroom. Lighting candles to make her room look soft and romantic, she headed back to the living room quietly to see Griff still sleeping. She stopped abruptly and stared at the sight of her ruined and discarded clothes on the kitchen floor. Smiling and chuckling to herself, shook her head as she stepped over them and grabbed 2 beers from the fridge.

Grabbing her iPod off of the counter, she took it and the beers back to her room. Faye popped her music on softly and stood back and surveyed her quick work. Perfect. Still naked, she headed back to Griff who was still out. Climbing back onto his lap she straddled him and leaned in, whispering his name. "Ian." Her fingers began gently tracing the part of the tattoo that showed below the sleeve of his t-shirt.

His eyes remained closed but his arms wrapped around her waist and he rested his hand on her bare ass.

She leaned back to look at him. He had the most gorgeous, lazy smile on his face. "Yeah, Sugar?"

Resting her hands on his chest, she laughed.

"What's so funny?"

"Well, the fact that I'm still bare ass naked and you are fully dressed, for one."

He finally opened his eyes and looked at Faye, melting her a little more. "Would you care to remedy that, Sugar?"

Biting her lip, suddenly nervous, she nodded. "Can I ask you a question?"

He nodded and smirked. "You just did." He laughed as she smacked him in the chest.

"Where in the hell did the gloves come from?"

Griff lifted his hands and looked at them as if seeing them for the first time. "It's like the Boy Scouts say: Always be prepared."

Faye giggled. Jesus, she wished she'd knock that shit off. Her smile fell and she grew solemn for a moment. She chewed her lip, steeling herself for her next question. "Uh, Ian, can you...would you stay tonight? I..."

In one quick movement he leaned forward and stood up, holding her tightly; one arm around her waist and the other one on her ass, Faye's arms slipped around his neck. He strode quickly to her bedroom and stopped short, taking in the scene Faye had prepared for him. He was blown away. She was an enigma. One big, he chuckled as he adjusted her in his arms, not so big in stature, contradiction. She appeared to be all hard edges but, much like a kaleidoscope, at each turn and at every angle she was different and more beautiful.

Rocking back a bit on his heels he realized that in the short time he had known her she'd managed to wheedle her way right through his carefully constructed walls, smashing them like a battering ram. Faye was unyielding in her loyalty; her quest to make things right never ceased to amaze him. For her to ask him to stay, to try and make this special, brought him to his knees. He knew she was strictly black and white when it came to her cop instincts, and he lived in the world of gray.

His hold on her tightened and she scanned his face, looking for his reaction. He gazed at her through hooded eyes, sheer unadulterated lust emanating from them. A sly grin played across his lips as he leaned in and kissed her tenderly. With a moan, she slid down his body. Not breaking the seal of their soft kiss, Faye pulled at the hem of his shirt, lifting it from the waist of his jeans. He stepped back and looked down at her, t-shirt stretched out front, still fisted in her hands.

Pulling the shirt over his head, she tossed it across the room, splaying her hands on his chest. Sighing aloud, she turned her full attention to the sexy as sin tattoo. She again began to trace it softly, following the pattern over his left pec, slowly traveling down his left arm, ending at his elbow. Slipping behind him, her fingers continuing to follow the tribal pattern. It was stunning, the barbed wire entwined through it looked as if it could cut her. In the soft lighting of her room she felt like it was moving under her touch like a snake undulating through the grass. It continued up and around the back of his arm to his shoulder, ending on his left shoulder blade. She went up on her tippy toes and replaced her finger with her tongue, sliding it along the bone.

Griff stood stock still, the feel of her light touch on his ink was electric, then when he felt the addition of her warm wet tongue, he couldn't help but groan. He'd had the tat for so long that he was barely aware of it anymore, unless he was staring at himself in the mirror. But with her touch, it felt brand new, alive. Groaning again, he turned around and pulled her close. Her hands slipped down his chest and unbuttoned his jeans. He cursed and gripped her upper arms, kissing her again, more forcefully this time.

Suddenly she was frantic for him to be naked; it was as if he read her mind. Taking a step away from her, he yanked off his jeans, then ripped the gloves off and tossed them aside. She swallowed hard as his erection sprang free, very happy to see her. Looking up at him, she felt flushed, the music echoing in the room along with their breathing.

Smiling, she launched herself at him. He caught her as she wrapped her long legs around his waist. Griff growled in her ear, "Damn Faye, you surprise the hell out of me."

He walked them to her bed, her body still clutched tightly against his, and laid her down gently. Gazing up at him, she was unable to put into words what she wanted from him or her feelings, confused as they may be.

With the music softly playing and the candlelight flickering around them, he made love to her. All of their couplings up to this point had been wild and rough and kinky. For Griff to show her this tender side was almost too much. Too confusing. She tried closing her eyes and turning her head away to close off the emotions threatening to spill over, but Griff gripped her face, kissed her lips and spoke against her mouth. "Eyes open, Faye. Watch me. Watch me take you again and again to the edge of pleasure and thrust you over the edge. I'll catch you, I promise. I'll always catch you... always."

He made her feel so much, too much and with that one whispered command her body shattered for him, yet again. Body wrenching sobs and tears of passion spilled from her eyes, Griff held her tight to his body as he spilled his essence inside her.

After their bodies settled from the pleasure rush, he pulled her so she was facing him. Tucking a strand of her hair behind her ear, his hand lingering on her cheek. “Faye.” Covering his hand with hers, she smiled at him. His heart leaped and he grinned as he leaned over to kiss the tip of her nose. She had no fucking clue how beautiful she really was. She was like a beacon of light that shone so damn brightly in the black of night, his never ending night, and shit... all that and she carried a gun. The woman was a walking wet dream. His walking wet dream, and damn, he really liked that shit.

“Mmmm, beer.” Faye laughed and rolled over to grab the bottles she’d set on the nightstand. She waggled one bottle in his direction and he took it with a laugh.

Leaning on his elbow, he took a long pull from his bottle. Faye sat all the way up and pulled her legs under her, Indian style, blushing slightly. He continued to stare at her as he sipped his beer and she played with the label on her bottle, unsure of his continued scrutiny.

Faye placed her bottle back on the nightstand and started to move off the bed. Before she could blink, she was flipped over on to her back and gazing up at him.

He didn’t even spill the beer still in his hand. “Where’re you going?”

Blowing hair out of her eyes, she laughed. “I was going to grab us some food. Damn, Gr-Ian, I’m starving. Sex with you ought to be part of the department’s fitness requirement.” She laughed again.

He angled his beer to take a swig, then leaned down and took one of her nipples in his mouth.

She arched into him as the cold liquid surrounded her nipple. “Mmmm. Is that how the kids are drinking beer these days?”

He sucked hard before swallowing the liquid. “No kids here, but that’s how I’m doing it from now on.”

Pulling him close, she kissed him long and hard until her tummy rumbled in protest. She laughed into his mouth and pulled away, his face so close he was almost out of focus. “So, dinner? I promise to come right back.”

He put his beer next to hers and rolled them both over. Faye now on top, looked down at him. “Is that a yes?”

He winked at her. “Well, I guess you’ll need sustenance. I’m not done with you yet.”

Rolling her eyes, she climbed off him and picked up his t-shirt.

He sat up quickly and yanked it out of her hands. “No.”

Cocking her eyebrow at him, she watched him scoot off the bed and take her hand.

“Let’s make this quick I have plans for you.”

As her hand made contact with the gauze on his injured arm she nodded, giving him a quizzical look. “You going to tell me what happened?”

He lifted her hand and kissed the back of it, then pulled her body flush against his. “It’s not really a bedtime story. I’ll save it for another time, okay?”

The sincere look he gave her made her stomach clench. Nodding, she pulled him towards the kitchen, dropping the subject, for now.

Faye began rummaging around looking for food when she heard him swear. Turning around, she smirked as she saw the remains of her shredded bra dangling from his index finger. She suppressed a giggle. A giggle? What the hell had gotten into her lately?

"Damn. I'll replace this." He scrubbed a hand down his face, trying to hide his own grin. "I should be shot for ruining this; it's damn sexy as hell." He continued to gather up her ruined clothes and Faye watched him move around her kitchen like he belonged there. After he dropped the remnants in the trash, he stepped up behind her and wrapped his arms around her waist. "I was a bit overzealous. I'll replace it all, Faye."

Twisting around to face him, she took his face in her hands. "I'm not worried about it. Let's take the food and go back to bed." She thrust a plate with a couple of sandwiches at him. "I don't have much, so peanut butter and jelly will have to do." As they headed back to her bedroom, Faye stopped suddenly and went back to the fridge. "But, I do have my favorite dessert." Her head popped up from inside the fridge holding a tin with the last two pieces of chocolate truffle cheesecake. A wicked grin spread across her face as she spotted something else, tossing it at him.

He reached out and caught the projectile in mid-air. Looking at the can, he grinned evilly. "Oh, you're in for it now, I know the perfect use for this and exactly where I'll be lapping it up from."

She shivered and nearly tripped on the way back to her room as he continued to explain in pornographic detail what he planned to do with the whipped cream.

***

She was warm and cozy and content. She rolled over into the arms of a hard, warm male body and sighed as she felt him grow even harder. But before she could guide him to paradise in a sleepy haze, a noise so loud and earth shattering caused Faye to bolt out of bed and grab her gun from the nightstand drawer.

Ian moved almost as quickly and Faye couldn't help a sly smile as she thought, not too shabby for two people who'd had all of two hours of sleep. He was scrubbing the sleep from his eyes and looking for his pants, yawning. "What the fu..." As he struggled to get into his pants, a pounding on her door made him growl and look around at her, but all she could do was offer a naked shouldered shrug.

"Ms. Kane? Ms. Kane."

His gaze on her turned predatory and amused at the same time. "You'd better not answer the door naked and packing heat. Don't get me wrong, I'm loving the visual but that poor bastard might just keel over."

She returned his gaze and couldn't suppress her sigh. He was standing on the other side of her bed, hair tousled, in only his jeans, which were distractingly not fastened. She couldn't help but recall their love making all night and blushing at the number of condom wrappers in the garbage can. Maybe she should take stock in Trojan...or, she shuddered at the mere thought, make a doctor's appointment for some birth control. Faye remembered the mess they'd made with the whipped cream. How they'd changed the sheets, sort of, showered and fell back into bed at the crack of dawn. She should be dead on her feet, but she felt energized.

Dragging her gaze from Griff's distracting image, she found a pair of yoga pants and a t-shirt. She threw her hair in a ponytail and stalked to her front door. The banging had yet to cease. Thank God she put her gun back in her drawer, poor Mr. Crenshaw would have had a coronary.

She pulled the door open, but before she had a chance to say a word the old man blurted, "Ms. Kane, your car... exploded...it's...," he shook his head, "on fire...flames as high as the building..."

Faye's mouth dropped open. She stared dumbly at him, stunned and unable to process the man's words, like he was speaking a different language. She jumped as Ian came up behind her, wrapping a protective arm around her waist.

Mr. Crenshaw crinkled his brow at Ian and then back to Faye who had yet to recover from the devastating news.

Griff grimaced, trying to figure out how to introduce himself. Images of the meltdown in his apartment flitted through his head and he swallowed hard, and extended his hand. "McManus. What seems to be the trouble?"

The elderly man hesitated only briefly, shook the male's hand and stammered, "Ms. Kane, Mr. McManus, you better come quick."

Faye nodded, turning away from the door, and headed in the direction of her bedroom.

Ian watched her walk away then looked back at Mr. Crenshaw. "We'll be right out." Shutting the door on the man's pained expression, Ian followed her.

He leaned on the doorframe watching her struggle into her sneakers. She hung her head, refusing to look up at him. "Faye, baby, look at me." She ignored him and continued mechanically putting on her shoes.

Not pressing her, he moved inside the room and found his t-shirt, slipping it on. Scowling, he looked around the small room for his boots. "They're in the living room," she whispered as she walked passed him.

He followed her out of the bedroom and spotted his boots, huffing out a hollow laugh as he realized he'd toed them off while he was holding her. Yesterday afternoon, it seemed like a lifetime ago.

Faye brushed by him again and this time Ian gripped her by her bicep, spinning her around, his expression fierce, bouncing between anger and confusion. "No way, Faye. You're not shutting me out. Not after everything. Not. Happening."

Pulling from his grasp, she grabbed for the door. Head hanging, she turned her face slightly, letting out a cynical laugh as a lone tear slid down her cheek. "Who were we kidding? Reality is a bitch." Without another word she quietly exited her apartment, closing the door with a soft snick and headed to the parking lot.

The cloying smell of acrid petrol fumes and burning rubber permeated the air around her and the entire apartment building. Faye heard her apartment door slam and her skin tingled as she heard him let out a string of curses. The churning in her gut turned quickly into an ache that spread all the way to her heart. She couldn't let herself regret the last 24 hours; he'd shown her a piece of herself she never knew existed. Yet, she knew their paths were vastly different, and no amount of sexual attraction, hot, sweaty sex or...whatever was between she and Ian/Griff was going to change that fact.

Faye snorted, thinking, "Me cop. You not." The parking lot was mass chaos: fire trucks, cops, her neighbors. Everyone was everywhere.

Once she was beyond the whitewashed trellis archway at the end of her garden walk, she froze when she saw her beautiful car engulfed in flames. Inwardly she raged so fiercely she scared herself while outwardly she stood frozen, gawking at the twisted, burning chassis of her precious car.

Her paranoia was her neighbors' saving grace. Always afraid someone would nick or scratch her baby, she made it a point to park at the furthest side of the parking lot; no man's land. Street lamps were almost non-existent on that side but she didn't care, she was armed so she didn't worry about muggers or carjackers. Her baby was safe there. A hysterical titter escaped her lips as she looked around at all the Mustang debris that littered the ground. Another crazy laugh snuck out. Nicks or scrapes; shit, there was no more car to nick or scrape.

A voice penetrated her psychotic haze and she turned to see one of the uniforms, Sonny, approaching her, his face a mask of relief. "Damn, Kane. We were afraid...this was about the time you leave for work. They've been searching for a body."

Faye reined in her anger. It wasn't his fault she was suspended or any of the crap that'd happened to her in the last few days. Sonny'd always been a good friend and even better cop. Hell, she'd even introduced him to his wife. She huffed out a breath and looked him in the eye. "What have you got?"

He shook his head. "Not a whole hell of a lot. The neighbors remember seeing a red Camaro in the lot last night, but no one can recall the license plate or description of the driver. Your neighbor, Mr. Crenshaw, said the vehicle looked familiar to him but didn't know why. Another neighbor mentioned seeing a shifty, her words not mine, man lurking by the dumpster, scoping the place out."

She dug her nails into her palms. That damn Camaro was Michael's. What the hell was he doing here? And a shifty male... well didn't that have Millie written all over it? She was getting deeper and deeper into the snake pit and there was no ladder in sight.

"Listen, Sonny..." She heard her name being bellowed from across the parking lot. It sounded like someone was in pain. She and Sonny looked toward her burning car. The captain was circling the wreckage, looking green. Faye turned her back on Sonny and strode across the lot, unable to hide her inner bitch. "No such luck, Cap." His title snapped out like a mousetrap on a rodent's neck. She folded her arms under ample breasts and rocked back on the heels of her sneakers, glaring at him.

All the color drained from his face as he turned to her. "Shit, Kane, what in the name of all that's holy is going on?" He whispered, "I'm glad to see you in one piece, kid."

Saying nothing, she scanned the surroundings for anything shady when out of the corner of her eye she saw Griff talking. No, she shook her head, no it was more like controlled screaming. Arms waving, he pointed and shoved at one male who looked like he was fading into the background, much like a chameleon might, and another who, even from this distance, was male model material.

She chided herself at how quickly he reverted to Griff in her mind. He looked far from happy, murderous was more like it.

The captain followed her gaze. "What is he doing here?"

She whipped her head back around and countered his gaze with a steely one of her own. "None of your fucking business."

"Watch your mouth, Kane."

"Or what, Cap, you'll suspend me? Too. Fucking. Late." With that, she turned on her heels and walked away.

She was too angry to cry yet, she was numb. Turning her back to the destruction in the parking lot, she jogged back to her apartment. With great difficulty, she managed to dodge cops, firemen and neighbors, all wanting to talk to her and ask her the same damn question. What happened? She heard whispers as she bustled past them all; words like 'bomb' and phrases like 'triggered accidentally,' jangled her nerves.

Back in her apartment, she sat on the edge of her couch with her face in her hands, torso folded over her lap. She was so focused on breathing in through her nose and out her mouth to keep herself from shattering into atoms, she didn't notice the door opening and closing. A pair of dusty motorcycle boots came into view and she raised her gaze to see Griff staring down at her. "I thought you left."

He crouched in front of her. "Faye?"

She blinked the tears away. She'd cried enough, it was time to figure out what was going on and try to salvage her much loved career. "Griff, just go."

"It's back to Griff, is it?" He grabbed her harshly by the shoulders and pulled her to him, kissing her to make her remember everything they'd shared mere hours before. Then, just as harshly, he pushed her away and stood up, heading to the door. He looked over his shoulder. "Griff that, Sugar." As he ripped the door open and stalked outside, he knocked over a delivery man holding a giant bouquet of flowers. Griff caught the flowers as the kid fell back on his ass.

Faye rushed to the door as the kid struggled to a standing position, explaining they were a special delivery from Martino Maliano.

Griff thrust the bouquet at her and muttered something unintelligible under his breath as he stormed down her sidewalk.

She threw the flowers to the ground and ran after Griff, coming to a halt at the end of the walk. At the same spot where she watched her car burn from beneath the arched trellis. She slipped to the side and poked her head around the corner as she watched Griff shake hands and do the manly "bump and barely hug" with the male model and made what looked to her to be an apologetic gesture to the great disappearing man. What was it with that guy? He looked like a mirage. She chewed her lip as she watched the troika drive off in a car whose license plates were obscured, intentionally making them unreadable.

When she got back to her apartment, Sonny was waiting for her and that's when the tears came. She crossed the room, Sonny met her in the middle, catching her around the middle as she fell to the floor in a heap, sobbing.

CHAPTER EIGHT

Dilly and Carpenter picked him up, even after the shoving and shouting match in front of Faye's ruined vehicle. They didn't like his behavior, but it was good to know they had his back, regardless. Hell, how could he explain to them what this clusterfuck was when he had no clue what he was doing?

He'd parked his Jeep Wagoneer down the block from her apartment thinking he was being stealthy. Well, shit. Maybe if his Broom Hilda'd been parked in the lot, her car... Shit, what if she'd been in the damn thing? Shit.

Dilly clapped Griff on the shoulder, startling him out of his morbid thoughts. "Hilda's right there man, you okay?"

"Yeah, thanks. Uh, thanks." Griff slipped out of the car and pounded the roof to let Dilly know he was out of the way.

Carpenter flipped him off from the back seat and Griff returned the gesture, unsmiling. Carpenter, the little twat, why he was on the team? Griff had no idea.

He hopped behind the steering wheel and brought the ol' girl to life. "Come on baby, we got a 'splanation to pound out." The tires squealed as he pulled away from the curb.

Griff pulled into Silk's parking lot, slammed the gear shift into park and flew out of the driver's seat as if his ass were on fire. He ran through the club and kicked in Millie's office door.

Millie looked up from a pile of paperwork. "Griff, always a ple..."

Griff circled his boss' desk and yanked the man out of his chair by the lapels of his thousand dollar Italian suit. "You blew up her fucking car? In broad god damn daylight?"

Millie smiled. "You've sobered up I see. If you'll release me, maybe we can speak as gentlemen do, not as the heathen you've become of late." Millie puffed out his chest, obviously pleased with himself. Over the past few months he'd been taking speech and etiquette classes to help him sound more civilized. When he was calm and able to think two words ahead, he sounded like a polished gentleman with some class. However, when he was frustrated, his inner thug still came roaring out.

Griff snarled at the shorter man then dropped him in his chair. Was he fucking for real? Did he really think talking like that made him sound like a gentleman? He sounded like a complete dick. As Millie straightened his suit, smiling to himself, Griff moved around the desk and sat in the leather wingback chair. It was the same chair that little bastard had been in when Griff dumped it backwards. He grinned at the alcohol flavored memory.

Griff sat back and banged his boots on the corner of the mahogany desk, knocking off some files and a crystal paper weight. He looked down at the spilled paperwork and snorted; like he was going to pick that shit up.

"I don't know what's crawled up your ass, but it'd better die a quick fucking death. No one, not even you, manhandles me. You want to keep those hands, you'd better remember that. Now, as for a car bomb," Millie sat back and spread his arms wide, smiling that shark-toothed smile. "Ain't gotta clue, kid." Millie grimaced and cleared his throat, as if those words tasted worse than the others.

Ah, there you are. You can't hide the sleaze for long, can ya'? Griff thought as he caught the man's slip. He folded his hands across his chest. "Is that why you had flowers delivered to the Kane bitch? Because you're that fucking clueless?"

"Watch that tone, boy. How'd you know about the flowers?" Millie narrowed his gaze at Griff.

Griff dropped his feet with a loud thud and leaned forward. "Did you forget you hired me to watch her?"

"Watch. Not touch, fondle, or taste. Seems you got your dick in a knot over my would-be girl."

"Would be girl? You fucking hire me to whack the bitch, and now you're courting her? You're fucking delusional *and* paranoid. I know you had a bomb planted, Millie. God damn it! Now if the bitch disappears, there'll be an investigation hotter than that Jag you drive. Am I still under contract or what? Cuz, fuck me, I can be doing other things besides babysitting your new little fuck toy."

Millie's filibustering seemed to deflate at Griff's words. He waved his hand. "Perhaps, I was a bit...hasty. I hired a, well, someone to get her attention. And maybe," Millie sing-songed, "he was a bit, shall we say, overzealous? She's an interesting distraction, however, the contract stands. You'll have to get creative."

Griff snorted. "Overzealous? Ya' think? Creative, great. Now I have to be Martha Fucking Stewart? Awesome. Look, she's coming to your damn party. She's even going shopping for a fucking dress, like it's prom or some shit." Griff inwardly gagged on the lie and hoped he could get to Faye before Millie did. He had to tell her about shopping for a dress, just great.

Millie smiled at that. "A dress, eh? I think we've got another to add to the Widows and Orphans Fund, whadda ya' think? She is on unpaid leave, correct?"

Shit. Just, shit.

Griff shrugged non-commitally. "Wouldn't know. How many you got on that fund to begin with? You've never shown me the books on that particular investment, not that it'd mean shit from shinola to me. I know when someone's skimming, other than that, numbers are useless." Griff started picking at his thumbnail as Millie watched.

Millie nodded. "One of these days, I'll show you the books. Then teach your limited ass to divvy out the funds but kid, you gotta control that hot head or you're the one that's going to get burned. Capisce?"

Griff snorted. "What the fuck was that? Did you sneeze? Did you get any on me? Need a tissue?" Griff feigned looking down at himself with disgust and checking for overspray. He gave Millie a sarcastic smirk and a wink.

Millie barked out a laugh. "Same ol' Griff, fuckin' off when you should be workin'. Now get out of here and do your damn job."

"I will, but let me *do* my damn job. Stop interfering. No more fucking car bombs." Millie scowled as Griff left his office, much quieter than when he entered.

In all the fracas of the morning, Griff had almost forgotten it was still morning. He squinted his eyes against the sun and tried to think of his next step.

***

Millie started counting to ten as soon as Griff shut the door to his office. Then he picked up the handset and stabbed the buttons on the phone. "I told you to watch his ass. What happened?" Millie listened to the voice on the other end of the line spit, sputter, and stammer excuse after excuse. He shook his head and used his middle finger to stab at a file for emphasis. "No. No. Now you listen to me, you little punk. Something's not right with that kid. What? I don't give a fuck how old either of you are. You. Watch. Him. I want to know his whereabouts 24/7."

Millie slammed the phone down so hard, the handset broke. He pushed his chair back, stood and straightened his tie. Turning around, he pushed his chair back against his desk and began pacing back and forth. Thoughts of jumping on his desk and stomping the crap out of everything that resided there consumed his thoughts. He stopped his pacing long enough to stare at the mahogany monstrosity. Taking a couple of steps towards it, he stopped in the middle of the room. Pulling his weapon, he checked the magazine then took aim. He squeezed the trigger and... CLICK... CLICK... CLICK. His anger management coach would be proud; he didn't load the chamber, or the magazine for that matter. He slammed the gun back in its holster, straightened his jacket, slicked his hair back with both hands, and took a long, cleansing breath. He prided himself on keeping his cool. He wasn't an animal, he was better than that. After all, he had men to do his dirty work. He was the coolest cat on the block, with the most cash. The Golden Rule at its most basic level. Whoever has the gold makes the rules and not only was he making the rules, he was breaking and redefining them at his leisure.

Just like with the Kane woman. He knew what she was the second he saw her, he made her for vice in the blink of an eye. Playing like she was a hooker. He laughed and shook his head. Damn cops never get it right. Street girls rarely had all their teeth, and sex hair was the name of the latest trend in hooker chic. Nah, Detective Kane was a bit more put together than the typical street walker. The working girls inside Silk came from his other investment: Velvet Escorts. He shrugged as if someone was watching him.

He had a thing for fabrics; his mother had been a seamstress when he was a kid. When he moved to this podunk little burg and opened the club and the escort service, he knew they had to be named for his two favorite materials. Those girls were trained on hair, make-up, poise, posture, demeanor, everything. No one would mistake them for the trash on the streets. And that feisty little bitch didn't fit the bill for those girls either. Too brash. He laughed when he thought about her interview tape for Velvet.

Man, the cops in this town were getting ballsy, trying to get one of their own inside the escort service. He laughed. They couldn't even get him for tax evasion; he paid his taxes on the place and all the employees. The shits couldn't get him for prostitution either; no money ever changed hands between the escorts and their clients. He gave himself a mental pat on the back for that one. He was untouchable.

Between Silk and Velvet, he single-handedly turned the struggling community of Pine Hill around. If not for him, the place would have blown right off the map. To hear them talk though, he was the evil to end all evils. So what if he had a couple of town officials in his pocket? That's politics. You want me to scratch your back, you pay me good for my services. And most of the businesses in town did, or they found themselves standing on the outside of a burning ash pile. The lucky ones. For the not so lucky, who knew? They were never found.

Millie made his way back to his desk, sitting with a heavy sigh, thinking again of Detective Faye Kane. If a cop's pay was diddly, then a vice cop's pay was diddly squat. He knew that. He also knew how much she cherished that car of hers. Having the thing destroyed put her in the position of needing some cash fast, and who better than good ol' philanthropist Millie to dole it out in exchange for a few favors?

Yeah, he told Griff there was an infestation in the organization and offered him the contract to take her out, but the fact was he still didn't completely trust the guy. There was something off about him he couldn't quite put his finger on. But, the one thing he wouldn't stand for was someone else putting their fingers, or any other part of their anatomy, on his property. At this time, he considered Faye his property. Whether or not she remained a living specimen, remained to be seen. God damn Griff and his perversions were sure as hell not getting anywhere near her living body, unless it was to fulfill the contract. Millie ran his hands over his head. "Jesus Christ, you sound like a damn fool." Fact was, he was in a twist over Faye. There was something different about her, he either wanted to choke the life out of her or marry the bitch.

He pulled a folder from the top drawer and he dumped the contents on his desk. Pictures spilled onto the surface. He picked up the most recent one, tracing the beautiful features with a loving caress. "You're mine. The sooner you come to terms with that, the better."

Griff kept calling him paranoid and could be he was right, too. But, he'd come too far to lose it all now because of some punk kid and his horny dick. Whatever Griff was up to, he'd find out and then he'd be sure to knock the shit out of him, sending him spiraling into oblivion. Millie'd greased too many wheels, kissed more ass than Jenna Jameson and shaken more dirty palms than a coal miner rescued from a cave in.

No. His world was not going to cave in. He'd die before he'd let that happen. He would take every one of them down. Every single person on his Widows and Orphans fund, he'd take them all down with him.

Just then Carl came running in, side arm drawn but down at his side. "Boss, we've been trying to call you. Somethin's wrong with the phone. Shit, you okay?" Carl looked around the room for an assailant, but his eyes only saw Millie sitting behind his desk, scowling.

Millie pulled his chair forward by gripping the sides of the desk. "Thanks for the concern, Carl. Bring me a new phone. Pronto. And holster that piece. What's so important you come bursting in with your weapon drawn?"

Carl nodded, clicked the safety on the gun and tucked it in the waistband of his jeans. "'Kay, okay. Phone? Uh, I'll bring the bar phone over until we can order a new one for ya, boss. Dino's back. He's pissed over what Griff did to him. And he's threatenin' to talk...about you, boss."

Millie narrowed his eyes and clicked his tongue. "Why don't you show your coworker into my office. Bring Johnny and Sherman with you." Millie waited until Carl left before he closed his eyes, running his thumb and forefinger over his eyelids, thinking it was time to kick things up a notch.

***

Griff threw his cell phone on the passenger's seat with a curse. He'd left Faye half a dozen messages to pick up, call back, fuck off, anything to get her to answer her damn phone or call him back.

In Millie's office, after dumping that file on the floor, he knew Millie had double crossed him. The contract Griff had taken on Faye was given to another hitter.

"Fuck that." Griff pounded the steering wheel; he needed to get to her first.

Pulling a U-turn, Griff headed back for Faye's apartment. Just as he completed his turn, the rear passenger window exploded. "What the fuck?" Griff swerved and ducked as more rounds exploded inside the vehicle. He stomped on the gas and blared the horn for traffic to get out of his way. Griff raised his head to try and get a look in his rearview at where the shooter was but each time a hair poked over the steering wheel, shots were fired.

“Sonofabitch!” Griff bellowed as his windshield exploded and the radio was blown out. “Cocksucker! Where are ya’, you coward fuck?”

Shit. Shit. Shit.

A bullet grazed one of the front tires and the radiator steamed. Ol’ Broom Hilda was losing power and quick; he needed to get her off the road and get his ass out of this hornet’s nest.

Up ahead. There. A concrete building loomed in his path, but the way the ol’ girl was limping along the shooter would be on him fast and, personally, he preferred his guts on the inside of his body. He was picky like that.

A siren sounded somewhere behind him. Shit, cops. He was screwed. Wait. A quick look in the rearview revealed a giant red fire truck. Thank the arsonist gods.

The shooting had stopped, thanks in part to the fire trucks behind him. It gave him time to get the jeep inside the parking garage for Connection Capabilities and Technologies, whatever the fuck that was.

Griff sat up in his seat to rip the ticket out of the little robot thing, impatiently drumming his thumbs on his steering wheel and stealing glances in the rearview, counting the number of fire and rescue vehicles passing. Finally, the security arm lifted and Broom Hilda screeched in protest as Griff pushed the accelerator. “I know ol’ girl, I know. I’ll get ya’ put up...” Tires screeched behind him and bright headlights appeared in the rearview. “Shit.” Griff pulled into the nearest open spot, left the engine running, and waited for the... Slam.

Ol’ Hilda rammed into the guard rail and Griff crawled over the bench seat, slipping out the passenger side door and onto the cement ground. He log rolled under the nearest car, then rolled again and again until he was at least five cars away.

He couldn't be sure if the driver of the other vehicle saw him get out. Breathless, he lay on his stomach in a puddle of oil and grime watching the dark SUV pull up behind the Jeep and blast the ever loving shit out of the classic beast.

"Holy fuck! What'd Broom Hilda ever do to you?" Griff whispered hotly.

The passenger side door of the SUV opened and a pair of black Italian loafers stepped up to the hunk of metallic Swiss cheese.

"Man, let's go. Cops and shit are crawling all over outside, let's go. We made our point."

"Gotta make sure he's part of the upholstery. You want Griff after you? An injured Griff is still more dangerous than you, even with that canon!"

The sound of distant sirens got the shooters attention. The passenger swore and jumped back in the SUV and they made a hasty exit.

Apparently the sirens were intended for another crime scene. Still, Griff counted to two hundred before rolling out from underneath his hiding spot and did a short circuit to his car. He scrubbed a hand down his face. "Ah, shit girl, I'm sorry." Damn it, he thought, he'd had her since he was 16 when he'd won her in a poker game. Walking over to the passenger door, he pulled it open. When he did, it fell off the hinges and landed with a crash at his feet. Griff shook his head. "Damn." He reached inside and grabbed everything out of the glove compartment, reached under the passenger's seat and pulled out the tool box. With maybe a hint of a mist in his eyes, Griff said good bye to the longest commitment in his life.

Emerging from the parking garage Griff set his possessions on the ground, taking a moment to shove the smaller stuff inside the tool box. He pocketed the smokes after fishing one out and lighting it. Standing slowly, exhaling a plume of smoke, he flagged down a taxi.

***

Griff sat outside her apartment building for an hour, waiting for her arrival. She was suspended so she really had nowhere to go, no schedule to keep.

"Jesus, Griff, creeper much?" he growled.

There. She pulled up in a taxi of her own with an armful of bags. As he approached, he watched as she leaned awkwardly over and paid the driver. Griff grabbed a bag from her and she smacked her head on the cab as she leveled him with a murderous gaze. "Give that back and leave."

Griff bent at the waist to look in the window. "Wait," he told the cabbie.

She ripped the bag from his hand and marched down her garden path; he followed at a jog. "No worries, Sugar. Just came to remind you the party's tomorrow and you need a new dress."

She stopped, swinging her bags around and nearly nailing him as she spun. "Dress? I don't do dresses, Griff."

"Better change that tune sweetheart, your new man's expecting his girl to be dressed to the nines. Carl'll be here at seven sharp." Before she could come up with a biting retort, he'd disappeared inside the cab, his cell phone already at his ear.

"You stay on her. Got me, Carpenter? I don't give a shit. Piss in a bottle, whatever, but stay on her. That's my contract, she's mine." He slammed his phone shut and leaned his head on the back of the seat, trying to figure out exactly what those last two words really meant. "What a fucking mess," he sighed.

***

After the taillights of Griff's cab were out of sight, but not out of mind or heart, Faye pushed her way inside her apartment and dumped her groceries on the couch. Suddenly exhausted, she plopped down next to the spilled produce. Leaning back against the cushions, she closed her eyes. "What a mess."

CHAPTER NINE

Faye gathered up the spilled groceries and dumped them on the kitchen counter. Sighing heavily, she started putting everything away, mechanically, her mind somewhere else; on someone else. She was in the middle of wondering how he managed to consume her every waking thought in such a short period of time, when she realized she'd put her milk in the oven and was trying to hang her bread on the coffee mug tree. Shit. She kicked the cupboard three times, cussing with each kick. "Damn it. Damn it. Damn it."

"Griff." She made herself say his name. "What is he, like Voldemort or something?" He'd touched her in ways that no other had. She knew she'd never loved Michael passionately, but he seemed safe, loyal, a good companion. Christ, she sounded like she was describing a fucking dog.

She grimaced at the memories as she realized he was anything but loyal or safe. Pfft, there was something to be said for unsafe.

Ian, ah yes, that was better. Ian had much less power, much like Tom Riddle was much less villainy than Voldemort. Still, she shivered, as she thought how he'd challenged and awakened feelings in her, some of which she never even knew were there.

He'd made her ache for what she didn't understand and, frankly, she wasn't sure she was ready to go spelunking for the deeper meaning behind those feelings.

She was usually so good at reading people, but lately she felt like she couldn't trust herself; Michael, Kat, and now the piece de resistance, Ian...Griff...Shit. She didn't even know what to call him.

Her gut burned.

Who the hell was he? And why the hell was she drawn to him, like a moth to one of those bug zappers; beautiful to behold but damned dangerous to your health to touch. There was just something about him that called to her.

After everything was put away, in the correct places-milk in the refrigerator, for instance-she grabbed the trash and headed out to the dumpster. Her nose twitched almost as soon as she opened her door. The lingering stench from the explosion wafted on the air. She felt sucker punched all over again. Angrily, she tossed the trash bag into the dumpster, growling out her frustration and slamming the lid down, shaking the metal receptacle in her anger. Once her tantrum ceased, she chastised herself. Temper tantrums were so out of character for her, yet of late, they were her new norm. Head on straight, she took stock of herself and realized the hairs on the back of her neck were tingling and had started a slow ascent to stand on end.

Instinct took over. Taking a deep breath, she sauntered over to her car's final resting place, scanning the area using her peripheral vision. There was no one visible in the immediate area.

The parking lot had been crazy for most of the day after the fireworks. Now it was a desolate wasteland. Literally. Especially with the scorch marks and debris that littered the lot. Faye walked the perimeter of the lot several times appearing to appraise the burn site from all angles; arms crossed over her chest, still using her peripheral vision to scan the area.

"Damn," she muttered under her breath. She couldn't see anyone, but could feel their eyes on her, watching her. Faye's head snapped around as a flash of red caught her eye. She walked over to a copse of crabgrass peeking up through a crack in the asphalt. Squatting down, she narrowed her eyes at the patch of weeds. There, in the middle, wedged between the blades of grass and concrete, lay a scarlet match book. "Of course."

Not wanting to touch too much and contaminate the evidence she reached out, fingers shaking, as she used her middle and forefinger as a pincer and lifted the small square out of the grass. She stood slowly, carefully, so as to not dislodge the matchbook from her precarious grasp.

Faye headed back to her apartment, resisting a very strong urge to look over her shoulder and flash her watcher the bird.

***

He slipped out of the shadows as she walked back down her garden path. He wondered what she'd found, but before he could ponder for long, his phone vibrated in his pocket. Fishing it out, he whispered angrily, "Hey, yeah, all's quiet. No, no problem. Yeah, I'll stick to her like flies on shit, man. Yeah, well come on, she's just one little cop. Hot as fuck, yeah, but just a chick cop. Don't get your panties in a twist. Nah, she didn't. Would ya' calm down, I got this. Chill." He snapped the phone shut and cussed as he realized he forgot to mention her little perusal of the parking lot. He shrugged. No biggie, he thought and slipped back into the shadows to become part of the scenery and settle in for another long haul.

***

Faye heaved a sigh of relief as she made it into her apartment without dropping the matchbook. She headed straight to her kitchen, dropped the book on the counter and dug out a plastic baggie. Slipping her hand inside the baggie, she used it as a makeshift glove, picking up the matchbook and unfolding the baggie from her hand and wrapping it around the little piece of evidence. Now able to examine it, she saw one word embossed in ebony on the face: Silk.

Faye grinned. Hot damn. She must be rattling Maliano's cage if he sent his minions to take out her car. Her poor baby, she felt her bottom lip pop out and immediately drew it back. What the eff was that?

Faye shook her head, swearing. She held up the baggie, thinking if she found out that Griff blew up her baby she was going to make him pay. And she did not mean monetarily. Her gut told her...Damn. Nothing. She hadn't a clue what to think, except she had to hide this little get-out-of-suspension-free card.

Looking around her apartment, Faye kicked her hip out and sighed. She supposed no place was better than the kitchen, she spent little to no time in the small space; Suzy Homemaker she was not. Deciding her best option was the freezer, she opened the door and tucked the baggie in the back corner, where leftover meatloaf and ancient ice cream lived.

Closing the door, she leaned against the refrigerator, folding her arms around her waist. Faye could trust no one. She knew she was in deep and she was determined to see this through, whatever this was, to the bitter end.

Typically, Faye was a one-woman team. Investigations, witnesses, evidence; she could handle it on her own better than any two man duo. But, lately, with this case, she'd been feeling the strain of doing it alone. Was it because of her relationship, for lack of a better word, with Griff... Ian... whoever he was? That damned male stirred up emotions in her she'd either buried a long time ago or she never knew she had, and they were confusing her, befuddling her brain. And now, it seemed like minute by minute the weight of the world was growing heavier on her shoulders; she longed to share the load with someone else. She scrubbed a hand down her face. Jesus, that was so unlike her. By definition, she was Miss Independent. Steadfast. Loyal. Damn, there she was describing a fucking dog again. As much as she might want to share the burden, in true Faye fashion, she held back. How could she put this shit storm on someone else? Nobody deserved it any more than she did. Shit, it was bad enough when she fell apart in Sonny's arms earlier. He was married with a baby on the way, and lately at every turn, Faye's name was synonymous with trouble. She would continue to shoulder the load alone and bury her feelings deep.

She found herself staring off into space, then realized, no, she wasn't staring off into space, she was staring at her phone. Crap. She really needed to contact her insurance company to get that ball rolling.

Huffing out a shaky laugh, she wondered if "Exploding Car Syndrome" was covered under the "Act of God" clause. She slid the lock to wake her phone up. Geezus she had a lot of texts. Her brother was demanding to know what was going on, threatening to hunt her down. Her mother was trying not to panic, but wanted to hear from her. Thank God for Leah; her colorful messages were laugh out loud funny.

Finished, she sobered. Everyone would just have to wait. No work. No car. No problem. But, the thought of replacing her car made her sick. She loved that car.

Grabbing an apple out of the bowl freshly replenished from her shopping trip, she pocketed her phone and decided to go shopping. Again. A glance at the clock on the microwave, she figured families were sitting down for dinner, so she might have some luck. In, out, done.

She needed a dress. Not just any old LBD. Nope, no average Little Black Dress would suffice. She needed a KAD. Kick. Ass. Dress.

When Griff's snide comments came back to her, she thrust out her chin and took a harsh bite of apple.

Grabbing her purse and her iPod, she plugged in only one ear bud and thanked her lucky stars she'd removed the technological musical wonder from her car or she'd be one cranky bitch. No wheels *and* no music? Hell hath no fury like a woman without a beat.

Pulling her jacket tighter, she headed to the el. She could enjoy her music and still be aware of her surroundings as she made her way to the elevated train. She'd slipped one of her extra pieces into her ankle holster; not unusual for a cop. Regardless of suspension, Faye was planning on protecting herself. She wasn't going to walk around with a giant red target on her back, not without some way of retaliating.

Walking briskly, scanning her surroundings, Faye sang along quietly to her tunes. She was walking at a good clip when she spotted the entrance. Her tail was with her; wouldn't he be surprised when she hopped on the train. Slowing her pace, she bopped her head along to her music and gave her hips a good shake. With a smile and a fancy spin-scan of her surroundings, still unable to see her tail, she shrugged her shoulders. They had no idea who they were messing with.

As she looked around, she soaked in the sights and sounds of her neighborhood, her safe haven. Who did they think they were, coming here, blowing up her car, trying to take away her sense of home and safety?

She could hear the train in the distance. She had to time it just right. She counted down in her head...3...2...1...Now! Bolting up the stairs, she slid through the turnstiles and looked over at Mimi, yelling, "Hey Mimi, how are those grandbabies?"

Mimi, the token taker, flipped on the intercom and winked. "Just fine, Detective Kane."

Faye gave her a wave and jumped on the train just starting to pull away from the platform. Heart pounding as she made it through the sliding door, the hem of her coat barely cleared the barrier before it slid shut on a pneumatic whisper. She looked out of the plexiglass window for her not-so-friendly-neighborhood-stalker. Her heavy breathing kept fogging up the window but she couldn't see him. Not that she could before, but she couldn't feel his eyes on her any longer.

Grinning like a fool, she slipped into a seat and gazed out the window. "Stupid ass," she whispered. This was her stomping ground. Faye tapped her fingers to the music as the train wobbled and sped through South Philly, dusk was falling all around.

***

The little bell above the door jingled as Faye entered Thread Bare's Dress Shop. The woman behind the counter didn't bother looking up. "I'm sorry, we're just about to close, we'll re-open tomorrow morning. Nine a.m., sharp." Faye moved past all the beautiful designer and bridal gowns that adorned the walls on either side of the small shop and made her way to the counter situated in the center of the store.

"You won't make an exception for a desperate cop you know and love?"

Leah looked up and laughed out loud. "Well, either hell is serving ice water, or you bumped your head. Which is it, girl?" She came around the counter engulfing Faye in a flourish of soft fabrics and spiced vanilla hug. Leah stepped back and looked at her. "So, which is it, because if you tell me you're marrying that creep, Michael, I will shoot you myself."

Faye barked out a laugh that came from down deep. "You have such a way with words. Those were some interesting texts you sent me."

Leah looked at her watch. "Let me lock up and we can chat."

Faye wandered around looking at all the dresses. Caressing some of the lush airy materials, wrinkling her nose at others, she busied herself while Leah locked the door, turned over the closed sign and dimmed the lights. The woman disappeared to the back of the shop and approached Faye from behind, tossing a Coke Zero over her friend's shoulder. "Think fast."

Jumping at the falling projectile, Faye snagged the can before it hit the floor. Popping the tab, she cocked her eyebrow over the can as she sipped. "I need a kick ass dress. I mean a show stopper, knee dropper, Leah. You know, one that'll have their tongues wagging and cocks begging." Faye smirked as Leah threw her head back and laughed. "But, it's got to be something I can move in if I have to bolt."

Leah gave her a conspiratorial look. "And you say I have a way with words? Guess where I learned it." She stood, grabbed Faye by the wrist and dragged her back to a dressing room. "Strip."

Faye gave her a doubtful look but at the fists on hips and cocked eyebrow attitude Leah gave her, she knew better than to argue. Undressing, she smiled as Leah threw her hands in the air, making the myriad of bracelets on her wrists clang and jangle. Then the woman left, squealing that she knew she had the perfect dress and the best Fuck Me shoes. Faye snorted into her Coke Zero, choking on the bubbles.

Leah continued to babble and coo while rustling through the gowns. From her vantage point, Faye could look around at the entire place that had been like a second home while she was growing up. Their mothers were very close and Faye's mom worked part-time here for forever. She and Leah played many a game of hide and seek in the shadows of the dress racks. Though they shared a common history, they were polar opposites.

Faye was knocked out of memory lane by Leah yelling, "So, Kat called me."

Outfitted in her bra and panties, Faye padded to where Leah was on her knees, digging in the back of a closet. "And?"

Leah squealed that she found said aforementioned perfect shoes and jumped up, nearly knocking Faye on her bikini clad ass. Steadying herself, she watched her friend scurry to another location. Damn, that woman was a whirling bundle of energy.

Suddenly she heard music playing through the dress shop. There was a pause, and across the loudspeaker Faye heard her name. "Come on, get your ass back to the dressing room. Wait until you see what I have for your sexy self."

Entering the dressing room, Faye jumped as Leah yelled at her to turn around and close her eyes. "How the hell am I supposed see what you've got for me if..."

Leah shushed her and told her to take off her bra.

Growling, she didn't wait for the next admonishment before she unclasped her bra and tossed it over her head.

"Are those whisker burns?"

Faye's hands flew to cover her breasts. Leah laughed and ordered her to put her hands up. She did as she was told and immediately felt the soft, airy material slide over her arms, settling gently on her bare shoulders. Leah fiddled a little with the dress and then told her to lift her feet one at a time. When Faye heard Leah's soft gasp, she slouched in defeat. "What, is it that bad? Damn it, I knew it. I'm just not the formal dress type."

Leah pulled her friend's hair out of its ponytail and ran her fingers beneath the unruly curls, fluffing out the silky waves. Grabbing her hand, she started to drag Faye out of the dressing room, eyes closed.

"Leah, whaaa, where are we going?"

"Hush we're just going to the front, ya' know, where the windows are? Along with the three way mirror and pedestal. Oops, step up there." A little more fiddling with the dress, then Leah finally stopped and told her to open her eyes.

She still wasn't facing the mirrors but Leah had the sweetest expression on her face as she grabbed Faye's hands.

"Before you turn around, to answer your question; when Kat told me what she'd done I told her she was a horrible friend, to grow the hell up and to lose my number. Then, I hung up, and promptly called that two timing asshole and told him he lost the best thing in his life."

Blinking hard, Faye stared at her. "I'm sorry I didn't call you, but things are...nuts, to say the least and well, I was embarrassed. You were right about him all along. You never did like him."

Leah squeezed her hands and smiled sadly. "I know. And, I also knew you would call when you were ready, but sweetie I heard from the beat cop that walks this area that you're suspended. I wish you would have called me."

Shrugging, Faye mumbled, "And my car got blown up today."

Leah squeezed her hands harder. "I know about that too and so do your parents. You should really call them. Your brother called me and I strongly suggested to him that he call your parents before your dad's contacts got to him. Geez girl. You need to stop shutting out your family, they only want what's best for you. Your dad quit interfering a long time ago."

Faye winced at her friend's chiding. She knew she was a coward, but she didn't want to deal with her family on top of everything else. She hoped to avoid them all until this case was wrapped up.

Then she would have good news to counter the fact that Michael was no longer around, as well as explaining no more Kat.

Her father absolutely loved Michael. In his eyes, he was perfect. Director of Internal Affairs, who could ask for a better potential mate for their career driven daughter? Could that be why she always held him at arm's length?

Psychology 101: when parents love your significant other, you run the other way. If they hate him, you run at him like a starving man after the last loaf of bread.

They loved Kat, as well. Same thing. Or was Kat as manipulative as Michael? She shook her head to get out of those thoughts and bring herself round to present. When she again opened her eyes Leah was still there, staring up at her with a mischievous grin.

"And girlie, when you can, I want the low down dirty deets on the rest of it, because I know those love bites and whisker burns aren't from that candy ass Michael. His smooth as a baby's bottom face wouldn't do that or..." Leah brushed a hand across her friend's blushing cheeks, "this." At her last remark, Faye laughed and Leah ordered, "Now, turn around and see how stunning you are."

Faye turned around and stared at her reflection. The dress was nothing she would have chosen for herself. Leah picked a simple Grecian style dress with a dramatic plunging neckline held together by a silver clasp, keeping the front sexy rather than sleazy. Though the dress was floor length, it had a thigh high slit on the right side.

Faye couldn't help but spin, taking in each angle and the way the dress billowed around her in a storm cloud of gun metal gray silk. What a color. Who knew gun metal gray could outdo the LBD? But this dress blew the definition of the Little Black Dress out of the water. The color was simply amazing, it took her breath away.

Leah laughed and reached around her friend's legs to pull back the fabric. "Look down, Tiny Dancer."

Faye's eyes about popped out of her head. Boots. The most killer boots she'd ever seen; black leather, stiletto heels, up to the knee with geometric cut outs and ties. The entire look was dynamite.

Knocking at the front had Leah cussing but she headed to the door anyway to give the idiot on the other side a piece of her mind.

"Wait." Faye climbed off the pedestal and ran to the dressing room to grab her gun.

As she emerged, dress billowing around her, cleavage bouncing seductively, a hint of hip and hand gun at the ready, Leah smirked at her. "Damn girl, you look hot. And look, your gun matches your dress."

Faye smirked back and nodded for Leah to go ahead and open the door.

CHAPTER TEN

A young beat cop stood in the doorway, mouth agape, eyes wide with shock at being held at gun point from inside the shop, holding a pizza box.

Leah laughed and waved him inside. "Hey Zi. Shut that mouth, flies are starting to gather." She grabbed the pizza box from his hands, which automatically raised, palms out to the sexy woman holding the gun.

"I just had dinner at Momma's. She noticed you were working late...again, so she sent this over." Leaning over, he whispered loudly out the side of his mouth. "You okay? You being stuck up for that dress?"

Leah looked back over to Faye and smiled as she was trying to find someplace on the dress to hide her gun. The look on his face was priceless, once he realized he knew the stunning blonde in the sexy dress. Although he looked familiar to Faye, she had yet to place him.

Leah smiled at the expression on his face. "Well girlie, I do believe this dress is a winner. Look at his reaction. Zi, honey, you're drooling. Get a napkin. Faye, you don't remember who this is, do you?"

Faye looked him over. He was a good looking guy and, of course, it didn't hurt that he was in his dress blues. She always had a thing for a man in uniform, though faded jeans, motorcycle boots, and tight black t-shirts were climbing the charts with a vengeance.

He grinned. "Damn, Pip, you sure grew up nice. And that dress? I'm not sure what you're trying to do, but you'll definitely bring them to their knees. You look...fucktastic."

At his mention of her childhood nickname, one she hadn't heard in ages, she rocked back on her heels and crossed her arms over her chest, gun still firmly in hand. "Nunzio Catalano, didn't you grow up 'nice' yourself?" She made air quotes with her index fingers around the word 'nice', pulling a face. "And stop staring at my boobs or I'll shoot your ass."

Laughing, he walked towards her. "There's the Pip I know." He hugged her close and she gave him a quick squeeze before she pushed him away, swatting him in the shoulder.

"The last time you tried groping me...."

He grinned like a fool. "You gave me a black eye."

Leah swept past them with the pizza box. "You two can jaw all night. Me? I'm starving and wasting Momma's pizza is a crime in this neighborhood. And with two cops in my shop, I ain't about to flout the law. Faye, get changed and hang the dress on the hook in the dressing room. That dress is perfect for you, you're taking it. I'll get it ready to travel after we chow. Chop, chop; Momma's pizza waits for no one. Move it, I'm famished."

Faye headed to the dressing room as the other two aimed for the back of the store where a small kitchen area was located to the right of the storeroom. As she dressed, she smiled at all the good memories she had here. She was glad she came to Leah; she needed a friendly face tonight after everything. Although she still wasn't sure about this outfit, she trusted Leah; she knew her stuff.

Faye felt uncomfortable in the luxurious dress, but judging from Zi's expression, she must have looked okay. After dressing and putting her gun in her ankle holster, she threw her hair back up in a ponytail. Jacket and purse in hand, she headed back to the kitchenette to mow some of Momma's pizza.

Growing up, Faye was weaned on Momma's food; her restaurant was the hub of the neighborhood. The food was great and reasonable enough for the middle class neighborhood. But more than that, when you ate there, it was like eating in your own mom's kitchen. It had been so long, too long, since she'd been to Momma's and now knowing her pizza was mere feet away, Faye's mouth was watering for a taste.

Zi's mom knew everyone and was loved by all. She never thought twice about giving a hug and kiss where one was needed, as well as a swat to the back of the head and a scolding where one was warranted. It mattered not if you were her child, brother, sister, or grandma. That was Momma Catalano for you.

Leah was eating and chatting Zi's ear off when Faye entered and grabbed a piece, taking half the slice in her mouth and moaning out loud.

Zi grinned at her. "You should come by and see my mom. She's kept up through your parents; she's really proud of you."

Smiling, Faye nodded as she chewed. "Fho She, I bign't oh oo cama shop." Faye blushed and hurried to chew and swallow and translate, even as Leah and Zi laughed their asses off. "Oh you two, shut the hell up. I said, So Zi I didn't know you became a cop." She stuck her tongue out at them and pulled a face.

Zi snorted. "Hell yeah, Pip. I watched you walk this beat and figured if you could make it past your first week, I could too. And I sure as hell did. And if I don't say so myself, I do it better."

Leah snorted as she sipped her soda, and Faye whipped her head around, narrowing her eyes. "What's so effing funny, Missy?"

Leah gave her an innocent look and rubbed her finger around the rim of the soda can. “Oh nothing, just remembering your first beat walk, and a certain thwarted robbery attempt.” Leah leaned back, holding her belly and laughing all over again.

Faye threw her napkin at her. “Shut up.” Zi simply smiled, looking between the two of them, chewing his pizza. “What? Come on, what?”

Faye sighed and rolled her eyes. “Fine. Fine! No, Leah it’s my story, I’ll tell it. Here, eat another piece of pizza and shut the fuck up.”

Leah howled with laughter, tears streaming her face as Faye summarized her first beat walk for Zi. “Okay, so my partner was a bit lazy and let me take the last stroll of the day. He was off flirting with Sara Theresa, your mom’s waitress at the time, Zi. I see a commotion through this shop’s window, and Leah Laffsalot here, freaking out at the customer who’s holding a gun on her.”

Zi swallowed dramatically, looking over at Leah. “Oh shit, you never told me that.”

“Anyway, I push the door open, no bell back then, and tackle the guy from behind. Not graceful, but I caught him by surprise.”

Leah’s face was red and the tears were flowing freely, she actually snorted and got up, running out of the kitchen. Faye looked concerned until she heard the bathroom door slam shut and more laughing. “Bitch. Yeah, so, I was pretty proud of myself, ya’ know, my first collar by myself and all, right? I was making sure Leah and ma were okay when the dude rolls over, knocking me off his back, and makes a run for it. I get up and grab his ankles and knock him into a display of mannequins.”

Leah's screams of laughter could still be heard in the kitchenette. Zi was smiling, looking amused.

"This time I cuffed the little fucker. Or, so I thought. Thirty seconds later, a vase smashes right by my hand. I turn and look up, and there's Leah standing over us with a big grin. She'd smashed a flower vase over the head of my collar, knocking his ass out. Apparently I didn't cuff the perp, so much as I cuffed... myself...to a dismembered mannequin arm."

Zi laughed so hard pizza shot out of his mouth. The sound of a toilet flushing and Leah's giggles announced she was returning. "Oh god, that's good shit." Leah wiped tears and continued to giggle.

Faye grabbed another slice of pizza and scowled at her so-called friends laughing at her misfortune.

Zi continued to laugh and cough at the same time, after nearly choking on his pizza. "Aw, Pip, that's freaking awesome. You remember when my mom pipped you? Hahaha, can't remember now why, but yeah, you're still the Pip I remember. Who'd've thought we'd end up cops with all the trouble we caused running this neighborhood."

After spending some more time walking down memory lane, Faye stood up, stuffed and feeling better than she had in days. This, this impromptu gathering reminded her how much she loved this neighborhood, and growing up surrounded by family and friends who were like family. She became a cop to protect this, to keep what she cherished thriving and safe. And she'd be damned if she was going to let some punk ass thug ruin it.

Hugging Leah, Faye gave her an extra squeeze, just because. Leah pushed her away, patting her shoulder. "Gotta grab your crap, cupcake."

"Leah, wrap it up good. Remember, I'm on the el since my car..." She let the sentence drop; she still couldn't wrap her head around the loss of her poor car.

Zi offered to drop her home.

"Are you sure? I'd appreciate it, but Zi I'm having a lot of, uh, let's say, issues, right now. You might not want to be seen with me."

He assured her it wasn't an issue for him, he was heading to his precinct to do some much needed paperwork. They headed to the front of the store and Faye grabbed her purse.

"'Kay, what's the damage?"

"Are you kidding me?" Leah shook her head.

"Come on, Leah, the dress and the shoes are gorgeous and expensive. I'm a customer, just like anyone else."

"You're not like anyone else, I'm not taking your damn money." She came around the counter and shoved the garment bag into Faye's arms, hugging her tight and whispering in her ear, "Be safe, be careful and be smart. Oh," giving her a conspiratorial smile, "I totally saw the red mark on your ass too. I'm guessing spatula." She wiggled her eyebrows. "Bring him by, any time."

Faye groaned, feeling her face flush with embarrassment, hugging her friend back, nonetheless. She whispered in her ear, the memory making her smile, "Spoon."

As they headed out, Zi asked Leah if they should wait and walk her to her car. Declining, she explained that since she needed to be back early for a dress fitting the next morning, she was going to crash in the apartment over the shop. Faye promised to be in touch soon and Zi ordered Leah to lock up tight, to keep her safe from random mannequin attacks. That quip earned him an elbow to the gut.

Other than her giving him her address, the short drive to her apartment was silent. He tried several times to talk about her circumstances, but she refused to allow him to get sucked into her mess. She could only imagine the rumors swirling around her suspension. It was never good to want to choke someone in IA, especially your ex.

She must have made a noise because Zi glanced over at her. “Care to share with the class?”

She couldn’t believe this was the kid that chased her and Leah around, yanking their pigtails. Never mind she gave as good as she got, Faye smiled to herself, probably better. “Nope, private joke. I’m up here on the right. Don’t linger, I have a tail. I shook him earlier but I’m sure he’s pissed and camped out waiting for my return.”

“Ah, that explains the gun when I knocked at the shop.”

“Yeah, I couldn’t risk it. I didn’t want to bring any of my shit to those I care about.”

He pulled up in front of her building, she hopped out and he grabbed her arm. “Don’t forget your dress, Pip.”

She opened the back door, grabbed the garment bag, and leaned in the window. “Thanks, Zi, it was really good to see you and catch up. I hope to see you around. Tell your family ‘hi’ for me.”

“Tell them yourself, Pip. Come into the restaurant.”

She smiled sadly. “As soon as I get things squared away, I will.” Giving him a little wave, she walked away.

He jumped out of the car and jogged after her, yelling, "Faye?" Stopping, she turned as he reached her. "Be careful, okay? I'm not sure what you've gotten yourself into but, be smart. You're a good cop and the reason I became one."

Squeezing his upper arm, she smiled and assured him everything was under control, then turned and headed down her walk. She didn't let out a breath until she was in her apartment. Without turning the lights on, she headed to her room and hung the garment bag in her closet. Heeding the flashing light of her answering machine, she pushed the button. Again, more messages from her brother; Sam was not a happy camper. Her mother's voice echoed, asking her to call them. They were concerned and realized she was a grown up, but a phone call was not too much to ask. Shoot, no one did guilt as well as her mom. Finally Sonny's voice filled her quiet apartment.

"Ah, Faye...got some intel for you, but, ah, keep this shit on the down low, okay? Yeah, okay...so, uh, you hear about a Jeep Wagoneer getting shot to shit about two blocks up and over from you? No body recovered from the scene. But, ah, Faye? That Jeep is, ah, registered to ummm...yeah, an Ian McManus, also known as Griff McManus? Enforcer for the Maliano family. That name mean anything to you?"

The machine clicked off and her room was suddenly filled with an oppressive silence rushing to close in on her with each tick of her clock. Lowering herself slowly, sitting on the edge of the bed, she spoke into the darkness. "That's the question of the moment isn't it, what does he mean to me?"

CHAPTER ELEVEN

It was Saturday afternoon and Dilly was standing in the middle of Griff's apartment. Arms crossed over his chest, legs akimbo and a smirk planted firmly on his face, he watched his friend, dressed in a thousand dollar charcoal gray Armani suit, run from room to room, cussing.

Griff held up a black silk sock and shook it at Dilly's face. "Help me find this sock."

Dilly pulled a face, trying to hide his grin. "Griff. I found it."

Griff stopped, turning his head this way and that like a dog trying to catch a scent. "Where? Where, damn you?"

Dilly ripped the sock from Griff's hand. "Right here, asshat."

"You suck. Not *this* sock, asshole, the mate to this sock. If you're not going to help, get the fuck out."

Dilly threw his head back and barked out a laugh. "What's got your panties in a twist? You're acting like you're going to prom and this is the night...ya' know...losing your virginity or some such shit."

Shaking the sock at Dilly, Griff growled, "Listen Injun Man, I called you here to go over the plans for tonight, not for your pithy comments."

"Better to be pithed off than pithed on man." Dilly smiled as Griff rolled his eyes and groaned. "Plans are set. The guys are all in place, waiting for the signal. We're still sayin' midnight, right man?"

Griff nodded. "Midnight, yeah. Uh, listen, make sure the guys steer clear of Faye. She's mine. Got it?"

Dilly smiled at the implication of Griff's words but rather than poke the bear any more, he simply nodded. "Got it. What about Millie?"

"What about him?" Griff, having found the other sock, sat down and pulled them on. He leaned forward, looking this way and that for his shoes and saw the toe of one Italian leather loafer poking out from under his sofa. Getting on his hands and knees, he yanked the shoe out, nearly over turning the couch, again. He needed to be careful, the piece of shit barely survived the shit storm he put it through. As it was, he had to trash most of what he'd destroyed.

"Griff, man, focus. Millie? Is he onto the operation or what?

Griff grunted as he stood, shoe in hand, looking around for the other shoe. "Help me find this shoe." As the smirk appeared on Dilly's lips and his hand reached out, Griff snatched the shoe back. "The other shoe, dickface. I didn't invite you over here for your damn sarcasm."

Dilly roared out a laugh and approached his friend, slapping him on the face with both hands, shaking the other man's head until he was sure his brain was rattling. "Fo-cus. Mil-lie. Op-er-ation?"

"Get off me, man." Griff yanked his face out of Dilly's grip, shaking his head much like a dog would, to get his bearings. "No, he's too busy worrying about this party. And before you ask for the millionth time, I don't have any idea what this party's about. He's playing that shit close to the vest. I do know he's planning on adding Kane to the Widows and Orphans Fund."

"Shit. What's the take now?"

"Like I fucking know. He said he plans on showing me the books, some time. No ETA on that. What I do know is, this fucking suit is uncomfortable as all hell and I feel like an idiot." Griff huffed and stomped out of the room. Dilly continued to stand in the middle of the room, with the same sarcastic smirk on his face, until he returned. Griff threw himself down on the couch and slipped his feet into both now recovered shoes. He pulled the laces so tight one set broke free of the eyelets. "Fuck me."

"You know, most people tend to take their clothes off in the same place and keep their shoes and socks in pairs. It's just a thought," Dilly muttered, swallowing a laugh.

"I'm not like most people."

"Don't I know it."

Griff sat back on the couch in another huff, squeezing his eyes shut and rubbing his eyelids with his index finger and thumb. "This night has got to go off without a hitch. But man, I gotta tell ya', I've got a bad feeling about it. Listen, you make sure no one, and I mean no one, moves until I give the signal. And, I take Kane, you got me? Anyone else lays a finger on her and they'll be shitting lead for the rest of their short lives."

Dilly nodded and repeated, "Wait for signal. Shitting lead. You got it, man. You ready to put the screws to Maliano?"

"Saddle up." Griff pulled his suit coat straight. "How do I look, seriously?"

"Seriously? Where's the corsage?"

The sound of the hammer of a handgun cocking right next to Dilly's ear had him holding up his hands in protest. "Take a fucking joke. Christ on toast."

***

"Ugh." Faye gave an aggravated sigh and threw the mascara wand at her reflection. "Fuck this girly shit."

Yeah, the dress looked just as hot as it did in the dress shop but the rest of her was a mess. Her hair wouldn't go in the damn friggin' clip she'd bought in the "As Seen On TV" aisle at the Walgreen's, she'd poked her eye with the eyeliner pencil and mascara wand so many times, the black shit was running down her face. Her cheeks were pink from her scrubbing them clean more times than she cared to count. She grabbed her phone and dialed a number she'd known her entire life. "Leah, fuck me."

"I don't do chicks, baby girl. What's the problem?"

"Makeup is bullshit!"

Leah barked out a laugh. "Oh baby, it's not that hard. You're gorgeous with or without it."

"Leah, come on. If all you're going to give me is attitude, I'll shoot you through the phone. Help me, god damn it!"

She had to pull the phone away from her ear as Leah screamed in laughter. "Okay, sweety, listen. You're making it more difficult than it has to be. Remember KISS?"

"The band? Yeah, Gene Simmons is hot, that tongue." She moaned as her mind wandered.

"No, not the band, for the love of god. KISS. Keep It Simple Stupid, some people say Sweety at the end but now you've gone and pissed me off." She laughed again.

Faye sat her elbow on the top of her bathroom counter, rubbing her forehead and listening to Leah's step by step instructions with a scowl on her face.

"Yes, I heard you. And no, I am not taking pictures, this is not the damn prom." Faye hung up the phone while Leah was still talking. She picked up the mascara again, and proceeded to do exactly as Leah had instructed.

Thirty minutes later, Faye sat back and nodded, impressed. "Not half bad, Kane. Okay, now to attack this mane of crap pretending to be hair." Faye fluffed out her tresses but the dress demanded the attention with the plunging neckline and even plungier back.

The back of the dress fell in a light swoop down to the small of her back. Any wrong move on her part could send the shoulders slipping and the entire dress would slip off her body to pool around her ankles. She thought briefly of taping the straps to her shoulders, but what was life without a little risk? "Ha. Someone else's life."

With a sigh she scooped her hair up off her neck and turned left and right looking, scrutinizing. "Not bad. Now, to find something to hold this mess up." She dropped the tangle of hair and started pulling out the drawers under her bathroom counter, then remembered, during some random shopping trip that she'd bought some combs, tossed them in a drawer and promptly forgot about them.

The last drawer stuck so she bent over, put one foot on the cupboard door and both hands on the handle of the drawer and yanked. "Arrrrr....guuuuuh...o-pen. Whoa." The drawer came flying out and Faye stumbled backwards against the wall, the drawer's contents raining down all around her, like shrapnel from an exploding beauty parlor.

Faye blew a strand of hair out of her face. "Didn't know getting ready to go out would be so hazardous. Oh gawd, please don't let my makeup be effed up, I can't go through that trauma again." When Faye pushed away from the wall her foot kicked a package across her bathroom floor to skitter behind the toilet. "Of course."

Retrieving the package, she had to laugh. The packaging had yellowed during its tenure. “Holy crap, when did I buy this?”

Twenty minutes later a blue cloud of brand new cuss words hung over her head and her hair looked relatively okay, hanging in wild curls around her bare shoulders. She’d managed to break each and every one of the plastic combs, unable to coax any of her hair to stay up. The look certainly wasn’t sophisticated, but it was sexy – ish. Though, considering she was her harshest critic, maybe she didn’t look half bad.

The subtle knock on the door alerted her to the arrival of her ride.

“Shit.” Rushing out of the bathroom, strapping her thigh holster into place, she checked her Glock and jammed the piece into the holster. She grabbed the handbag that Leah wisely thought to include with the dress, throwing her keys and cell phone inside it, she snapped it shut and ran to the door.

Carl was leaning his hand on the brick next to her doorframe, head hanging, twirling a toothpick in the corner of his mouth when she whipped the door open. “Whoa.You look...whoa. The boss is going to cream his jeans.” He stood up straighter and watched her race past him to the end of the garden walk.

He jogged up behind her and opened the back door to the limo, practically salivating as the slit in the leg came open and gave him a great shot of the inside of one of her smooth, creamy thighs.

Faye looked up at him, waiting expectantly for him to shut the door but he continued to stare. “Uh, thanks. Am I supposed to tip you or what?”

“Oh shit, uh, sorry. Yeah. Buckle up.” Carl took a step back, turned back to her, then smoothed his hair, and straightened his jacket. Then, finally, remembering to shut her door and scurry to the driver’s seat. “Holy shit,” he whispered to the steering wheel.

Faye sat back in the supple leather seat and laughed nervously and talked out loud to herself, “Alrighty then, I must look sort of decent, then again,” she wrinkled her nose picturing Carl’s leering expression, “that can’t be saying much, considering the source.”

***

Griff paced the foyer of Millie’s mansion, his shoes making an annoying click on the Italian marble floor. He’d been put on security duty, checking guests as they arrived, for weapons and invitations. The main room was already bustling with early arrivals and the wait staff passing around amuse bouches, whatever the hell those are, he thought bitterly.

The door opened to yet another group of six or seven guests. Why they had to arrive in clusters, he’d never know but he put on his charming smile for the ladies and intimidating scowl for the men. “Okay, you know the drill.” Leaning over to one older female, he whispered in her ear, “Spread ‘em.” She giggled like a school girl, hurrying to obey. Several passes with the wand and each guest was cleared to enter the party. What was Millie being so secretive about? He’d thrown parties before and didn’t have half as much security.

“Damn it Millie, what the hell’s got you so damn paranoid?”

Griff had his back to the door when it opened for the thousandth time. He took a deep, steadying breath and put on his best smile. “Welcome. Present your invitation first and your purse and other valuables for inspection.”

When he completed his turn his throat closed and his mouth dropped. Faye was standing in the door looking good enough to eat, again.

***

A blush colored her cheeks but she kicked her chin out at him and stepped through the threshold. As she approached, all she could think was, “Damn it, we look like we’re going to the prom together.” Well, that, and the unwanted moisture that dampened her panties. Great, she thought, now I’m not going to be able to sit down. Awesome.

Griff scrubbed a hand down his face before stalking up to her, using his body to push her against the wall. “Hey there, Sugar,” he growled and ran his finger between her breasts, making her shudder, “Missed you.”

Her body arched into his touch as his hands traveled down her sides, over her ass, down to her legs. He pulled one of her thighs up to his waist, his hand caught on the black strap of the holster. “What’s this? I was wondering where you’d be hiding a piece in this sexy little get up. And don’t get me wrong, this is sexy as hell.” He kissed her cheek as his hand manipulated the holster, releasing it from her leg.

“Damn,” she whispered. His body pressed against hers, she could feel his hard length rubbing against her core and she moaned. She hated the fact that as soon as he was anywhere near her, all coherent thoughts were swept away.

“We need to take this some place a bit more, private,” he growled.

CHAPTER TWELVE

Griff gripped Faye's bicep and marched her to the coat closet. There'd been another lull in guests arriving so he didn't give a shit about taking a break. He gave her a quick shove, took one last look around the foyer, and closed the door.

"Damn it, Griff. You can't just man..." Her tirade was cut off by his mouth clamping down over hers, her tongue automatically seeking his.

His hands cupped the sides of her face, one moving around to caress her neck. With a force stronger than the big bang, Griff pulled himself away, panting for breath. He leaned his forehead against hers. "Have I said I've missed you yet?"

She laughed through panting breaths. "Yeah, I believe you have." Christ, listen to them, they were acting like two giddy school kids. Why in the hell did her brain evacuate every damn time he came in contact with her.

"Lift your arms, Sugar and hang onto that rod up there," his voice was a gravelly growled command.

"Griff, I don't think we have time for..." She was actually discussing this, contemplating...WTF? A sharp slap to her ass cut off her speech, as well as her thoughts. She raised her arms.

"That's your problem, Sugar, you're always thinking. Take two seconds to feel." He used the side of his finger to skim down her arms to her neck, back to the valley between her breasts; he barely touched each of her erect nipples. "No bra? Are you wearing panties under this thing? I'll be careful not to ruin your dress."

“Griff,” she whispered as his hands blazed a trail of desire every place he touched.

The hand that had been sliding up her thigh stalled and his warm breath was gone from her neck. “It’s still Griff? Let’s see if I can make you say Ian...or better yet, Sir.”

“Sir? Are you fucking nuts? Okay, this game is done.” She was pissed but she made no move to get around him or, his lips curled in the darkness, remove her hands from the bar overhead.

“Stay still, Faye.”’His hand moved up her thigh and did an inspection of her almost non-existent panties. He chuckled as his fingers found the satin ribbon ties on the side. “Can’t wait to see these on you but for now...oops...they fell right off. I’ll just hold onto them for later.” Pulling the tie free on both sides, he slid the material against her dampened core. But rather than tucking them into his pants pocket, he stuffed the airy material into his breast pocket, tipping his head and taking a deep inhale.

“G-give those back.” Her voice was a harsh whisper, her body trembled, and a fresh gush of her juices spilled forth, soaking her thighs. The thought of seeing him walk around the party with her panties for his suit kerchief was a turn on like no other. She seriously thought she must be losing it. Then, he ran his fingers through her slick folds and she jerked against the rod. She could have let go at any time; she wasn’t tied down, or up, as the case may be. But she couldn’t bring herself to walk away from the mind-blowing euphoria he was providing.

“That’s it, feel. You’re so wet I can smell you. My mouth is watering for a taste of you. I can’t get enough. I’m addicted.” On the last word he shoved two fingers inside her tight, wet sheath.

Faye's head lolled back and a deep groan emanated from her parted lips. "Ian, please."

He growled his pleasure. "Now, we're getting somewhere." Pulling her dress to the side, he freed one of her breasts and laved his tongue across one distended nipple, blowing across the moistened nub. His other hand continued to pump in and out of her quivering core, his thumb circling her clit. "Oh, you're so close. Quiet now. No one can know we're in here." He leaned over again and clamped his teeth down on her nipple. Her body jerked, her core clamped down on his fingers. "Come, Faye."

Tingling tendrils of pleasure shot through her body as he commanded her release. Back arched, she bit the inside of her lip to keep from screaming. Her hands tightened on the closet rod and her body shook, trapped in its own private earthquake.

Griff gripped her around the waist and pulled her body to his. "Gorgeous, I love to make you come." He kissed her forehead as she laid it on his shoulder. "Party time. Got your land legs back?"

Party? What party? Her brain was still basking in the orgasmic euphoria and the electrical system was trying to spark back to life; she'd almost forgotten where she was. Nodding, she pressed her lips together and patted Griff's shoulder. "Party. Ready."

He chuckled as he escorted her out of the sex-scented closet. Looking around, he saw the foyer was empty and moved with her to the large double doors leading down into the main room where the party was in full swing. Letting her go down into that sea of sharks was one of the hardest things he'd ever had to do but he had a job to do tonight. He'd seek her out later. "Be careful."

She turned to him, hand on her hip. "I want my gun back."

"No. Don't forget this." He handed her the leather clutch then turned around and went back to his post at the front of the house.

Taking the purse, she stared at it as if she'd never seen anything so compelling. She was confused. Where had he gotten the purse? Oh yeah, the closet. She'd dropped it when he pushed her inside. Damn him. How could he turn hot and cold with just the snap of his fingers? Though Faye did have to admit she was feeling much more relaxed than when she first arrived.

Stepping down into what she presumed was a living room, except there was no furniture beyond the two bars facing each other on either end of the room. People milled around smiling, giving air kisses and munching on some delicious looking snacks.

Faye grabbed a champagne flute from a passing waiter with a long jet braid. Narrowing her eyes as he passed, she could have sworn she'd seen him somewhere before. But before she could puzzle it together, a hand closed on her elbow. She turned her head to look at the hand then raised her gaze. "You're lucky it's you touching me. I almost knocked you on your ass."

Millie laughed. "Always a delight to see you, Detective. My, don't you look ravishing." He leaned in and gave her a peck on the cheek. "And you smell exquisite, what is that scent?"

She'd been taking a sip of her champagne and choked at his question. "It's soap."

"Soap smells quite enticing on you, Detective. Tell me, have you met the mayor?" He pulled her over to the local dignitary who smiled at her approach.

"Yes, we've met. Whenever there's a police funeral he's sure to show his face for the photographers."

"Now now, Detective, be polite. He's a guest in my home as much as you are." He laughed as he pulled her around and continued to introduce her to more politicians than currently in DC.

Millie turned as Carl approached. "Sir, your next appointment."

"Ah yes, please excuse me, Detective. A businessman's work is never done. Please continue to mingle. Try the crab puffs, they're delicious."

Okay, that's weird, Faye thought. The host is making appointments on the night of some party that no one knows what's going on? She needed to figure out what he was up to.

Turning around, she caught Millie heading out of the large room, clapping a hand on the shoulder of one of the politician's she'd just met.

Looking around the room, everyone was too busy drinking and chatting to notice; not Faye. She set her champagne flute down and started to follow the two men. Just as Millie and Arthur LaFontaine, Town Councilman, disappeared behind a marble column, Faye ran into a brick wall. When she looked up, she discovered it wasn't a brick wall but a very large, mocha skinned male. With her heels on, the top of her head barely reached his shoulders and he was at least three times her body width.

"Holy shit," she breathed as she looked up at him. Then clicked into place, this was the man from the club guarding the VIP area the other night.

The male's voice boomed out in a deep rumbling laugh, "Well said little lady. Now, why don't you have a seat at the bar and wait for the boss."

"Damn, I'd tell you to join me but I don't think there's a chair big enough to hold you."

Again, the male laughed and it reminded Faye of a thunder storm; she half expected a bolt of lightning to strike right next to her.

His hand was quite gentle as he placed it at the small of her back and guided her back to the party. A snap of his fingers and another glass of champagne was in her hand before she was fully seated.

"I shouldn't have this. I've had way too much all ready." She'd formulated a few contingency plans in case she was caught being sneaky. Looking like she'd been drinking all night was one of those plans.

"Millie says his girl's to have as much as she wants, she just has to stay put." He raised his eyebrows at her. "You gonna stay put?"

Faye smiled and took a sip of champagne. "I'll stay put, uh Gigantor? What do I call you?"

"This genial fellow is affectionately called Brick." Griff showed up, giving the giant a punch in the arm Faye was sure must have felt like a gust of wind to a man Brick's size.

"Griff. How the fuck are ya'? How's the welcoming committee detail?" Brick gripped the smaller man around the shoulders and shook him, then gave him a bear hug that made his spine crack.

Coughing and grunting as Brick released him, Griff squeaked out, "Fuck you, Brick. You're payin' for my chiropractor bill."

Brick leaned his head back and laughed, clapping Griff so hard on the shoulder his knees buckled. He had to grab hold of the bar to stay upright.

Faye choked and spit her champagne as she watched Griff lose his balance.

He looked at her and winked. "You think that's funny?" He reached over his chest to touch the panty kerchief in his breast pocket. While still looking at her, he asked Brick, "Do you need a hanky to wipe your face?"

Faye gasped. "You wouldn't."

Griff raised his eyebrows, grinning. "Wouldn't I?"

Though Brick didn't know what was going on between the other two, he laughed, grabbing a stack of napkins from the bar.

The three continued to chat amiably, Griff stealing surreptitious brushes of her bare skin whenever he could. Faye's body reacted with each secret touch, and all she wanted to do was grab him and drag him back into that closet and not come out until doomsday.

Before the words could form on her lips, another male joined their small group, Millie. He'd returned from one of his secret meetings, taking up post in the empty bar stool on Faye's right. He immediately placed a possessive hand on her thigh and gave each male his shark tooth smile. "I see you've got quite the fan club, Detective. Care to add one more?" He leaned over and sniffed her neck.

Faye swallowed a mouth full of bile but gave him the best innocent gaze she could manage. "I have no idea what you're talking about, Millie. You're the president of my fan club, aren't you? With all rights and privileges thereto." She laughed drunkenly, swaying in her seat.

A muscle in Griff's jaw ticked as he watched Millie's hand caress Faye's thigh. He looked like he was fantasizing about breaking each of Millie's fingers one at a time, slowly, when Millie snapped his fingers in Griff's direction. "The detective and I need to have a chat. You should join us."

Faye hopped off the barstool and stumbled, laughing, "Oops. Need my land legs and another glass of champagne. Millie, you need one too. I don't li-like, 'scuse me, to drink amone...er...alone." She grabbed two glasses from that same waiter with the long black braid and stumbled up the stairs. Griff gripped her elbow to keep her steady.

"What are you doing?" He hissed in her ear.

She swung her head to him, made a slight pucker with her lips, winked and then continued after Millie. He opened his door and held it wide, allowing them both to pass.

CHAPTER THIRTEEN

Faye staggered over to a large leather wingback chair and plopped down, the champagne nearly sloshing out the top of the glasses. She leaned forward and placed one on the corner of Millie's desk, sipping out of the one she hoarded to herself. "Millie, this champagne is wonderwall... waterfall... wonderful. I'm a beer drinker, but damn." She licked her lips.

Millie smiled at her. "Only the best, Detective." He picked up his champagne glass and moved to his side of the desk. Griff stood just behind Faye to the left, chewing on his tongue and looking around the office. Something was off. "So, my boy, I've asked you back here to be a witness, of sorts. The detective here has consented to join our Widows and Orphans Relief Fund, and I believe it's time you learn the system. Each of the members of the WORF have their own witness, it keeps everyone," Millie opened his hands, tilting his head from side to side, "shall we say, honest." Millie took a long swallow of champagne, pushed away from his desk, and went to a bookcase.

The case must have been on casters or something, Faye thought, as she watched Millie swing the large piece of furniture easily away from the wall. She half expected to see a secret door or a safe behind the panel, but the wall was just a wall.

Millie counted books from right to left and top to bottom, until he finally pulled one free and dropped it to the floor. Satisfied, he stepped away from the case and pushed it back against the wall. When Faye looked back at the bookcase to see from which shelf Millie had pulled the book, she furrowed her brow. None of the other books looked disturbed. Even though the book Millie was carrying back to his desk was large, red leather bound, and old, there didn't seem to be a space on any shelf large enough to house such a tome.

When Millie saw her expression, he simply smiled at her and winked. "Some secrets are best left as that, Detective, secrets." He looked over at Griff. "Don't just stand there, get your ass over here; you need to see this too."

Griff walked stiffly towards Millie, not wanting to leave Faye's side. Rounding the desk, he leaned over, resting his weight on his hands. As he looked at the open pages before him all he could make out was gibberish. The ledger was filled with rows and rows and rows of numbers, no names.

"No names," Millie read Griff's thoughts. "Each WORF member is assigned an account number. Very corporate thinking on my part, don't you think? Only I have the ledger key. See these last six entries? They're new, that's why you're only seeing one disbursement. These columns are the percentages each member receives. Don't make the mistake of thinking because a member is new to the WORF that they receive a smaller percentage. Each member's talents are what decides their take. Capisce?" Millie looked up at Griff, who simply nodded.

"How the hell am I supposed to know who gets what without knowing who these fucking account numbers belong to?" Griff grumbled. "This is just a bunch of Klingon bullshitese." Griff pushed up and away from Millie's desk, stalking back to the other side of the office. "Thanks for nothing. Am I free to go?"

Millie laughed. "No. Like I said, I have the key to all this, back at the club." He waved his hand over the pages. "This is all you need to know, for now." Millie picked up a pen and began writing in the ledger. He laid the pen down, folded his hands over the pages, and, lacing his fingers, smiled at Faye. "There you have it, Detective, you're now a proud member of WORF."

Faye was confused. She hadn't signed anything or really even said a word almost the entire time they'd been in his office, all she could do was nod dumbly.

Millie came around the desk, champagne flute in hand. "Shall we toast your good fortune?" He tipped his glass to hers, clinking them, then emptied the liquid into his mouth. Faye followed suit, with a small smile. Griff continued to scowl.

"Let's rejoin the party. I still have an announcement to make." Millie held his hand out to Faye to help her stand, and guided her to the door. "Griff, you gonna stand there like a statue all damn night or are you going to have some fun? You remember fun, don't you? Maybe I should have invited one of your back alley sluts to put a grin on that ugly mug." Mille smirked and Faye cringed.

"In a minute. We need to talk. Send her out with Brick." Griff whispered dangerously.

Millie's expression darkened but he nodded once. He moved to the door and pulled it open, to see Brick's profile standing sentinel to the right of the door. "Big Man, take my favorite detective here back to the party and ply her with as much alcohol as she wants."

Faye laughed, then affected a pretty convincing pout. "What about you? I don't like to drink alone."

"I'll be there before you finish your first one." He patted her on the butt and watched as Brick's giant hand spanned the small of her back. He turned back to Griff, scowl firmly in place. "What's this about?"

***

Griff swallowed the bile that rose in his throat as Millie swatted Faye on the ass. Get it together man, he thought. He turned his back on Millie and wandered deeper inside the large room before slowly spinning around, throwing his arms out to the side. "Care to tell me why my ride broke out in a serious case of lead pox?"

Millie stood stock still, shoving his hands in his trouser pockets. He dipped his head then raised his mud brown eyes to Griff. "You've got a real bad habit of playing with toys that belong to others. I don't share."

Griff narrowed his eyes at Millie. "What the fuck are you talking about?"

Millie pointed at the door. "That is what I'm talking about. I haven't caught you in the act yet, but your brain is in hump mode with my would-be girlfriend." He shrugged. "I needed to send a message; Tinker and Nova were all too happy to volunteer for the job. They weren't as discreet as I'd hoped, but they did make my point, didn't they?"

"She's a hot piece of ass, I'll give you that much. But, Millie, man, any thoughts about her have uh, gone down the drain, if you know what I mean. You set your sights on her, then all bets were off. That was no reason to shoot up two city blocks and my truck. Man, I've had Broom Hilda since I was sixteen. Wait...fuck, man that's why the cops didn't show. How many you got in that book?"

"Enough. We're clear then?"

"Crystal."

Millie nodded, then swept his hand before him, waiting for Griff to cross to the door. He clapped his enforcer on the shoulder as he came up beside him. "By the way, nice suit hanky."

Ice water filled Griff's veins and his stomach swooped, but he looked at Millie with a smirk. "Gotta love those back alley sluts."

Both were engulfed in laughter as they left the office.

***

Out of the corner of her eye, Faye saw Millie and Griff approaching, laughing and chatting congenially. A flash of anger swept through her and she picked up her champagne glass and took a long drink, slamming the glass on the bar. Millie clapped Griff on the back, then they went their separate ways. Mille headed for the front of the room and Griff to the bar to stand next to Brick, who was standing next to Faye.

Faye realized he was keeping his distance physically, mentally, and emotionally. The combined taste of defeat and mourning was a bitter pill to swallow, making her stomach clench; the need to retch became all encompassing. She forced the feeling aside as Millie raised both his hands in the air, calling everybody's attention to focus on him.

"Good evening. How is everyone feeling tonight?"

"Horny." Someone called out and the room filled with laughter.

Millie laughed too. "I'm sure we can come up with a cure for that affliction. I'm glad to hear my friends and colleagues are in good spirits this evening, I certainly paid enough for those spirits." Millie smirked as his eyes scanned the room. "I suppose you're all wondering why I've called you here this evening. It's a coming out party for me. I'd like to announce, that with many of your generous contributions, I will be running for mayor of this fine city of Philadelphia. And, with your continued support, I'm sure I'll be running this town in no time." Millie's expression was one of amusement, however, the emotion didn't quite reach his eyes. His shrewd gaze continued to scan the room, randomly stopping at various points, holding one person's attention for a few seconds, before sliding to another and then another. Satisfied he'd made his point, he left the makeshift podium, waving at the guests.

The room erupted in cheers and whoops of congratulations. Faye nearly choked on her drink and when she looked at Brick he was absorbed in a quiet, animated conversation with Griff.

Turning back to the crowd, she noticed not all the party goers were whooping it up. The current mayor had turned the color of ash, a well-known criminal court judge's jaw was set in a grim line, and the local union president couldn't stop shaking his head, like he'd just come down with some sort of palsy.

"Shit," Faye whispered. Millie was buying the mayorship, but how?

Millie was shaking hands and smiling as he made his way back to the bar. He grabbed her face in both of his hands and planted a kiss on her lips, to which he received more whoops from the crowd.

Faye pulled away and laughed. "I don't think I'm drunk enough for that, Mr. Maliano," she handed him a glass of champagne, "and neither are you."

"You may be right, Detective," Millie chuckled as he tipped the proffered drink to his lips. A band started to play, guests began to dance, and Faye continued to drink.

The night wore on with conversation and much hand touching on Millie's part. He started slurring his words as he spoke to each of his well wishers.

He'd taken up post at the bar, next to Faye, keeping his hand on her thigh, even as she crossed and recrossed her legs, trying to ditch it.

"Dance?" Millie's rough, slurred voice whispered in her ear.

Faye turned her face to his and smiled. "Sure." She set her glass on the bar and grabbed her purse as she hopped gracelessly off the stool.

They both staggered to the dance floor and Millie immediately had both his hands firmly on her ass. She promptly stomped on his foot. "I'm soooo drunk and such a klutz. You sure you want to dance?"

"Yeah. You ever hear of the horizontal mambo?"

Faye laughed and swatted Millie in the shoulder. "You're so bad. No wonder I like you." She took his hands and led him off the dance floor, then stopped suddenly and looked around. She felt those invisible eyes on her again and her skin crawled.

"Lose your way baby? Let me show you to paradise." Millie pulled her along behind him. With each step, Faye continued to look behind her, sure she'd finally set eyes on whoever was watching her.

Millie stopped before a closed door and, as Faye was not paying attention, she slammed into his back. Stumbling back, she nearly knocked over a hall table, covering by laughing drunkenly. Millie gripped her elbow and hauled her against him.

"Careful baby, the only bruises I want on this fine porcelain skin are ones I make." He spun her around, hands firmly on her hips, and marched her forward in front of him. "Open the door."

As ordered, she turned the knob and pushed the door forward. The room was Millie's room; done in dark woods and every shade of brown known to man. This was definitely a male's room.

He pushed her forward with his hips and she looked around the room. A mammoth four-poster bed made of some dark hardwood with intricate carvings on each post took up almost one entire wall of the room. There was a door to her right, which she thought must be the master bath, and a giant flat screen TV hung on the opposite wall from the bed.

"I can't wait to get thish-hmmm-this dress off you." Millie shook his head and ran his tongue through his mouth. "Thass word...world...weed..." He started laughing, a high-pitched giggle, and ran his hand over his forehead, covered in a heavy layer of sweat.

Faye cocked her head and gave him a concerned look. "You okay?"

"Mmmm fine, baby. Now less get you on the book." Millie snorted and laughed again, moving toward her, staggering, pushing her backwards toward the bed. He reached up and pushed one of the straps off her shoulders and she assisted by pushing the other one down.

As the garment fell to the floor, she deftly covered her naked breasts with her arms and gave him a coquettish gaze. "Millie, you dirty boy..."

Millie swayed where he stood, his eyes rolled in his head and then he fell forward, pushing her down on the bed.

Faye gasped as he fell, relieved the bed was close enough behind her to break her fall so she didn't break her ass. Millie's head rested on her collarbone, dead weight. She lifted it by his hair, his eyelids opening from the force of her grip. All she could see were the whites, the irises were rolling, the pupils dilated.

"It's about fucking time, I slipped you that roofie over an hour ago. Ugh, get off me!" She slithered back, the flesh on Millie's face sliding along her body, distorting his features so he looked like a flat Quasimodo.

When she finally reached the end of where Millie's body touched hers, she scrambled backwards, too quickly. The edge of the bed was closer than she anticipated and she toppled over backwards, narrowly missing hitting the bedside table with her forehead. "Ouch, shit. Millie, you suck." She stood and moved quickly, not knowing how much time she had. Removing her boots and throwing them across the room, Faye watched them land in separate locations. Then, moving around to the other side of the bed, she started tugging on Millie's shoes, pants, suit jacket. Although initially hoping to get him mostly naked she decided after a few minutes of struggling, maybe half in and out of clothes would be more convincing.

After about fifteen minutes of work, Faye stood back and nodded. "Okay, looks like a quickie to me." She'd managed to get his pants down around his ankles, his jacket lay on the floor in a heap, his tie still around his neck, but his shirt was askew, buttons open to midline. For that, she'd had to straddle his back and work the buttons loose from behind with him laying on them.

Satisfied with her work, Faye moved around his room looking for something to put on. She found a black silk robe hanging on the back of the bathroom door. Perfect. She slipped it on, tying the sash as tightly as she could. Finding her bag on the floor, she thought about taking the whole thing, but the only thing she'd really need was her phone to take pictures.

Moving quickly, she grabbed her phone, tossed her bag, then went to the bedroom door and turned to make sure Millie was still out cold. Convinced, she opened the door to go back to his office. "Time to go to work," she whispered.

CHAPTER FOURTEEN

The problem with parties was that there were always people everywhere, even where they shouldn't be, like on a flight of stairs. How the hell was she supposed to sneak downstairs when she kept running into people, all of them giving her a knowing smirk and wink.

Keeping up appearances, she gritted her teeth and smiled at them, muttering to herself, "The next one who gives me that look is getting their balls kicked into their tonsils."

The bottom part of the stairs curved towards the party room. Could this get any better? At the fifth step up, Faye gauged the distance from the banister to the floor; she could make it. Gingerly, she climbed over the railing, trying to keep her private parts private. Balancing her toes on the outside of the steps, she took a deep breath, and jumped. It was only about a three to four foot drop, but it still made her stomach swoop. Silently, she landed on the balls of her feet and looked around, laughing at what she saw. Too many drunk people on the ground level to give a shit about a flying, half naked chick.

Keeping to the shadows, she looked behind her to see if she was being watched or followed, but she was alone. Millie's office door appeared in no time. Reaching her hand out, half expecting it to be locked, she turned the knob and the door opened easily.

Faye's heart was hammering in her chest. Was this a little too easy? "Fuck it, I'll take it any way I can get it." She moved quickly through the door and shut it, quietly. Heading directly for the bookcase, she messed with a couple of the books, until finally finding the right lever to open the case and pull it away from the wall.

The back of the case was actually another bookcase. It had shelves filled with books of all shapes and sizes, boxes, and folders. Not seeing the book she'd come for, she peeked around the corner. Had Millie left it on his desk? WTF? This was getting too weird. Before she closed the case, a folder caught her attention. It had been shoved into a spot so haphazardly, part of it was bent and the papers inside spilled over the top.

Did someone just come in? She swore she heard someone open and close the office door. Looking around the edge of the case, she couldn't see anybody and paranoia set in. Hurriedly, she grabbed the folder, slammed the case closed, and ran over to Millie's desk.

She set the folder and her phone on the desk, scanning the office again. "This cloak and dagger shit is for the birds," she whispered to the room. Then she opened the red book, which was so conveniently left on Millie's desk, to a random page and, as much as she didn't want to admit it, Griff was right; the shit made no sense. Faye ran her finger across the rows and down the columns, unable to make either heads nor tails of the ledger. Picking up her phone, she snapped a couple of pictures of the pages, hoping that'd be good enough to justify a warrant and a more thorough search. Several numbers were repeated within the same cycle, at least that's what she thought it was, a cycle. She narrowed her eyes. A couple of the numbers looked vaguely familiar, but she couldn't quite figure out why. Faye stopped on one set and tapped at it. "Where have I seen you before?" It wasn't the entire sequence of numbers that was familiar, only the last four digits.

"Kane, what are you doing here?"

Faye gasped and stood up quickly, clutching her phone to her chest with one hand and reaching under the robe for her gun with the other, swearing aloud when she realized Griff had taken it from her. "Fuck." Her eyes focused on the intruder and she breathed a sigh of relief. "Cap? You scared the ever loving shit out of me. What the fuck are you doing here?"

Captain Jensen smiled at her and moved around the room, scanning the area as if looking for someone. "You alone?"

His voice sounded tight and shaky. Faye nodded. "Yeah."

"For someone who claims not to be in Millie's pocket," he pointed at her robe, "you seem to be filling the role quite well."

"Fuck you, Cap. I'm here to find something on him. He's buying the mayorship, I know it. If I can just find...Cap?"

He'd moved around the room and drew a weapon, letting it hang down by his thigh. "Kane, hand me that folder and your phone."

Faye's eyes traveled back to the desk and the folder she hadn't had a chance to look at yet. "Why, Howard? What's in there?"

"It's Howard, now? So disrespectful, and that mouth of yours. Someone should have taught you some manners a long time ago." Reaching his non-weapon wielding hand out to her, he shouted, "Hand 'em over!" Faye jumped.

"Jensen. I told you once your ass was mine. Drop the weapon and move away from her. Now." Griff's voice was an ominous growl in the darkness.

Howard turned towards his voice and Faye reached forward grabbing the folder off the desk. Opening it, she scanned the first document, her eyes filling with angry tears. She ripped the first page out and focused on the second page. Her breath caught, her hand flew to her mouth; the folder and papers spilling to the floor. She looked up at the two men in an armed standoff.

"Faye, listen..." Griff turned his focus on Faye for a brief second, until a soft click had him whipping his head back around to Howard.

The other man had his weapon trained on Faye. "Kane, you don't understand..."

BANG!

***

Millie startled in his bed. "What the fuck was that?" His head felt heavy and groggy. He tried to lift his hand to his face but it felt like there were invisible weights tying him down.

Carl burst into his room. "Boss. Whoa. Sorry. Uh, we have a situation."

"Don't I fuckin' know it? Get over here and help me up, I feel like shit."

Carl ran over and helped his boss stand and, in a comedy of awkward errors that Carl would soon be repressing, had Millie presentable to head downstairs.

Millie, hanging on tightly to Carl's considerably smaller form, staggered into his office. The scene before him could only be described as chaos.

Brick had Faye around the waist. She was screaming and kicking, trying to get to Griff, who was armed and wearing an expression of pure feral rage. A body lay prone on the floor, bleeding out from the head.

"What the *fuck* happened here?" Millie shouted before he gripped his head and swayed, proceeding to throw up on Carl's shoes.

Faye screamed and pointed at Griff. "Your fucking pet there killed my boss. I'm going to rip his dick off and shove it up his *ass! Let me go!*" Faye struggled against the python sized arms wrapped around her waist to no avail.

Carl's face turned pasty white and Millie gripped his shoulder tight for balance. "Fuck. God damn, fuck. Brick! Get her the fuck out of here. Five...take her to five."

"No. No, I'm staying. Fuck you." Faye continued to fight and struggle as Brick heaved her over his shoulder and marched out of the office.

Griff started after them, but Millie held up a shaking hand, swallowing down bile before he was able to speak again. "Explain."

Griff watched as Brick left, a hissing and spitting Faye draped over his shoulder. Panic poured into his veins like water through a wheelhouse. He'd never been to safe house five, fuck. He glowered at Millie. "Your fucking mess, that's what happened here. You've had way too many fucking hands in the cookie jar and one of them had too many nuts. Translation: Howard here lost his marbles and was going to kill your girlfriend. I killed him first. You should be thanking me. What the fuck's wrong with you? You look sick or some shit."

Millie pushed off Carl, who immediately ran from the room, hand over his mouth. Millie staggered to the leather sofa and sat heavily, holding his sweat soaked head in his hands. "Fuck. Did she get anything?"

"She saw the fucking hit file, Millie. The file I've been telling you to take better care of. What the fuck's wrong with you?" Griff was raking his hands through his hair, trying to work out a way to get to Faye.

"Get me a glass of fucking water," Millie grumbled.

"I'm not your god damn servant."

"Do it." Millie swayed, even though he was sitting, then vomited for a second time, sending Griff hauling ass out of the office.

As soon as he shut the door, he pressed his finger to his ear. "Abort...Abort...Abort! Code 4-1-7...ABORT!"

Several waiters, a bartender, and a couple of the guests faded out of the party as if they'd never been there. They moved so stealthily that no one but Griff saw them exit.

"Fuck, Millie." He growled to himself as he stalked out of the mansion and watched Brick stuff Faye into the front seat of a Hummer. Grinning and shaking his head, he ran to the Ram, his temporary ride. "Big mistake, big boy."

***

"Now be a good girl," Brick said, "or I'll tie your ass up and stuff you in the trunk."

Faye tried bolting out the other side of the Hummer, but one of Brick's hands easily encompassed both of her ankles and she was halted mid-vault. "Fine. *Fine*. Let me at least sit up."

Brick looked at her doubtfully. "You going to play nice, sweet thing?"

"Yes," she hissed.

The giant released her ankles and Faye scrambled to the passenger's side, sitting up and crossing her arms over her chest with a scowl, tears running freely down her face. Never had she felt so betrayed in all her life.

Howard...Griff...Howard...Griff...their names kept echoing in her head.

"Buckle up for safety, sweet thing."

"Fuck you," she spat.

Brick leaned over her, grabbed the seatbelt and snapped it into place before reaching up and grabbing her chin to pull her face towards his. "Last warning girly," he growled. He started the vehicle and pulled out of the driveway with ease; one of the advantages of owning a Hummer was that no one parked near you and when they saw you coming, they cleared a path.

Faye was lost in her own turmoil and anger when she noticed a change in Brick's smooth sailing. Looking up and over at him, she whispered, "What's wrong?"

"What?" Brick was watching his rearview.

Faye turned and looked behind them, but all she saw was headlights from about a dozen or more vehicles; nothing stood out to her. "What's wrong?" she asked again.

"We've got a tail."

"You're sure? How can you tell?"

"Fuckin' right, I'm sure. Now, sit back." He stomped the gas and Faye was thrown back in her seat.

***

Griff knew how to follow someone so they didn't know they were being followed but at this point, he didn't care if the fucker spotted him. He had to get to Faye, she was in more danger than she could even fathom.

He watched as Brick changed lanes and made a right turn from the left lane. Tires squealed, horns honked, and people yelled curses. Griff followed Brick's path and enjoyed the same negative applause as Brick's driving received. The Ram weaved in and out of traffic, following the Hummer through back alleys and crossing intersections against red lights.

"Shit." Griff stomped on the brakes as a city bus moved through the intersection, cutting off his pursuit of the Hummer. He drummed his fingers on the steering wheel, shaking his leg, waiting for the lumbering metallic beast to move out of his way.

Stomping the gas pedal, the Ram fishtailed and Griff swung his head from side to side looking for any signs of the Hummer. He slowed to a crawl, scanning. "Where... where... where..." There. Yes. But, there was something wrong. The Hummer had pulled from a side street, turned right, then swerved to the left, then to the right again.

"What the fuck?"

The Hummer came to a stop in the middle of the road, took off again, then swerved to the right at a traffic light, and then came to an abrupt stop, one tire up on the curb.

Griff couldn't help the grin that crossed his face; he knew what was coming next. Sure enough, the passenger's side door flew open and out hopped Faye. Still wearing that black silk robe, barefoot, she tore ass down the sidewalk, slipping into the shadows of an alley.

"Good girl," he said to his steering wheel.

The Hummer sped around the corner, slammed into park, and the giant driver stormed out, slamming his door so hard the whole vehicle shook.

Griff laughed as he drove passed. Nobody could get a male's ire up quite like his Faye, thank God for that, he thought.

CHAPTER FIFTEEN

If Brick said they were being followed then Faye had to believe him. And, just who would be following them? Had to be Griff, and if Griff caught up to them, what would he do to her? She had to get out of this death trap.

"Pull over, I think I'm going to puke."

Brick looked over at her, a look of revulsion on his face. "Not in my ride, no way sweet thing. You push that shit back down."

She shook her head dramatically, placing her hand over her mouth. "I c-can't...stop."

"Fuck that."

Faye leaned over and tried to grab the steering wheel, but Brick pushed her back to her side. Turning her head towards him, she gagged in his direction. At which point he leaned away from her, causing the Hummer to swerve, again.

During all the commotion inside the vehicle, Faye unbuckled her seatbelt. When she leaned toward Brick, she managed to unclick the door lock button without him noticing. She spun in her seat and used her heel to kick him in the nuts.

Folding forward, he huffed out a breath. Faye took that opportunity to grab the steering wheel and yank it to the right, throwing the gear shift into park and hauling ass out of the vehicle.

Faye tore down the sidewalk and took a quick respite in a side alley, hiding behind a dumpster. Doubled over, she rested her hands on her knees, breathing heavily, and trying to decide where to go. Who could she trust? Fresh tears flowed down her cheeks. "What a fucking mess." Her voice echoed back to her from the darkened alley.

Taking a few deep breaths, Faye finally recognized her surroundings. Shit, she knew where she was. This wasn't her neighborhood, but she'd been in the vicinity a few times. Steeling her emotions, she pushed off against the wall, looked back at the main street, but headed deeper into the alley. She might be half naked but she could still kick ass. Coming upon the back of the familiar building, she wasn't sure if this was the best of ideas but she didn't have many alternatives.

Smoothing her wild tresses, she wiped the tear streaks from her face, not realizing she'd smeared every last bit of make-up she'd put on and caused the black streaks from her tears to go full-on wrecked kabuki style makeup.

Pulling open the door, she padded down the back hallway and thought she'd be able to pull open the first fire exit door. She swore as she yanked on the handle and found it locked. "Damn. Fuck." She had no choice; she had to go by the front desk to reach the elevators. She really hoped the security guard wouldn't stop her.

Putting her head down, she tucked a strand of hair behind her ear and power walked through the main lobby of The Artisan apartment building. The place had a Boho feel; the settees, mismatched throw pillows, knick knacks placed in haphazard but artfully appropriate groupings, and overstuffed chairs with handmade afghans thrown over the back.

The security guard was sitting behind the desk and grinned as he saw her trying to skip by. "Get locked out, miss?"

Faye's stomach flip-flopped; she swallowed hard but nodded. "Yeah, uh, thought I had a spare set in my car." She smiled inwardly; he was new, hot damn. "Penthouse 5LH?"

“Of course.” He dropped his feet from the desk and moved to the elevators jangling his keys. He pushed the button for her and, when the doors opened he leaned in to put his key in the slot and push the button for the 5th floor. “There ya’ go, miss. Next time, try to remember your key, I’m not supposed to do this. Have a good night.”

The doors shut on his smiling face and Faye breathed a sigh of relief. She hadn’t figured out how she’d get up to the apartment without a key to the elevator but now she was home free. Maybe.

A few painfully slow moments later the elevator binged, the doors opened and Faye stepped into the hall. There were three apartments on this floor, the one she wanted was the last one at the end of the hallway, around the corner from the other two.

Walking was taking far too long, Faye started into a light jog. Something heavy in Millie’s robe pocket banged against her leg, but she had other things on her mind besides some random object. Finally standing before the familiar door, she was not gentle in her knocking. She pounded on the wood as if her life depended on it, it very well might.

“Open the fucking door. Police.” She wanted to laugh at that one.

The door was opened mid-knock, her fist still moving, hit nothing but air.

“What the fuck? Faye?”

“Let me in, damn it.”

The door opened wider to allow her entrance and she ducked under the arm to immediately start pacing the living room. When the door slammed Faye startled, and again, instinctively reached for her gun...that Griff still had.

“Want to explain to me what you’re doing here, looking like that, in the middle of the night?

Faye collapsed on the overstuffed couch, folding over, and putting her face in her hands. She looked up, shaking her head back and forth. “I’m in trouble, Michael.”

***

“Where the fuck did she go, man?” Griff poked Brick in his massive chest.

“Like I know. She jumped out and ran. I mean, who does that? Seriously? And quit poking me before I take that finger and put it someplace where you’ll never see it again.”

Griff’s head fell forward and he took a deep breath.

“Man, you should have seen her run though. Hauling ass like a cheetah after its dinner. I’m tellin’ ya’, she needs to get somewhere and quick. A half naked chick runnin’ around that part of town?” Brick shook his head. “She ain’t gonna last too long, man. Where would she go?”

“Fuck if I know. That part of town’s like a bipolar neighborhood. One end is a step above the projects and the other end is top dollar condos and apart...ments. Shit. I think I know where she went. Gimme your phone. What, mine’s dead.”

Brick groused, “Don’t mess up the ringtones, man. I just got ‘em the way I want ‘em.” Brick thrust the phone into Griff’s gut, grinning as he huffed out a breath.

“Fuck you. Don’t tell anyone a damn thing until I know for sure.” Griff pulled up the white pages and typed in a name. “Sonofabitch.” He tossed the phone back to Brick and took off down the street toward his loaner truck, pointing behind him. “I want my ringtone changed, big man.”

***

Millie paced his office, poorly; the after effects of the drug he'd been slipped still had a hold of his equilibrium. "That *bitch*!" he yelled then held his head. "She fucking dosed me. You find her...you find her and bring her back. I want her on her knees in front of me, begging me to kill her."

Carl nodded, a little green around the gills from all the vomiting he'd witnessed, nodding anyway at Millie's orders. Millie stopped and looked at him. "Did she get anything? I can't tell. Fuck, I feel like cock lint."

"No, not that I can tell. Everything's as it should be. And Griff and Brick are already trying to locate the woman, sir. It seems she slipped away from Brick on the way to the safe house. He called Griff for backup." Carl saw there were missing pages, but what the fuck did he care? He was going to be getting what he really wanted, and soon. He just had to be patient and then, game on.

Millie sat heavily in his chair, wiping the greasy sweat from his brow. "Good...good. Those idiots will pay for letting her get so fucking close to me. I'm going to drag her stomach up through her nostrils. *Capisce*! Because of Griff's fuck up, we're going to have hell to pay. Killing a cop in my office during my election bid. *Fuck!*"

Carl could only nod silently at his boss' tirade.

"Out! I need some privacy. Make sure the guests didn't hear the fucking gunshot. And Carl? Be disfuckingcreet, got it?"

***

Griff sat behind the wheel, tapping his fingers and singing under his breath. "A little bit of Monica by my side. Shit. Whatever the words are. Fuckin' Brick and his god damn ringtones."

He looked up at the apartment building, shaking his head. "Ah Faye, why'd you come here of all places, Sugar?" Heaving out a resigned sigh, Griff slipped from the car and jogged across the street, into the lobby of the exclusive apartment building.

The security guard looked up at him from behind his desk, a bored expression on his pock-scarred face. "Can I help you?"

"Sure thing. I need to see Michael Dieter, asap."

The kid shook his head. "No can do. No visitors after nine pee...em." He exaggerated the fact that it was evening and past some weird apartment building curfew.

Griff hung his head, nodding, then lifted his gaze, along with the Glock, training it right between the kids eyes. "Let's try this again. I need to see Michael Dieter, asap!"

Swallowing hard, the kid reached for the phone. "L-let me just an-announce you...*Ow*!" Griff smacked the kid in the forehead with the side of the gun. "None of that. Let me upstairs or you'll have lead vision from now on. Got me?" Griff had to give it to the kid, he moved pretty quick, even with the good sized goose egg forming on his head. The keys jingled more than normal in the kid's hands as he let Griff into the elevator and turned the key for the penthouse floor. As the doors closed, Griff said, "Better have a doctor look at that bump."

***

"Let me get this straight," Michael paced his living room, running his hands through his hair for the hundredth time, "You were running a scam on Martino Maliano? You've been humping his enforcer *and* you drugged Millie to find information on him. And Howard's dead? Dead. What the fuck happened? Fuck, Faye!"

"Michael, listen. You suspended me. Howard was...on the take. Those numbers I recognized, they were all jumbled up with other numbers but I know now...badge numbers, Michael. They were badge numbers; dozens of them. Griff just came in and, and shot him." She ran her hands through her hair, lacing her fingers together behind her neck, bending forward as she tried to breathe.

"Okay, okay. Let's figure this out." He swiped his thumb and forefinger down the corners of his mouth. "Okay, Howard was dirty. I know, he was under investigation. We couldn't finger him, though. I suspended you, Faye, to protect your stubborn ass. I might have been a shit boyfriend, but I know my job."

"Mike? Mike, who was at the...shit."

Faye's head snapped up and jerked around at the sound of the female voice coming down the hall, then back to Michael. "What the fuck is she doing here?"

Kat stopped at the end of the hall, tying a sash around Michael's brown satin bathrobe, her long dark hair spilling over her shoulders. "Ah, hey...Hi...Faye."

Well, at least she had the grace to look embarrassed. "This night just keeps getting better and better," Faye gritted through clenched teeth.

Before Michael could say anything, a loud, harsh banging on the door brought all their heads around.

"Open up. Faye, I know you're in there. Open up!"

Faye stood and backed behind the couch, pointing at the door. "Don't you open that door, Michael."

He turned to give her a disdainful look. "Like I even considered it."

Kat moved to put her hands on Faye's shoulders but a steely look kept Kat where she was.

Just then, the door flew inward, wood splintering everywhere. Kat screamed and covered her face with her arms. Faye fell to the floor behind the couch in the bomb shelter position kids were taught back in the day.

Michael simply stood his ground and growled, "What the fuck do you think you're doing?"

"Asshole, remind me to kick your ass later. Right now, I need to talk to Faye."

Michael stepped up to him. "This is my house, asshole. She's not here. I'm going to take the cost of a new door right out of your ass."

A door slamming had two cold male gazes turning their heads towards the sound.

Michael moved to Kat, placing a gentle touch on her arms. "Hey, baby, where'd she go?"

Kat pointed, with a shaking hand, to the balcony. At first, Michael didn't understand, and then comprehension set in. "The fire escape? Shit."

"Shit," Griff agreed. Running the direction Kat was pointing, he saw a door on the other side of the kitchen and burst through, kicking in the second which led to the fire escape. He ran to the edge to catch a wisp of blonde hair and the trail of a robe disappearing down the steps. "Faye, stop!" He started down the stairs, but she moved too quickly. Already two flights below him, she'd be hitting the ground before he even made it one level down. God damn, his girl could move. He smiled to himself, impressed and frightened at the same time.

He was right, though. He saw her jump to the ground and turn and look back at him, flipping him off before she started toward the street. He couldn't help but laugh. Starting to run down the steps again until screeching tires had him hauling to a stop.

Griff leaned over the railing and looked out to the street. A large, dark panel van had jumped the curb. "Shit. *Shit! No! Fuck!*" Scrambling down the stairs as fast as he could go, he stopped on the last landing and looked back to the street.

A large male was struggling backwards, hand over the mouth of a struggling woman in a black robe. He watched as her legs flailed, kicking, trying to find purchase, but the male backed his way inside the van, which screeched away as the door slid shut. Griff ran out of the alley and down the street chasing the van, cussing with every step.

"Sonofabitch." He stopped in the middle of the road, folding over and resting his hands on his knees. "Shit, Millie. Just shit."

CHAPTER SIXTEEN

Faye's head kicked back from the third or fourth slap, she'd lost count. All she knew for sure was her lip was bleeding and her eye felt like it was going to fall out of the socket.

Millie was sitting in the chair opposite her, leaning forward on his elbows, fingers steepled. He nodded to Carl, who landed another blow.

Calm facade now gone, his face appeared inches before hers; eyes crazed, his lips curled into a sneer. "When he gives me the word, we're going to have some *real* fun." Faye spat in his face. Carl gripped her by the chin and landed three closed fist strikes to her face, his firm grip making her face take the full impact of the blows.

"Enough, Carl." Millie's voice was eerily calm as he gave the command.

Stepping away from her slumping form, Carl took up post to Millie's right. He stood with his legs spread and arms crossed over his chest.

"Okay, Detective, time to talk. If I like what I hear, I'll make sure Carl kills you quickly. If you spew shit at me, then," Millie shrugged, "he gets free rein of that body."

Faye raised her eyes to Millie, licking her swollen and bloodied lips, she smiled. "Fuck you."

"I thought that's how you'd reply." Millie sat back and dropped his hands, lifting one, he waved offhandedly to Carl.

Carl moved towards Faye, a sneer on his lips and pure insanity in his eyes.

***

Griff ran through the office building and burst through a set of glass doors. The man behind the desk dropped the file in his hands, and peered up at him over the half moon spectacles sitting at the end of his nose. “Can I help you?”

“It’s almost fucking midnight, what the fuck do you think? Where’s the team?” Griff started frantically dialing numbers on his cell, then chucked the thing at the wall, remembering it was dead.

“I’m here,” Carpenter said, sliding from the shadows.

The door clicked shut and Griff spun to see Dilly undoing the braid in his hair. “Present, Mr. McManus. Can I get my spanking now?”

“Shut the fuck up. Where’s...shit.”

Music could be heard in the quiet of the outer office and

Dilly started shaking his ass. “Hey, Mambo No 5. Love this joint.”

Brick breezed through the door. He moved easily and swiftly for a man of his size. “What’s the hubbub?”

Fuck. He’d hoped that at least Brick had caught up with her. But the whole team was present and accounted for. No Faye. Griff couldn’t settle his nerves. Faye was in danger and he needed to get to her and quick. “Porter, we’ve got a local vice in the hands of Maliano. We need to get her out, like yesterday.”

The man behind the desk, Reverend Porter, named after his maternal grandfather who actually was a man of the cloth, took off his glasses and laid them on the desk. He pinched the bridge of his nose. “McManus, you aborted the op. Now you want a search and rescue put together in," he checked his watch, "ten minutes? Explain."

"Brick knows where she's at; safe house five. I've never been there. As one of Millie's bodyguards, Brick's been to all of them. Flash-Bang, we're in and out and done. We can recover the evidence during the snatch and grab. Dilly and Carpenter can go back to the mansion to get what we need and Brick and me and can go to the safe house."

"Brick and I," Dilly corrected.

Brick looked around the room, the jovial smile he'd had on his face quickly changed to something dark and ominous. He shook his head from side to side and spoke to the floor. "Five's bad business, man. Five's no safe house, it's a kill room." He raised his chocolate brown eyes to the deathly silence of the other four men in the room. "If she's not dead now she will be, soon. And, I hate to tell ya', man, but, I've never been there. Begged off each time the place was brought up. Got a few people away from that mess, but not enough. Not enough." As large as he was, whatever the thoughts roaming around in his head had him retreating within himself.

The sight was unsettling and Griff had to turn away. Griff swallowed bile as he listened to Brick. Pointing at the giant, he spoke in a dangerous whisper to Porter, "See? We've got to move on this, now." Turning, he stalked back to Brick, poking him in the chest as he spoke. "How the fuck did I not know about that place, man? Kill room, are you shitting me?"

Brick grabbed the front of Griff's shirt, raising him up on his toes. "You didn't know because you didn't need to know." He shook the smaller man, whose teeth rattled in his head. "Besides, the place gets used for special treatment from what I hear. Five is usually reserved for traitors, snitches. It's all very Dante's Inferno or whatever. You know

Maliano prefers most of his hits to be a tad more public and during times where there's lots of folks who can vouch for his whereabouts." Shaking Griff a second time he went on, "I ain't never been there."

Before Griff could unscramble his brains to muster another argument, Porter put his hands up. "Enough. One dirty cop..."

Griff swung his head around, eyes rolling. "She's not dirty. She was putting on an act. If I would've fessed up, she wouldn't be in this mess."

"Fessed up? You killed her superior officer. I want a report on that ASAFP. Nobody, but nobody, is to know of this agency. We are secret, we move through the shadows. We are only a rumor, like the Men In Black, except we're the men in the dark. Got it?"

"Christ, Porter. Everyone knows about the BCI," Carpenter chimed in.

"No, they only think they do." Porter looked to Griff, who looked as if he wanted to pace, but due to the fact Brick still held him by the shirt front, pacing was a bit out of the question. "Brick, drop him."

Brick dropped Griff and leveled Porter with a condescending look. "Just how in the hell are we getting to an uncharted safe house?"

"GPS might be an option." Carpenter's soft voice came from the back of the group.

Porter looked over at the nondescript male. "What do you mean 'might be an option'?"

Carpenter stepped forward and gave a Griff a withering look before lifting his chin at Brick. "Were you able to get her phone in her pocket?"

For the briefest of seconds, Griff seriously considered kissing another man. He ran his hands through his hair, then swiped down over his lips. "You're a fucking genius. Creepy, but a god damn genius. Every cop has the GPS on in their phone." Griff's attitude toward Brick shifted from pissed to grateful as fuck. "Let's hope the fuck she's still got it on her. Porter, pull that shit up. Like now."

Porter raised his eyebrows at him. "One of these days, you boys'll learn some manners." He pounded his keyboard and waited with his hand hovering over the keys. "What's her number?"

Griff fed him the number from rote and waited. The silence inside Porter's office was palpable, weighing down on them as the seconds stretched on interminably. What felt like an eternity, turned out to be a mere forty-seven seconds.

Porter finally lifted his head and waved Griff over, pointing at the coordinates. "There. She's there. In the middle of fucking nowhere right by Bum Fuck Egypt. Get this thing done, quietly. Brick and McManus, you go to the safe house; get her out, no casualties. And keep your hands to yourselves, would ya'? Dillinger and Carpenter back to the mansion. Uh, hey McManus, there's something you should know. Background checks on that Carl Thibedoux make Bundy look like Santa Claus."

Griff ran for the door on rubbery legs when Porter's words caught him in the solar plexus. "Carl? Meek and trembly at a gust of wind Carl? You sure?"

Porter nodded solemnly. "Absofuckinglutely."

***

Blood dripped out of her mouth, joining the rest that had puddled and congealed at her feet. Both of her eyes were black and swollen, her throat raw. She was sure she'd have finger marks on her throat. Added to that, she was sure her hand was broken.

It seemed little Carl had a thing for strangling and torturing females. Only Millie's invisible leash on his control kept her alive.

"Detective, I'm tired, and hung over from that not so nice little mickey you slipped me. Now, Carl is getting a little twitchy over here. Are you ready to come clean?"

Her eyes rolled as she laughed, her voice hoarse. "I'd love a bubble bath."

Millie nodded at Carl. Sneering, he drew back his fist and struck her so hard the chair tipped and crashed to the floor. Falling hard enough her head knocked with a sharp crack and she saw a blinding flash of light that made her eyes and ears hurt.

Suddenly, the room was alive with activity, people shouting but their voices sounded far away, like a radio that wasn't tuned it to the right station.

She tried getting up but her body felt heavy, her head pounded. A face appeared before hers and her stomach dipped, from fear or elation she couldn't tell. The face grew strong arms that lifted her and held her in a firm, warm embrace. She laid her head on the shoulder attached to the arms and face. Closing her eyes, she welcomed the peaceful, painless darkness.

***

"Drive! I don't give a fuck! Don't give me that look. Call 9-1-1 and get the locals out here. We need to get her to the hospital."

Griff and Brick were running from 'safe' house five which turned out to be a shack in the middle of nowhere that definitely had more in common with a house of horrors than the name would indicate. Entry and rescue over, the details sifted through Griff's mind falling into order.

Brick had thrown the flash-bang grenade and Griff burst through the front door. Kicking Carl in the kneecap from the side, incapacitating him, he kneed Millie in the nuts and grabbed Faye, carrying her out of that hell hole. The whole operation was complete in less than five minutes.

Now, Griff was settling into the backseat of the Hummer, bitching at Brick, who was kvetching about leaving the men behind without securing them.

"I don't give a fuck about them right now, Brick. Drive this god damn hunk of junk before I put my boot up your ass."

Brick humped into the driver's seat, turning to glare at Griff. "You diss Lucille again and you be walkin'. 'Scuse me while I make a phone call." Brick cleared his throat and dialed 9-1-1. When the operator came on, Brick's typically melted chocolate smooth baritone became a snotty frat boy whine. "Yeah, I was trying to get it on with my girl and some idiot was setting off fireworks. It's not even Fourth of July. Yeah, Route 292, it's the old Hilldale Sugar Shack. Yeah, yeah. Damn baby, gotta go, my girl's about to get a mouthful." Brick threw the phone in the passenger seat and hauled the Hummer out onto the main road, catching Griff's reflection in the rearview. "How's she doing, man?"

Griff was stroking her hair, blood caked in the blonde bangs. Her face was swollen but she seemed to be breathing okay. “She’s knocked out but she’s breathing. Just keep breathing baby, you hear me?”

Lights and sirens brought his head up to stare in disbelief out the front window. Miraculously, the locals had flown past them mere minutes after the 9-1-1 call. Griff and Brick stared open mouthed at each other as car after car whizzed by them. The reason for their sudden appearance loomed up ahead. More lights and colors and sounds of what looked like a carnival. Carnivals always had a police presence. Griff had somehow missed it on the way to the shack. No surprise, his mind had been on getting his Faye out, safe and in one piece. He’d never been happier to see a carnival in his entire life. “Go get ‘em boys,” he whispered.

***

Thirty excruciating minutes later, Brick pulled up in front of the hospital. Griff slid out of the backseat, Faye’s unconscious body clutched tightly against him. He ran through the emergency room doors, yelling for a stretcher. “Someone get the fuck out here. Move it,” he yelled at the three nurses who came out to direct him to a room with a bed. They asked him a barrage of questions, to which he only knew all of two answers. “Faye Kane.” First and last name.

The medical team ushered him out to the waiting room, instructing him to sit in one of the plastic chairs and wait. So, he waited. He even ignored the myriad of texts and calls to his cell phone from his team. His team.

He’d been a member of BCI since its inception in this part of Philly. BCI stood for Bureau of Criminal Investigation. An agency designed with undercover activity in mind for those cops who felt that walking a beat just wasn’t their cup of tea. Yet, it was more than that, more than even Griff knew but then again, he didn’t ask questions, he simply did his job.

It took Griff many years to put his past behind him; several years of being homeless. Then some of the worst foster homes in the system, some you just hoped didn't really exist, and then, predictably, juvie.

He'd been picked up by one cop so many times the guy started to seem like family, and though he was too old to be adopted, the cop and his wife treated him as if he were one of their own. At eighteen, he legally changed his last name to McManus and Declan and Iseult became Griff's parents. High up in the BCI, Porter had the power to manipulate his juvie records so anyone doing a background check on him would find the McManus name, not his given name, Rinker. He shuddered at the thought of his birth name. His biological parents were drug addicts themselves and...he closed off the rest of those memories, unable to bring himself to think about his bios. Not now, not ever again. Then again, being in the ER waiting room brought back other memories.

His adoptive father, Declan, was killed while off duty. Stopping to pick up a gallon of milk, he was caught in a robbery. The would-be thief was just a kid himself and Dec was just trying to talk him down. The kid was hopped up on meth or something according to the cashier and, when Dec tried to talk to him, just started shooting. From that point forward, Griff had worked hard to get into the academy and take down every criminal in his path, at all costs.

Now, here he was, in another emergency room, waiting to hear about the prognosis of another loved one. He couldn't take it anymore. He looked at the clock, he'd been waiting for five hours. My how time flies when suffering, he thought. Pushing himself off the plastic chair, he began to pace.

Griff absently rubbed his left arm, the arm with the tattoo. To the casual observer it was nothing more than a nonsensical tribal tat with barbed wire, but to him the barbed wire represented his years of abuse and neglect. It was a reminder that while the past was painful, there was no point in dwelling; the sun would still shine. After finding the ancient depiction of the sun in a book he had the artist combine it with other hidden information in and among the twists and whirls, particularly Declan's and Iseult's names which were preserved in old Gaelic glyphs. He'd gone to the tattoo parlor, Ink Wells, in New Jersey and sat for five hours to have the partial sleeve done after his father's funeral, needing the physical pain to subvert the emotional trauma. Unable to take the silence any longer, he shouted at several nurses, a physician's assistant, and a med student foolish enough to wander his way.

Finally, a doctor appeared. His white and gray beard stood out in stark contrast to the shoe polish black of his hair implants. "Sir, I'm going to have to ask you to calm down."

Grabbing the physician by the lapels of his pristine white lab coat, he glared at him. "I'm going to have to respectfully decline. How is she?"

The doctor cleared his throat. "Assaulting a physician is a federal offense. You know that, right?" Griff shook the doctor three times before the man relented and pointed at the door he'd come through. "Back there, room fifteen. She's sitting up. Refused pain meds."

Griff laughed. "Of course she did." Dropping the doctor, he stalked back to the room, ignoring the concerned looks from the medical staff. Room fifteen was all the way in the back and only one of three rooms to have an actual door rather than a curtain. Griff knocked lightly before he pushed the door open. His breath caught in his throat, his heart hammered at the sight of her. Ugly red and purple patches covered her swollen face. Carl and Millie were going to die for this.

***

Faye was fan folding the sheet one handed then straightening it, smoothing the material. Aware of Griff the moment he entered, she couldn't bring herself to look up at him. Her face hurt, her heart was broken, and her soul was bruised, and he was here for her. Uncertain how she felt about that, she only knew she was frightened. Sensing her unease, he stayed at the end of the bed, pacing back and forth. He was speaking quickly and not making much sense. She couldn't bring herself to focus on any of his words; all that had ever come out of his mouth had been lies and she felt like such a fool for believing them. A few nights of hot sex and amazing orgasms and she thought she was in...she shook her head. No, not even going to think it, so not going there.

Her head snapped up and she immediately regretted the action, he'd stopped pacing and babbling. He'd asked her a direct question. Staring at him, she listened as he said it again. Her lips moved in a whisper barely loud enough for him to hear. The breath he sucked in had her mind and heart screaming to take it back. When she looked up, the door was closing and the first tear rolled down her bruised cheek.

***

He couldn't have explained it any better, he didn't know what else to say. When he asked for her to say something, he hadn't expected her to say that. Storming out of the hospital, he'd almost knocked down Dilly.

The sun glinted off his shiny black hair, the ever present smirk was nowhere to be seen when he caught Griff's dark expression.

"Hey, man, how is she? Did you talk to her? What'd she say?"

Griff snorted bitterly, thinking about what she'd said as he descended the steps.

Dilly jogged down after him, landing in front of his friend and, putting his hands up, halted Griff's momentum. "What did she say?"

Griff stepped around him and said only one word, "Red."

CHAPTER SEVENTEEN

She flinched as the door clicked shut. Though it barely made a sound, to her mind it echoed loudly, reverberating endlessly inside her head. That click caused her breath to hitch and, suddenly, the finality of that sound broke the dam. Tears streamed down her battered face. It even hurt to cry, the salt from her tears literally stinging her wounds. She tried desperately to control it, but the flood gates were opened. Body wracked with pain, her sobs were the only sounds to permeate the small drab hospital room.

How had it all gone to shit so fast? How could she feel such a sense of loss for a man she barely knew? Michael's betrayal hurt her, but for all the wrong reasons. She knew she'd never really loved him. But, this? She absently rubbed her casted hand over her heart. This was a pain she'd never felt. She was in love with Griff...Ian...damn.

Faye attempted to curl into a fetal position as she continued to cry. A sharp exhale of breath escaped her dry, cracked lips as a stab of pain struck her. Trying some shallow breaths, she attempted to calm herself.

She needed to get out of this room. Faye could feel the ugly institutional green walls closing in on her. She didn't want her family or friends or even her enemies to see her like this. Hell, *she* didn't want to see herself like this. Christ, her family. Her brother Sam was going to go ballistic. She had no doubt his department had heard by now; a dirty, dead captain and another cop, albeit a suspended one, hurt bad enough to be hospitalized. Not to mention her dad was going to pull in some big favors when he heard about Howard. They went way back.

While she'd been gasping and sobbing, she'd missed the door opening. Though she did hear a curse, grimacing as she recognized his voice. Slowly, she lifted her head, her hair hung around her battered face as her gaze met his. "What are you doing here, Michael?" Faye clutched her bad hand to her waist as if it could protect her.

"Damn, Baby Do-er...Faye, what did they do to you?"

She lifted her chin in defiance, like she always did, jutting it out. "Nothing I couldn't handle."

He moved closer to her, wincing as the extent of her bruises became more clear. "Here, you deserve to have these back." Michael reached into his pocket and placed her gun and badge on her lap.

Her eyes slid down, narrowing as she watched him, suspicious of what he was up to. Raising her gaze, she cocked her eyebrow. "Catching on a little late, aren't ya'?"

He smirked at her. "Forever the smartass."

She put her hand on her badge, her fingertips tracing over the raised letters and numbers. "What can I say, it's a gift."

"Faye, look at me." He waited for her to raise her eyes to him once again. Mouth set in a grim line, eyebrows furrowed, his voice was a dangerous whisper, "You need to finish this. There's an impromptu..." he tilted his head to the side as if searching for the right word, "gathering, I suppose you could call it. Today. In about an hour and a half. I suggest you drag your ass out of that bed and into some clothes, something less drafty in the back. Let's just say that this 'suggestion,'" he made air quotes, "is more of a direct order. You didn't hear this from me, Kane, but they're looking to nail a scapegoat to the cross for this fucking debacle, which you were a central part of." He held up his hand to stall the argument he could see brewing in her eyes. "I'll be damned if I let them make it you. Surprised?"

Putting his hand in the inside of his suit coat, he pulled out a crumpled pile of papers and tossed them on top of her badge and gun. Her eyes widened as she realized what they were. A rogue tear escaped. Michael cleared his throat. "There's no use crying over spilled milk, Kane. I can't change our personal history, but, professionally? You're a damn fine cop. And if you repeat that to anyone, I'll deny it and suspend your ass for insubordination."

Her spine stiffened at his back handed apology. "Too bad you spilled said "milk" inside my former best friend."

Michael huffed out a frustrated breath. "I called Leah. She's on her way here with some clothes for you."

As soon as those words were out of his mouth, Leah swept right in the room as if on cue. Faye had to give it to her, the woman never even blinked when she looked at her ruined face.

Leah pointed to Michael and ordered him, in some very colorful language to leave. Shoving the door shut, she cursed the pneumatic door for not allowing her to slam the door on the prick's uptight ass. Leah hustled to the bed where Faye was sitting, picked up her gun and badge, and put them on the bedside table. The woman was a force of nature as she whipped the covers from Faye's legs.

"Alright girl, let's get you dressed."

She helped Faye slide her legs to hang off the side of the bed, every muscle in her body screaming in pain. She stifled a groan and Leah froze.

Lips tight, Leah turned, crossed the room and grabbed the garment bag she'd brought. As she unzipped it and removed the clothes, she caught Faye out of the corner of her eye attempting to stand and winked. Returning, she laid out the kick ass suit she must have found in the way back of Faye's closet; the damn tags were still on it.

Faye leaned on her friend, grimacing at the suit. "You picked that?"

Leah laughed and hugged her friend carefully. "Yes, you fashion criminal. Your closet looks like a throwback to an 80's hangover. For today, you need to scream 'I mean fucking business and I'll cut your balls off and use them for batting practice.'"

Faye groaned as she tried not to laugh. "Shit, Leah...don't...ouch...make me laugh."

Leah grinned and leaned down to fish out Faye's favorite boots, holding them up. "And, to finish off your kick ass ensemble."

Leah's grin froze in place as she watched the hospital gown fall to the floor as she struggled visibly to hide her reaction.

Faye had to give Leah credit, she was expecting a full on tirade as she watched her friend's eyes grow wide as she gazed at her battered body. Like a boss, the woman didn't miss a beat. Quickly and gently, she helped Faye dress. When they were done, Faye felt as if she'd just run a marathon.

"Now, for the most important accessory." Leah dug in her purse, reminding Faye of Mary Poppins and her bottomless carpet bag. When Leah pulled her hand out, holding it up in triumph, Faye had to stifle another laugh to avoid the pain. Leah handed Faye her holster.

As Faye attempted to wrestle the damn thing on through gritted teeth, her attending nurse arrived with a tray of meds and a full on scowl at the scene before her. Obviously, she was appalled that her patient was out of bed, and armed. Faye looked at the formidable woman's name tag. "Rachel? I have a meeting. It's life or death, which, I'm sure you can appreciate. No narcs for me." She tilted her head at the tray of vials and syringes. "Perhaps a Motrin or twelve before I go?"

The nurse was ready to argue but as she watched Faye slide her gun in and clip her badge to her waist, she winked at her patient. "Let me see what I can do, Detective."

Faye walked gingerly to the closet, opened the door and faced her reflection in the full length mirror.

Leah came up behind her and helped her with the jacket, completing the ensemble. The charcoal gray suit fit her as if it were made just for her. The suit had been an impulse buy, she'd found it on a clearance rack. Faye snorted. If Leah knew what she'd paid for the thing she'd definitely rap her upside the head. Where and when she got the frilly white blouse she had no idea but all together, the outfit worked. She had to admit she looked less severe, though the bruises complimented the gray suit nicely. Faye painfully pulled a face at her hair, a cotton candy nightmare. "Can you do something with my hair, Le?"

Leah nodded and, again, dug into the Poppins carpet bag extracting a brush and scrunchy. Looking up from the gaping maw of the purse, she asked, "Do you want makeup to hide the bruises?"

Faye regretted the action as soon as she'd made it but shook her head vehemently. "Nope, let them see. They'll hurt them much more than they're hurting me at the moment."

As Leah dragged the brush through her hair and tied it up into a loose bun at the top of her head Faye thought, even her hair hurt.

She sighed in relief as she saw the reflection of the nurse returning with a little medicine cup holding four extra strength ibuprofen. Faye took them, greedily downing them with the water the nurse handed her. As she handed it back, the nurse smiled and pulled a sling out of her pocket.

Weaving a bit Faye tried to put her boots on. Leah chuffed, shoving her friend by her shoulders to sit back on the bed. The nurse rolled her eyes and set the water down on the bedside table before applying the sling. It took some dedicated teamwork to get the thing in place around the holster and to get her arm settled comfortably against her body. Faye hoped the throbbing in her wrist would ease some, and quickly.

The nurse sternly advised her to contact her family doctor as soon as possible, leaving just as Michael re-entered.

"You ready, yet? Time's ticking and I just got word they're about to start."

Faye pocketed the papers Michael had given her and started to gather her stuff. "We have to stop at my place for a minute. Don't give me that look, I'm in the mood for some ice cream."

Leah kissed her cheek and took over. "Go. I'll drop all this off at your place on my way back to the shop. Call me as soon as you get home. I'll be there with Momma's Pizza and wine by the bucket."

Nodding, Faye walked out. Michael moved to grab the door to follow but Leah stopped and grabbed him by the sleeve, pointing a well manicured nail in his face. "Michael, if you fuck her over again, there will be no rock you can hide under where I won't find you. Batting practice will be a holiday compared to what I'll do to your balls. Do we understand each other?"

He stepped back, yanking his arm out of her grasp and wrapped his hand around the door handle. "Yeah, yeah, Le, I know."

***

The car ride was short but excruciating, every nerve ending in her body felt has if it were on fire. Needing her head to be clear for this, Faye put all thoughts of Griff on the backburner. She promised herself a full-blown pity party after she got home, one with pain meds and her bed.

As they headed into the precinct she could feel all eyes on her. Steeling herself, her back ram rod straight, she told Michael she would meet him on his floor. His facial expression relayed his unhappiness, but he nodded and stepped onto the elevator.

She waited for the doors to close on his scowling face, then headed to her desk. After much cussing and painful gasps, she finally fished her spare key out from under its hidey hole and opened her bottom drawer. Grabbing the file, she went over to the copy machine and made duplicates of everything, including the pile of papers Michael had given to her. She slid the extras, along with the crimson matchbook from her freezer, into a manila folder and wrote Sonny's name in large black print on the outside. As she passed her fellow officers she kept her gaze straight ahead, never looking her coworkers in the eye. When she reached the desk sergeant, she shoved the envelope at him and told him to deliver it ASAP.

Trying not to slump, she headed to the stairwell. At least there were copies of everything, just in case the ones she handed over to IA accidentally "got lost" or something mysteriously and tragically happened to her, like death. Sonny would know what to do.

Slowly, she climbed her way to the third floor where Internal Affairs was located. When she approached the conference room she took a steadying breath, gripped the doorknob, and glided inside. Audible gasps and cusses were heard throughout the deathly quiet room. “Well, I see you were going to start this party without me. I’m crushed. After all, what’s a party without the guest of honor?”

Faye tossed the file on the table and it slid directly in front of Michael, seated at the head of the oval table. Rocking back on her heels, she took her first good look around the room. Not only was every seat at the table occupied but there were even some additional spectators hiding in the shadows in every corner of the room. Several high profile faces dotted the crowd. Doing a double take, she spotted Sam sitting in one of the chairs. She guessed they wanted someone from homicide due to Cap’s murder. Her brother being there gave her a little extra backbone. He winked at her.

Someone else offered her a seat. She tilted her head, her gaze sliding in the man’s direction with a dangerous glint in her eyes. “Thanks, but no. The last time I was offered a seat, I ended up tied to the fucking thing with a face full of fist. Something tells me I don’t think you gentlemen and ladies would be as polite.” She cocked an eyebrow at Michael as she heard him groan. “Shall we get this...,” she gestured with her good hand, “so-called debriefing under way?”

Michael cleared his throat and shot her a warning glare to keep her mouth shut before he proceeded to lay out the entire case, including Captain Howard Jensen being on the take of Philly’s latest crime boss.

Faye narrowed her eyes as a man stepped out of the shadows. Leaning over Michael, he picked up her file, then stepped back into the shadows and started leafing through it.

The man's entire bearing screamed uptight Fed, his expression nonplussed at what he read though his salt and pepper brows furrowed with each turn of the page. His dark ultra-conservative suit and bland tie gave him a look of vagueness, like you'd not remember him once seeing him. But his eyes, there was something about his eyes, like he'd seen far too much and participated in way worse. She watched him with rapt interest as Michael's voice droned on around her.

When Michael paused, the man stepped from the shadows once again, this time demanding attention of everyone in the room. His eyes locked on hers as he introduced himself. "For the record, my name is Reverend Porter, Agent In Charge of the Bureau of Criminal Investigation. I'm not a real reverend, but I believe I've prayed more over this damn fucking operation, than I have in my entire life." Addressing, Faye specifically, he caught and held her gaze. "Detective Kane, you really gave us a run."

She blinked and tried to contain her anger. "Well, sir, I'm sure you already heard, I tend to flout authority." She shrugged her shoulders and glanced at Michael, who was rubbing his temples. "What can I say? It's a gift." She gave her brother a quick glance; he just shook his head and suppressed a grin. She turned her attention once again to the AIC.

Porter stepped towards her, repeatedly slapping the file in the palm of his hand. "You're very thorough, Detective, and a pain in the ass."

Faye narrowed her eyes at the new and unknown player in the game, trying to discern if she'd seen him before or knew him from somewhere. Before she could decide if he was familiar or not, movement out of the corner of her eye caught her attention. Turning her head, she recognized the man from the fateful party.

Heaving out a sigh, she did a double take as her eyes settled on a lone figure in the far off corner. Not so well hidden as Porter, it wouldn't have mattered anyway; that face could be seen from the space station in a blackout. Gorgeous hair hung in a plaited braid down his back. Gasping, she ignored the confines of professionalism and stalked over to him, leaning oh so casually against the wall. His arms were folded over his broad chest, his expression amused, like he was at a party instead of a lynching.

Her body screamed in protest at her aggressive approach, but she refused to show any weakness. She stopped right in front of him and he grinned down at her. Son-of-a-bitch, she thought, it was as if the gods had shined down on him and poured all the beauty of the world and heavens into this one being. Native American by descent and just too damn gorgeous for his own good, the bastard clearly knew it.

The roaring in her ears was so deafening she nearly staggered backwards as things began to click into place. She must have swayed because he reached out to steady her. Stumbling back, she pulled away before he could touch her. Through gritted teeth, she hissed, "Where?" She scanned the room for the one she knew without a doubt would be missing from these proceedings.

One by one, men stepped from the shadows. Most she recognized, with the vagueness of a remembered dream, while others, well she was seeing...red. She knew these men, and her temper rose as the men approached her. All the while she continued to seethe, silently raging at the pretty boy before her.

Reverend, sensing danger to his men's favorite body parts, appeared at her side. He started to place a hand on her shoulder until a whip of her head and a glare stalled him mid-motion. With a polite cough, he stated, "My team, Detective. I see you've met, Jon Dillinger. Though, most of us call him Dilly." Another little cough as her steely gaze didn't soften, and he motioned to the male slightly taller than her and somewhat out of focus, like he wasn't real or something. "This is Carpenter, he's been your shadow."

Another try at a smile and another arctic blast from her. Clapping the last man on the shoulder, though he had to reach above his head to do so, Porter finished the introductions. "This is Nolan House, or Brick as you might know him. You made him run. He doesn't like to run."

She turned her head to each man, eyes scanning the shadows for the last one, waiting, unable to breathe, for Griff to appear. When she turned back to face Reverend, she poked her finger in his chest, jutting her defiant chin up to him. "Where the fuck is he?" When Reverend didn't answer, she shoved him as hard as she could, her entire body screaming in agony. "Where, god damn you, where?"

Pretty boy laughed out loud. "He always said she was a handful. Color us dumb for not listening."

Michael stood up, pounding a hand as a makeshift gavel. "We have other more pressing issues to deal with at this time. Shall we proceed?"

She turned her back on the lot of them and started towards the conference room door. Stopping with her hand on the knob, she turned back, her eyes finding Michael. "Captain Jensen was dirty," her gut roiled at saying the words, but she moved forward. "There is no doubt in my mind there are others, some that we considered above reproach are on that list. It's all there in that file. I did my job and it nearly broke me. If you want to punish me for taking a beating while you sat with your thumbs up your asses, well, so be it." She nodded toward the file. "I'll let you get to deciphering that mumbo jumbo but, while you do, you can hold those fucking assholes for kidnapping and the attempted murder of a police officer. Those charges will keep their lawyers busy for a while, especially with my written and sworn statements."

Her gaze swept to the mayor who stood beside Michael as if to remonstrate her for her language, but Michael held up his hand and the man's face turned purple as he choked back his words. Bitterly, she jerked the door open, pausing to give Sam a quick look, his only response was a nod.

Before the door closed, she heard Michael call to her, "That'll be a fifty to the swear jar, Detective."

She couldn't help the laugh that erupted, but she didn't stop walking until she was free of the building. Hustling into a neighboring alley, she unclenched her fists. The piece of paper Dilly had slipped into her hand was crumpled and moist from being wadded into her palm. She had so many questions; a few answers had started to form into a solid picture as she looked around that room at the familiar faces, yet so many were left hanging in the ether there was no way to catch them without the right net.

Lost in thought, she didn't notice she'd been followed, her focus was on the address written on the slip of paper.

"You should have stayed. The shit's hitting the fan, hardcore. The mayor's doing more double talk than he did on his last campaign."

Looking up, startled and ready to fight, she relaxed as she watched Dilly, his long braid swaying as he came closer.

She shrugged. "I've had enough bullshit to last me a lifetime. Let them kill each other for all I care."

"You're quite the ball breaker, Kane. Not his usual type."

"Tell me, how did he find me?"

"Your cell phone. GPS."

“You’re lying. I didn’t have my phone. I’d have called 9-1-1 if I did.”

“Brick dropped it in the pocket of the robe you were wearing. Tell me something, Kane, he ever mean a damn thing to you?”

She whipped her head up. Fixing him with a glare, she gritted out through clenched teeth, “Fuck you.”

He quietly blew out a long breath. “Yeah, that’s what I thought. Whatever. Listen, he’d kick my ass for even talking to you. You’ve been a thorn in his dick since the second you fell into our op. He’s a great agent and an even better friend.”

She held up her good hand to silence him, all the while shaking her head as if to clear Griff...Ian from her mind, body, and soul. Turning her back, she walked away without another word, crumpling the paper in her fist and tossing it in the nearest dumpster without missing a stride.

She walked for blocks, miles; the entire way to her apartment. All the while her mind screamed, almost as loud as her bruised and battered body. Barely upright, she stumbled into her apartment and locked the door. She made her way to her bathroom, slowly undressing and wrapped her casted wrist in a plastic bag retrieved in a brief sidestep into the kitchen.

She scrubbed her body, trying to wash away the kidnapping, the beating, the last few weeks, hoping all the shit would fall off her bruised body and just swirl down the drain.

Damn it, she’d been so out of it; Carl the Beater had done a number on her. Still, she remembered Griff...Ian, battering his way into that cabin. Unwilling to think what it meant, she remembered feeling his rage and anger. At the time, she thought, god, she thought he was pissed because he wasn't the one doling out the beating. Then, when he tried to explain at the hospital she'd still been in a pain-filled fog.

Covering her face, she couldn't hide from the look in his eyes when she whispered Red, the safe word he'd given her. Sliding down the tiles, she sobbed and hiccoughed as everything crashed down around her.

Déjà vu danced around the tiny bathroom as she remembered all the god damn events that spiraled her, no, really launched her, into a man who would show her what it truly meant to be deeply, crazily in love.

Finally, she staggered out of the tub and gingerly dried off. Finding his t-shirt that still smelled of him, she slipped it on and climbed into her bed, drying tears stinging the cuts on her face. Burrowing herself deep in her bed, she closed her eyes, giving into the sheer exhaustion and gratefully fell away.

CHAPTER EIGHTEEN

3 weeks later...

She thought she was still dreaming but that aroma. Moaning, she whispered, "Coffee."

The bed dipped and her eyes flew open so she was staring into Leah's beautiful green eyes. Her friend's fiery red hair spread out on the other pillow reminding Faye of all the blood spilled, both physically and emotionally from the gaping wound in her soul.

She blinked repeatedly to make sure she wasn't imagining things. Faye wasn't even sure what day it was; she'd barely left her bed except to use the bathroom. Food was like sawdust in her mouth, so she mostly sipped from a water bottle she kept at the bedside. After several hours, or was it days? However long it was, she started thinking J.K. Rowling was right about those damn Dementors; she felt as if all the happiness had been sucked out of her.

Leah popped the coffee under her nose. "Shower, girl, and this will be your reward. If I don't see you in twenty, I'm outta here." Tears leaked out of the corner of Faye's eyes, Leah didn't miss a beat. "Your eyes are watering because you reek!" She smacked Faye's ass cheek through the sheet. "Come on girl, time to get up."

Faye dragged her sorry ass out of bed with an irritated huff. But, once she was in, she had to admit the shower felt orgasmic, not that she remembered what *that* was after all this time. She laughed at her bad timed sense of humor. Done cleaning herself, she slipped into yoga pants and a t-shirt for comfort. Then, once she saw the shape her bed was in, she pulled a face. Declaring them "gross," she immediately changed her sheets, slipping her piece back under her pillow where it lived now. After she was done, she made a mental note to burn those sheets; there was no salvaging them. Feeling mildly human again, Faye padded to the kitchen, barefoot and hair still damp.

Her cast had come off three days ago but her wrist was still sore and stiff. Now she realized why the doctor had looked at her the way he did; she'd been damn scary looking and quite pungent.

The doctor had debated leaving the cast on for another week, but Faye promised to continue to use the sling and take it easy. Her bruises were nearly gone, some turning a nice jaundicey coloration as they healed. Most of the cuts had shrunk to mere shadows of what they once were. It was a shame the effects of her mental battering was lingering far longer than the physical one. She doubted she would ever sleep without her gun under her pillow.

While Leah was cooking Faye listened to her voicemails on both her house and cell phones. Her messages runneth over, but she couldn't bring herself to give a shit about any of them though. Sam was livid, yet even under his anger she could hear how proud of her he was. She would have to remind him he so owed the swear jar. Hell, even her dad's message warranted a hefty deposit into that damn jar.
Leah handed Faye a cup of piping hot coffee and smiled wide at her. "Much better. I can actually smell the food I'm cooking instead of that stench that surrounded you."

Faye took a sip of the coffee and flipped her off with a small smile and wink.

Leah threw her head back and laughed. "I've got that covered, thanks for the offer though. Sit. I'm cooking you something to eat, it's fatty, greasy and good for the soul. While you were wallowing in your filth I bought groceries. Perhaps in the future, when you're kidnapped and beaten, you could at least have a full fridge for those of us who are stress eaters. Oh, and that you're alive, that's important, too." Winking back at her friend, she set a plate of bacon, omelet, home fries, and toast before her. Taking the seat across from Faye, Leah set her chin in her hands. "Do you know how many calls you've gotten? How many *I've* gotten? Shit, the national debt's nothing compared to my phone bill right now."

Faye shrugged. "Sorry."

Leah stabbed at the omelet Faye was playing with and not eating. Faye dropped her fork, shut her eyes, and sipped her favorite coffee.

"You want to talk about it, girlie?"

She blew out a long hard breath. "What's to talk about? The whole thing was a clusterfuck. I couldn't tell the good guys from the bad."

Leah pointed at the omelet with her fork. "Eat, it'll help. You have decisions to make, and if I have to kick your ass to get you to make them, I will. I've done it before, won't be any skin off my nose to do it again. Don't give me that look. God damn it, Faye. You know it's bad when I'm getting calls from Michael. Michael! Faye, no good deed goes unpunished, and...well, Michael!"

Faye smirked and forked some of the mushroom and cheese omelet in her mouth. Leah, bless her, made her favorite. The bitch, she thought lovingly. She really hadn't realized how hungry she was until she took that first bite and, then promptly went on to devour every last morsel on her plate, then downed all the juice.

Looking up, Leah was grinning at her. "That's my girl. Now here, take some ibuprofen. Your ribs and wrist must ache like a bitch."

Downing the pills with the last of her coffee, Faye felt almost back to normal. "Thanks."

Leah stood and started clearing the dishes. "Well, it was time for you to get up. Shit, you've been hibernating for weeks. Enough is enough."

Faye was somewhat shocked. "Weeks? No fucking way. I left the bed seventy-two hours ago to get my cast off." She lifted her wrist to show her.

Leah rolled her eyes. "That was for less than two hours and it doesn't count, oh eloquent one. I was tired of fielding calls for you. You can't hideout forever."

Over the next quarter of an hour, Leah filled her in on all that Zi and Sam had disclosed. Faye didn't think she could be any more stunned than she all ready was, but she was wrong.

So many names were on that list she'd risked her life to get: the mayor, Lister and Barnett from Vice. Holy shit, the names spewed on and on. Some she recognized as public figures, there was even someone from IA on the list. Holy shit!

Leah came back and pulled a chair close to hers. "Listen Faye, Sam also told me something that's being hushed up. You really should have taken your brother's calls, girlie. Your captain? Yeah, he was...uh...paid to kill you. I honestly don't know what went on in that room when he was... er... died, but girl, that man saved your ass."

Faye was staring at her lap. Fuck, this nightmare never seemed to end. Griff...Ian saved her life? Just thinking his name took her breath away. She had been hiding for weeks, unable and unwilling to process much, if any of it. Taking any portion of that time to examine it under the microscope was too confusing and painful.

"So, I've been quite the busy little bee since you've been incommunicado. I had a visit from a very sexy agent." Faye's head whipped up and Leah chuckled. "No, not your sexy agent. This one was too gorgeous for words and had much better hair than either of us." Faye smiled sadly at Leah's blatant mention of *him*, whispering that he was not hers. "Well chickie," Leah went on undaunted, "this hottie was looking for you. He seemed surprised you didn't utilize some address he slipped you. What's that about? What address? Anyway," she waved her hand, "apparently, he and many others have been here," she pointed her finger down on the kitchen table for emphasis, "and, you appeared to not be. He was under the impression that you'd taken his not so subtle hint. But, since his friend is still miserable and a wee bit crazed, he realized you hadn't. I don't know him, but I'm agreeing with him on this. What in the hell are you waiting for?"

Faye felt beaten down emotionally. She'd loved more in their short time than most do in an entire lifetime but shit, it also scared the holy hell out of her. Instead of trusting her gut, she chose to wave the white flag, or in this case, the red one. She hung her head and whispered, "I made him go. I said the one thing that was sure to send him away. I didn't trust him...me...us. Shit," she cursed softly.

Leah watched her friend wrestle with her emotions; she'd never seen her so lost. Slamming her hands down on the table top, she made Faye jump. "Where's Pip, the terror of Pine Hill? Where's the girl that grabbed life by the balls, consequences be damned? Dig down. You were right about that scum Maliano. You didn't let your job deter you from what your gut told you, you brought him down. What's your gut telling you now? Come on, stop being a god damn pussy. Stop letting what happened with Michael cloud your judgment. Talk about pussy, shit."

Faye raised an eyebrow at her. "Yeah, my face, ribs, wrist, and other divots in my armor thank me loud and clear for following my gut. Oh...and fuck you very much for bringing that up."

Leah barked out a laugh, leaning over to squeeze her hand. "There's my sassy bitch."

Relaxing for the first time in weeks, Faye sighed then smiled. "Can I borrow your car?"

Leah jumped up. "Now you're talking, girlie. Hell yes! Although, you probably shouldn't be driving. Go right ahead, I won't tell. After all, that might get you spanked." As Faye gasped and blushed, Leah laughed and waved her off. "Besides, I have a date tonight with one gorgeous agent and I told him to pick me up here." Leah wiggled her ass. "Maybe I can get a spanking of my own."

Faye stood up, still blushing but laughing so hard she had to grab her ribs. "Oh shit, that hurts. You're going on a date with Jon Dillinger?"

"Did I say 'date'? Silly me." Leah winked and did a hoochy dance in Faye's kitchen as Faye tried again not to laugh.

***

In the four point two seconds that she looked at the address Dilly had given her a few weeks ago, she'd memorized the dumb thing. Maybe memorized wasn't strong enough of a word. That address was emblazoned on her brain, burned into her corneas, tattooed on her short and long-term memories.

Hastily, she dumped some clothes and toiletries into an overnight bag with Leah's help. Meaning, Leah went behind her and folded the wadded clothes, then snuck in some sexy items Faye wouldn't have chosen if she'd been paid.

It seemed fitting she was headed towards one of her favorite places. No matter where she was on this earthly plane, the beach made her feel centered. How poetic that the beach was where he was holed up. She cranked the music and drove towards her destiny.

According to what Dilly told Leah, Ian was staying at a place right on the beach in Ocean Shores. Faye was familiar with it, she'd gone there as a kid. She loved how tranquil the place was even with the tourists; the constant sound of waves crashing no matter what time of year it was.

The simple act of driving over the 9th Street bridge and breathing in the salt air somehow made all her troubles blow away with the light ocean breeze. She smiled just thinking about the water lapping against the sand, the sounds of the street vendors hawking their wares, and the myriad of scents from the restaurants on the pier. Basically, she clung to anything to keep her mind off of him.

She'd pushed him away, would he do the same? How would she feel when she saw him again? Faye blew out a long sigh and focused on her drive, her body wound tight and still a little sore.

The early spring day was one of those where the sun shone high in the sky. The air was still and chilly, and as she crossed over the bridge onto the island, she shivered, though she wasn't sure if it was from the weather or anticipation. She guided Leah's car towards 50th Street, taking her time driving through the main part of town taking in all the sights. The small shops with the quirky owners who were spraying the sidewalks, the boardwalk with joggers and cyclists, and the ocean view that still took her breath away.

Inevitably, her thoughts drifted to the man she'd come to confront. Looking for an upside, she figured if things didn't work out she'd find a place to crash for a few days, lick her wounds. But then what?

Before she left she'd called Michael letting him know to tell whoever was in charge at the station she was going out of town for a few days. And when she returned she wanted to take out the trash, do her part to clean up her department. She also told him she was ready to testify against Maliano. She also called Sam. Her brother gave her more shit than she expected. She let him have his mad, if the roles were reversed, hell she would have stormed his place by now. He always knew when to back off and when to come in gang busters. Also, she begged him to hold her parents off for just a little longer. Faye had been informed that she owed him, big time. When he tried to inquire about the agent who rescued her she feigned another call coming in, promising to be in touch soon.

Faye figured they'd be uncovering messes for months to come. She was still having a hard time believing her captain had consented to do the hit on her. God, her head hurt. She knew, well, she thought she knew, that Griff was also supposed to do the hit. Until she learned that all the while he was actually protecting her, even from herself.

Man, she had really fucked it all up. Every last piece of info that'd been sent her way since that violent night in the "safe house" only made her see that he had been trying to keep her out of harm's way while still trying to do his job. Somehow she wished she would have known they were on the same side, yet she understood why, now, that there was no way for that to happen. Hell, her boss and co-workers were dirty. How could the BCI agents know she wasn't just as dirty? Especially after she'd agreed to be Millie's toy and gotten unwittingly put on his payroll.

"Fuck," Faye sighed as it all finally penetrated. Sometimes, she was too thick for words. At the end of the day, Faye *was* her job. She should've known she wouldn't fall for someone that didn't play by her rules.

She chuckled softly into the wind. Well, he mostly played by her rules. Shivering, she remembered how his hands felt on her body, all the interesting things he'd done to her body. Slowing down, she began looking intently at the numbers on the houses. She blinked several times as she spotted the beautiful, isolated Victorian house up ahead. The house stood at the edge of the street at a dead end, dunes protected it on one side, while the other side was piled high with shrubs.

Whoever owned this place must have bought a double lot. There were no houses, or skeletons of decaying houses, on either side. The only one of its kind, the house was a cornflower blue with white shutters and a wraparound porch. Another deck jutted out on the second floor. The view would be breathtaking from either, she thought. Her gaze was still on the house as she parked the car and got out, head tipped back, blinking in awe. Faye ducked behind some tall shrubs and found her way up a winding driveway.

Heavy metal music assaulted her ears and she followed the screaming of a lead guitar to the open garage door. Mouth dropping, she beheld the most beautiful sight. Without thinking, she walked through the garage and slid her hand over the gorgeous, slick red 1967 Mustang convertible GT. Damn, if the thing didn't make her ache for her incinerated baby. Except for color, the car was an exact replica of hers; a Phoenix rebirthed from its fiery death. The color made her think of that god damn safe word and her last contact with Griff... shaking her head, Ian.

She continued to walk around the car, caressing the silky smooth metal as she moved, afraid if she stopped touching it, it would disappear. Gaze transfixed on the car, she missed the form sticking out from underneath the chassis and stumbled. Suddenly, there he was to catch her before she fell.

He blinked several times as if uncertain she was really there. Pulling her elbow out of his grip, she took a few steps back. He moved towards her, reaching her in one long stride. His intense gaze swept over her body, making her shiver. Damn him, how'd he do that? Stopping, his eyes lingered on all of her still healing physical wounds. Reaching out, he grazed her cheek with his knuckles.

Then, swiftly, he reached around and undid the clip holding up her hair, letting it spill around her face. Faye looked up into his eyes as he cupped her face and very carefully kissed her. His lips brushed over every bruise, cut and blemish that marred her face.

She sighed against his stubbled cheek. He was so gentle with her, yet the intensity of his actions made her ache desperately for so much more. From habit, her newly healed wrist had been pressed protectively against her chest when he grabbed her. Now, it lay sandwiched between them, touching both hearts. Dropping before her, he knelt, gently wrapping his arms around her middle, trying to not hurt her. She could feel his breath coming in short, choppy, pants as she ran her good hand through his hair. It was longer than she remembered; she liked it.

Every time she'd been with him, he'd carried an air of danger swirling around him like a cloak, always there, ever present. Right now, today, he seemed almost vulnerable, bare to his soul.

When he stood back up she kept her hand tangled in his hair. He still had yet to utter a single word. Yet, somehow, it was okay, just the hint of intimacy at their reintroduction spoke volumes.

Not able to handle the silence any longer, she stood up on her tippy toes and pulled him closer by his hair to whisper in his ear. "Nice car." She smiled up at him. Her first genuine smile in ages, it came from the very depths of her soul. Ian's laughter boomed through the small space, his body vibrating with it. Pulling back from their embrace, he winked at her as he pulled keys from his pocket and dangled them in front of her questioning face. He tugged her hand out of his hair and pressed the keys into her palm.

Opening her palm, she looked at the keys and burst out laughing. Her old keychain blazed bright yellow in her hand. CAUTION: I Like To Get Drunk And Hump Things.

Wait. How did he find this keychain? Surely it wasn't hers; not the one from her baby.

She looked back up at him, his gaze penetrating. Tucking an errant strand of hair behind her ear, he kissed the tip of her nose. "Go have a look inside."

Her senses were on hyper-drive. Suddenly, he was too close, the music was too loud, the sun was too bright, everything was too much. She pulled away and climbed in the driver's side. As she slid in and looked around she was stunned silent. It was the same year, after all, so she shouldn't be shocked at the similarity to her baby. But, to find another car was one thing, to find one with impeccable interior was something all together different and difficult, if not damn near impossible.

Faye ran her hand over the dash, which was smooth as silk. Closing her eyes, she inhaled the faint scent of lemon mixed with leather and let out a soft groan. Her eyes flashed open as the garage went dead quiet.

Leaning forward, Faye turned the ignition, closing her eyes as the engine growled to life. The radio boomed, making her jump at first, and then she began to sing along quietly, bobbing her head with the beat of the latest Rhianna song. Ian slid in the passenger seat and quietly watched her, smiling. She was joy incarnate and he basked in her glow. Finally, she opened her eyes again, and turned down the radio, laying her head on the steering wheel to face him. "This is some sweet ride, she reminds me of the one I lost."

Turning off the engine, she attempted to hand him back the keys but he waved her off, with a mysterious smirk. When he was no more forthcoming, she rolled the key chain between her fingers. “Where did you get this? Is it mine? I thought I lost it. I mean, I’m sure thousands of these were made, but is this one actually *mine* mine?”

Ever silent and stoic, Ian slipped out the passenger side and walked to the front of the car. Helpless against her body’s reaction, her eyes tracked his lithe movements through the windshield. Damn, that boy’s gorgeous, she thought. Just one look from him made her body quiver. The tight black t-shirt fit like a second skin, the sexy as sin tat peeking at her, daring her to come for another lick. The old pair of jeans hung off his hips making her wonder how many pulls it would take to yank them down. His hair hung loose, curling around his ears and almost touching his shoulders. But, those eyes. Those fucking eyes sucked her in from the beginning.

Standing at the front of the car, he watched her through the window. He still looked like he did on that fateful night in the bar, exuding power, intensity and something so much darker. Difference was, she knew, now, that there was goodness, a sense of justice in him that she somehow doubted before. She should never have let him, no, pushed him, away.

She blinked, and like a ray of light breaking through the clouds, she realized he was home, her home. Faye turned off the car and exited. Again, the silence was louder than the music it replaced. It was her turn to stalk over to him. She stood right in front of him. “You didn’t answer my question, Ian.”

He cocked his eyebrows and grinned. “I see you’re wearing your bossy pants today, Sugar.”

She poked him hard in the chest and he gazed down at her, his eyebrows almost disappearing into his hairline. He began to walk towards her, forcing her to walk backwards. The backs of her legs came into gentle contact with the front bumper. He pressed his body against hers until her ass rested on the hood of the car. Her finger still pressed into his chest, he growled. "I took it."

Confused, she blinked up at him. "What? Why? Why would you even care?"

He shook his head. "That night, that first night, after you ran out of my truck. When I returned your keys. I thought for sure you'd rip me a new one for stealing it. And besides," he shrugged, "I figured it was less conspicuous than stealing your panties...oops, I forgot, you weren't wearing any. And, as to why, that little saying summed you up, my sexy little smart ass."

She stared up at him. He was so damn close she could feel the heat emanating from his body. Leaning down, he licked the shell of her ear, whispering, "You can have it back, Sugar."

She stared down at the keys and chain in her sore hand. Then, realizing what he was saying, Faye gaped at him, flattening her palm against his heart. "The car? It's mine? I send you away and you...you buy me a car. Why?"

Closing her hand around the car keys, squeezing them, silent tears slid down her face, she could feel his heart beating wildly under her hand. She bowed her head until the top rested against his chest.

***

He watched as her emotions flitted across her face. His gut told him he would see her again. After he climbed out of the tenth or hundredth bottle of Jameson, he had about twenty platefuls of Hangover Helper and several Dilly lectures that all boiled down to the same thing: Get your fucking head out of your ass. Ian decided it was best if he took some time off and went away. Dilly strongly suggested, with a couple of uppercuts, and crotch punches, that he go to the one place that truly was home to him, the beach. He loved it here; he'd dumped all his savings and spare time into this haven. Dilly may have been a pain in the ass but the guy helped with the planning and construction. So, Ian conceded, he might be right, though he'd never admit it out loud.

Except for his team no one knew it was his; all records to the house were buried and, if anyone did go snooping, they'd find the place was in escrow hell battling between two off-shore banks and two very rich families. The place was completely off the grid.

As for the car, well, that was easy peasy. As soon as hers went up in smoke he'd put feelers out. Carpenter, that sneaky little fuck, could find a needle in a stack of metal shavings, in the dark. Son-of-a-bitch found this car in a matter of hours. Ian had the car delivered here. And why the fuck not? He was already here licking his wounds and waiting. He figured he would give Faye some time to heal as well, emotionally and physically, and then, he'd go to her. Tell her he wasn't giving up on her, on them. He'd tell her they were made for each other. He grinned a little, as if he could tell her anything.

She, as usual, blew him away showing up here. He should have figured if she didn't listen to him, she sure as hell wouldn't listen to the doctors. He'd have to knock Dilly around a bit, make his teeth rattle in his skull for not giving him the courtesy of a heads up that he'd disclosed this location to her. GQ cocksucker was the only one that knew where he was currently. Lost in his thoughts, he was pulled back by the absence of her touching him. She'd slid back inside the car, he could hear the radio. Smiling, he shook his head; her and her music, well, wouldn't she be surprised.

Suddenly, the radio grew louder and he realized she was getting out of the car. Damn fickle female. He blinked at her as she moved into his personal space, tucking her body against his. Well, shit, if that didn't stroke a guy's ego. Happily, he wrapped his arms around her and felt the vibration of her voice as she sang along to the song. Her eyes fluttered closed and she held on to him tightly, gripping the front of his shirt with her good hand. Together, they swayed to the song as the sun sank below the horizon. Holding on, he squeezed her in reassurance, letting her know he understood. He knew what it took for her to come to him, to try and tell him how she felt.

The song finished and she looked up at him, tears still on her beautiful face. "Will you be my home, Ian?"

As he stepped away from her, he heard her small intake of breath. He looked over his shoulder at her as he leaned inside the car to click off the key, silencing the music. He'd upgraded the sound system to include an iPod dock to accommodate her music fetish, so before he stood back to his full height, he'd grabbed the iPod and handed both it and her keys to her. Before she could say anything, he smiled wide, then scooped her up in his arms.

She gasped, ready to argue, then, miraculously tamping down her damn stubborn streak, sighed as she laid her head on his shoulder.

He hoisted her up and kicked in the adjoining house door. Kissing her roughly, he spoke against her lips. "I already am, Faye. Always."

Ian walked quickly through the house and to the back porch. Using his hip to open the French doors, he hugged her closer against his warmth as he stopped at the railing to watch as the sun set over the water. Her arms snaked around his neck and a sense of calm washed through him the likes of which he'd never felt. It'd always seemed he was running from this thing to that thing, hiding here and there and always on the razor's edge of danger. He always had to watch his back, was always waiting for the next shoe to drop.

The two things in his life he was the most sure of, the plot where he built his house, and her; he knew the second he saw them both they belonged to him. As soon as he saw the plot, he'd envisioned from the start what he wanted to build here. He never realized how complete he'd feel to have someone with whom to share the space. Squeezing her ever closer, he kissed the top of her head. "You hungry? I've got a great kitchen, want to take a gander?" He felt her nod against his chest. Then, turning his back on the sunset, he walked back through the French doors to the kitchen. He sat her carefully on the bar stool at the kitchen island and, kissing her on the forehead, he walked around to the other side of the island and leaned on his hands. "How about I dig us up some grub and we can eat on the deck?" She nodded again. He smiled. "You ever going to talk to me, Sugar?"

The smile she gave him lit her up from the inside out. "Can I take a look around?"

He pushed off the island, spreading his arms wide. "Mi casa es su casa."

As she slid off the stool to wander around the house, she gingerly rotated her wrist. The doctor warned her to take it easy, but encouraged her to start using it, telling her it could cut down and possibly completely rule out physical therapy. She wanted no part of any type of therapy, physical or mental, as either would further delay her return to active duty. The pig-shaped stress ball, which almost crapped when he was squeezed, did give her a few hours of entertainment and was a much better alternative than any damn therapy.

Walking past the sofa, she glanced up at the vaulted ceiling. God, the floor to ceiling windows framing the fireplace were gorgeous. As her gaze was still trained towards the ceiling, she noticed an inside balcony peeking out from the second floor. She could hear him slamming cabinet and refrigerator doors, she turned her tilted head towards the kitchen. "Hey, I'm going to go poke around upstairs." He called back that was fine.

The entire house was decorated in earth tones. Head slowly moving from side to side so as not to miss anything, she climbed the steps one at a time, taking a second at each step to appreciate her surroundings. Having reached the landing, she looked over the balcony, down into the living room and kitchen. Ian was pouring wine. She couldn't help but smile at how domestic this all was.

Continuing her trek up the stairs, she started nosing around the bedrooms. When she reached the last one, the fourth, if she counted correctly, the master suite. "Holy shit," she sighed as she pushed the door open. The walls were a warm, soft beige, the floor covered in deep, plush carpeting the color of which would have made the sky envious.

Apparently, the owner of this place had a thing for French doors, she thought as the ocean view caught her attention out of the corner of her eye. When she raised her hand to push the doors open, she realized the song she'd been singing wasn't actually in her head, but coming through invisible speakers inside the room. She laughed out loud, man she loved this place.

The view off the second floor deck was simply breathtaking. Leaning against the railing, she closed her eyes and lost herself to the sounds of the waves crashing against the shore, inhaling slowly, taking in the scent of her favorite place.

She smiled as she felt him behind her. When she turned, he handed her a glass of wine. Grateful, she took a long pull. "You must know some pretty special people or they owe you big time. This house is amazing. House on the beach, music piped into every fucking room. Damn, Ian, it's my wet dream."

He barked out a laugh nearly spitting out his wine. "Faye, Sugar, this is *my* house."

A soft breeze moved her hair and he tamed an errant strand by tucking it behind her ear. His hand lingered, caressing her cheek. "Other than my team, no one knows about this place. Dilly's the only one who's ever been here. However, that invitation may be rescinded. Fucker doesn't know how to keep a secret. He is kind of handy with a hammer, though, he helped with some of the ground work and painting."

She grinned like a fool. "I must have misunderstood him. I thought you were crashing at a friend's. Ian, it's amazing." A blush raced up her neck, coloring her cheeks. Bowing her head, she looked up at him through thick lashes. "Can I just say, I want to..."

Not waiting for her to finish, he took her mouth in a heated kissed with a fierceness that left her panting. He growled against her lips. "Oh, Sugar. I'm going to fuck you in every. Room. Of. This. House...Twice."

She shivered. "You took the words right out of my mouth." She backed away from him with mischief in her eyes; even battered and bruised, she was still the sexiest damn woman he'd ever laid eyes on.

He was aching to be inside of her, again. Absently, he rubbed his free hand over the front of his jeans while the other squeezed the wine glass. When he heard the glass squeak in his hand, he knew it was time to set it down.

She was slowly walking backwards, her eyes trained on his hand continuing to move over the bulge announcing its presence inside his jeans.

As she sipped at her wine, she snaked her pretty tongue out, teasing him. Turning away from him, she made the last few steps inside the bedroom. Eyes glued to her ass, he watched as she swayed her hips in blatant invitation. He whistled loudly.

CHAPTER NINETEEN

She looked over her shoulder. "You going to stand there ogling my ass or you going to come and get it, big boy?" For the first time she noticed the bed. Beautiful and huge, it was an oak sleigh bed, king size if the king was from the land of giants. She thought she might have to start jogging again just so she could make it across the bed without passing out from exhaustion. With a smirk she walked to the side and ran her hand over the navy blue plaid bedspread, the beiges, light blues, and hints of yellow accented the room perfectly. Hell, the whole scene was like something written in one of those damn romance novels, good thing this was reality, she thought.

Ian came up behind her and wrapped his arms around her. Careful not to squeeze too tightly, he settled a kiss on her neck. Melting against him, she felt his warmth wrap around her, his scent intoxicating her, making her dizzy for him. As much as she knew they had much to learn about each other, about adapting and compromising, Faye knew down to the very depths of her soul that they belonged together. She turned in his arms. "I'm sorry I sent you away."

"Shh, no apologies Sugar. You're here now, we're here now, together. Shit, if we're starting down that whole 'sorry' path, I'll have to start a fucking list; we'd be here for days." Hooking his finger under her chin, he tilted her face up to his. "It makes me sick they got their hands on you, but, it's time to move forward. Later, we'll hash it all out. Tonight, let me throw out the welcome wagon."

Tenderly, he wrapped his hand around her injured wrist, bringing her fingers to his mouth to kiss each of the pads one by one. On some sort of timer, the bedside light clicked on, illuminating the table where he'd placed their wine glasses and a small tray of snacks for them to nibble on. Who the hell was this guy? There was an assortment of cheeses, fancy crackers, fruits, and shaved deli meats.

He noticed her staring at the platter. “Do you want to eat?” Tugging her a little closer, he gripped the bottom hem of her t-shirt. Pulling it over her head, he tossed the thing over his shoulder. “Or, we can just stay right here.” As he grazed the back of his hand over her hardened nipple, he raised an eyebrow and gave her that telltale smirk. “No bra?”

Breathless, she swallowed hard at his touch, shaking her head. “I still can’t get one on without help.”

“Well, I think I’m going to enjoy your limitations.” Bending his head, taking one peak into his mouth, Ian swirled his tongue around the hardened nub. Taking it between his teeth, he gave it a good nip.

With a groan, Faye’s head fell back. Both nipples beaded tighter and a warm gush of fluids pooled between her legs in the same place that began throbbing, demanding to be filled. He gave her other nipple equal treatment while massaging, pinching and pulling the other nipple.

She could tell he was trying to be gentle with her, acting as if she would break. Then he picked her up and laid her gently across the bed, gripping her hips and shimmying her yoga pants off along with her panties. Her scent filled his bedroom and he growled, ready to devour her in one greedy feast.

Bared to him, vulnerable, naked down to her soul, she didn’t bother trying to cover the fading bruises scattered over her torso. His gaze raked over her body as he peeled his shirt off and dropped his jeans to the floor. Noticing her eyes lingering on his tattoo, he grinned. “I’m glad you like.”

Giving a slight nod in agreement, she softly sang the lyrics of the song piping into the room; words that reflected her need for him to stay, always. He grasped her hand and tugged her to a sitting position. Then, with little encouragement he moved back, her following, a questioning expression on her face. Ian settled on a settee in the corner of his room, pulling her onto his lap.

Ian gripped the base of his cock as she straddled his legs. Laying a steadying hand on her shoulder, he gave her a wicked grin as he swept the broad head across her slick folds. With a hiss, Faye sucked her bottom lip between her teeth. Gripping her by the nape of her neck, making her bend to him, Ian leaned up and took her mouth in a crushing kiss. "Tell me what you want, Sugar."

Impatient, Faye panted against his lips. "Fuck me, damn it."

"Oh, that mouth of yours," he chuckled, then leaned back and gave her a slight nod.

Knowing his intent, she lowered her knees, slowly impaling herself on his long, smooth shaft. Her head lolled back at the stretch and burn, sighing at the pleasure and pain of having him inside her again. Her movements were slow and deliberate, she wanted to feel every inch of him, every vein, every scrape against her walls massaging her internal bundle of nerves until she was breathless and begging for satisfaction.

His hands splayed across her back as his mouth ravaged each of her breasts in turn. He moaned out her name as she arched her back, her breast disappearing further into the warm cavern of his mouth.

They moved as if they were dancing. The moon lifted over the water, shimmering, as their moans and sighs filled his room, drowning out the music. Arms around his neck, Faye tried to quicken their pace as he filled her, stretched her.

With a soft placement of his palms on her thighs, he told her without words to slow down.

Ian twined his fingers in her hair and brought her face close to his, stealing another soul searing kiss, connecting their bodies in every way, desperately pouring his feelings into her. As his cock thrust inside her she thrust her tongue inside his mouth, matching his frustratingly slow and sensual rhythm.

Still trying to be gentle with her, Faye chuckled and sighed at each extra sharp nip or squeeze of his strong hands on her thighs and ass. No matter how he touched her she felt cherished; each time they made love she experienced something new with him.

Placing both hands on his cheeks, she pulled back from the kiss. "You know I'm not going to break, right?" Even though she was gazing into his eyes, her hands framing his ruggedly handsome face, she never stopped gliding up and down, savoring every slow stroke. The knowing smile that settled on his face made her laugh.

He leaned forward and nipped her bottom lip. "Don't worry, Sugar, as soon as you're one hundred percent I'm going to give you the spanking of your life."

Dropping her hands on his shoulders she brought herself up, and eyes locking, ground down harder. The pace changing, she wanted to show him she was real, here, and could handle whatever he dished out.

***

He felt her mood change; she was trying to push him over the edge by moving faster, a wildness filling her eyes as they locked with his. It sickened him that someone hurt her and, damn it, he wanted this time to be gentle. He didn't want to hurt her more. He loved her spirit and he really loved that she was willing to let him take over. And, son of a bitch that he was, who was he to deny her what she wanted?

"Sugar? That keychain of yours...is that saying true?" He grinned at her confused expression.

Confusion turned to disdain. Panting, "I...mmm...don't know...is that...oooooh...really important... right... ahhh... now?"

"Mmmm, yes, very important. You see, if you only hump things when you get drunk, you're going to be an alcoholic by the end of the weekend."

Stopping her movements, Faye tilted her head and gave him a lopsided grin, then threw her head back, laughing hard. She wrapped her arms around his neck, kissing his cheek. "Oh my god, I love you." As soon as the words were out of her mouth, she gasped, her hand flying to her mouth and hopped off his lap. Backing away, she shook her head in obvious panic.

In one swift movement he stood up, stalked over to her, making her walk backwards until she hit the wall. He took her hand away from her mouth and put each hand behind her back, locking them in place being mindful of her sore wrist. Then he kicked her feet apart with his, pressing their naked, sex flushed bodies together so as not even a breath of air could squeeze through. He hooked her chin with his index finger, lifted her blushing face, her lips swollen and berry red from their kissing. "What did you say, Faye?"

She shook her head from side to side, looking every bit a frightened animal. She was trying to hide from him, but he decided that from this point forward there would be no hiding. “Nope, no closing off. We’re done with that little game. Now, what did you say?”

Blinking up at him, her voice a barely audible whisper, she spoke again. “I said...I-I love you, Ian.”

The silence bore down on them and, again, she looked absolutely terrified until he nodded. “Good. Now, that spanking I promised earlier? Yeah, after each smack, do you know what you’re going to say?”

The smart ass comment came without any hesitation. “Thank you, Sir, may I have another?”

Ian threw his head back and barked out a laugh. “No, Faye. The last thing I want to think about when your sexy little ass is over my knee, is Kevin Bacon. No, you’re going to say, ‘I love you, Ian,’ until the words don’t sound like words anymore and your ass glows in the dark. Shall we have a practice run, at let’s say, level one?” He pulled her body against his, her arms still locked behind her back, and his hand came down on her ass in a none too light smack.

The sting to her ass quickly turned into a comfortable and very throb inducing burn that settled in her already sensitive clit. Faye’s voice turned husky. “I-I love you, Ian.”

Smack.

“A little more conviction.”

Smack.

“I love you, Ian.”

“Better. Now, shall we finish what we started?”

In one fluid motion he picked her up, encouraging her to wrap her legs around his waist. Without guidance, his cock immediately found its way back inside her. They both groaned and froze briefly, savoring that first stroke all over again.

Balancing her with one arm, he moved them to the bed, reaching around her to grab the edge of the bedcovers and rip them aside. He brought his knees to the side of the bed, climbing on, still resolutely inside her.

She wiggled, groaned, and pouted up at him from his lack of movement, making him smile. "What's the matter? Did I ruin your plans? Did I take away some of that power you white knuckle?

Grinding her core against him, she whispered breathlessly, "Some of my best orgasms have been when I've relinquished control to you."

And just like that, hearing this woman admit that she trusted him enough to control this aspect of their world flipped a switch in him.

Growling in her ear, nipping at her lobe, he laid her flat on her back, still connected by their sexes. He pulled her legs up into the crooks of his elbows and began to thrust into her. Lost in her, he watched her head thrash from side to side, lifting her hips to meet his, stroke for stroke. The sounds she made because of what he was doing to her had his sac tightening against his body and the telltale tingles in his lower back had his fingers tightening on her thighs.
He could tell from her breathing that she wanted to let go, her body demanded release.

"Ian, please..."

Leaning down, pushing her knees to her shoulders, he swiped the sweaty hair off her face. Her blue eyes sparkling like gems, he kissed her forehead, the tip of her nose, each cheek. "What, tell me what you need."

"Come, please...I...need to feel it."

"Damn, how can I refuse such a pretty pout?" He trailed his tongue from cheek to the shell of her ear. "Come for me, Faye. Let me hear you scream."

And scream she did. His name came tumbling out of her mouth over and over as she went spiraling over the precipice of bliss.

As soon as he felt her walls flutter and clamp down on his cock, he promptly followed her over. His thrusts became harsh and erratic, a deep rumbling growl erupting from his chest as the pleasure flowed through him and he bathed her walls with his hot seed.

Ian pressed his forehead into hers, peppering her face with soft, chaste kisses, savoring the beads of sweat from her temples and upper lip. Not wanting his weight to crush her, he rolled them over and she settled her head over his heart. Pressing a kiss to the top of her head, Ian stroked her hair."By the way, Faye, I love you too."

She nodded, mumbling, "Good." He felt the moment she let go of consciousness and her breathing leveled off and deepened.

Stroking her hair, he smiled into the darkness. Well, didn't his little Sugar turn him into a big old sappy pile of goo? Not that he'd admit that. No, he'd keep that little tidbit to himself.

His final thought, before sleep claimed him, as he hugged her warm, sated body against his was simple. MINE.

***

The sun shone through the French doors, the golden rays kissing her skin gently, as a lover might. She rolled over and stretched, feeling sore all over and a slow smile crept across her face; it was a delicious kind of sore.

Eyes fluttering open, she spotted her overnight bag laying on the settee; oh that settee. Grinning wider at the memory, she contemplated jumping in the shower. Then the aroma of coffee came drifting into the bedroom and all other thoughts fled her brain.

Faye groaned as she slid out of bed. Ian's shirt lay in a heap on the floor and she thought, what better negligee to wear than that? Slipping it over her head, she inhaled his musky scent, sighing and feeling more relaxed, lighter, than she had in a long time.

Padding to the stairs, she stopped and looked over the balcony. Damn, she loved this thing. Then she spied him out on the back deck drinking coffee. He was wearing nothing but shorts slung low on his hips, his hair pulled back into a ponytail. From the back, he was all muscle and sharp lines, powerful. His tattoo danced in the sun, the barbed wire looked as if it slithered like a snake.

And she thought to herself, MINE.

Faye continued down the stairs. He must have sensed she was near. As he turned his gaze was predatory, hungry. Though now his expression was one of joy, with a hint of amusement, as usual.

Meeting her in the kitchen, Ian wrapped an arm around her waist, and kissed her. "Hey, you sleep okay?"

"Yeah, I really did. First time in weeks, no nightmares."

She grabbed at his cup, but he pulled his away with a smirk. "Watch yourself now. What do you think this is, some kind of partnership or something?

She gave him one of his own smirks in return, tilting her head and setting her hands on her hips. "Yeah, partners in crime. Now coffee me, damn it." She tried again to reach for his cup and he swatted her hand away.

Then, turning to the cupboard, he dragged down a second mug and pointed with his head towards the garage. "Okay, sassy pants, you go see if I left my wallet in the Mustang and I'll get your damn coffee."

"Sure." She saluted, grabbed the keys off the counter, and turned on her heel to march towards the door, his laughter at her back.

Jogging down the front steps, she noticed he'd moved Leah's car into the long driveway. Barely able to contain her excitement over her new car she skipped, shit, how did he do this to her? She fucking skipped to the car, *her* car, and climbed in, breathing in the scent of leather.

Looking around the interior, she pawed under both seats trying to find his wallet. Not seeing it laying out in the open, she leaned over the passenger's seat to check the glove compartment. No wallet, but there was an envelope. With her name on it. She rested her weight on the seat as she furrowed her brow at the envelope, then sat up slowly, staring at it. What was this? Something clunked her on the back of the head as she straightened up. Looking around, she saw a delicate silver chain hanging from the rearview mirror, and on it, the most beautiful ring she'd ever seen. Cupping the thing in her hand, she stilled its momentum so she could get a better look at it. Platinum, with intricate scrollwork. Upon closer inspection, she could see it was a rose. Diamonds made up the petals bordering the side of the ring, and at the center, a pink diamond twinkled up at her.

Blinking in confusion, she looked around the car again, back at the piece of jewelry, then out the windshield. He was leaning over the side of the deck, coffee cup clutched in both hands, watching her. Realizing that her other hand still clutched the envelope, she reluctantly released the ring, setting it to swing again, the sun glinting off the diamond.

Opening the envelope, she slipped the paper out and unfolded it, eyes glued to Ian's curious expression. He nodded towards her, hinting she should maybe look at the paper in her hand. She recognized his writing.

A single word was scrawled in the middle of the sheet. Faye's heart was beating wildly as she wiped the tears from her face. Sitting in the car that he'd replaced for her, in the sun shining at her favorite place on earth, she smiled at him and nodded.

Letting the paper flutter to the floor, she slipped the chain off the mirror, pushed out of the car, and, without shutting the door, ran to him. Clutching the ring in her palm, she threw herself into his arms.

He squeezed her tight and whispered the word he'd written, "Always."

EPILOGUE

6 months later...

The air was brisk and chilly. Glancing around at the decorations, she hurried along. Faye loved this time of year; Halloween was one of her favorite holidays.

Parking the truck in the shadows, she glanced at the time before she shut it off. Late again, he was going to bust her chops, and redden her ass. Again. She hadn't meant to be late for dinner, but she'd stopped at their apartment to change out of her work clothes.

Grinning, she hopped out, giving his surprise a last once over. He was going to shit. Damn, her other vice was creeping out too.

Since her promotion she'd been trying to curb her punctuality issues, along with her potty mouth. She wanted to set a better example and, damn, that shit was hard. One good thing that came from her colorful language, her swear jar was usually always full to brimming. Those funds helped pay for the repairs for the ungodly mess of Ian's current surprise. She'd put all that money to good use, once Dilly was able to locate it. He must have searched every junkyard in the city. She asked him once why he hadn't asked for Carpenter's help and Dilly gave her a million dollar smile. "Wanna make sure the thing is legal, babe." When he asked her to meet him here, she laughed said sure. It was their five month wedding anniversary, and this is where it all began. Where, in one glance, he managed to tilt her world on its axis, eventually proving to her that he was her home, always.

She patted the truck one last time and turned to leave the alley, pausing again, debating if she should use this entrance. Grinning at the memories she had of this particular alley, she decided to go around front; she would try to be classy tonight. Then she snorted, thinking of her attire, the reason she went home to begin with. She'd dug out those jeans, that red bustier, and those red sky high fuck me shoes. And decided to go sans panties. She figured he might want to christen the hood of the truck like they did her Mustang.

Smiling to herself as her heels clicked on the pavement, she stopped and looked up at Stammers' flashing sign. If she'd only realized that fateful night how her entire life would change. That all the pain and drama would be worth it in the end, and she'd end up happier than she'd ever been in her life, maybe she wouldn't have fought against him so hard.

Pulling open the door, she hustled inside. The place was unusually dark. Blinking furiously, she tried to adjust to the lights as they flashed super bright.

"SURPRISE!"

She about pissed her pants, automatically reaching for her weapon. That she'd left at home, great cop she was. Her eyes adjusted rapidly, and her body relaxed as she spotted the sign over the bar:

CONGRATULATIONS CAPTAIN McMANUS!

Gaping, she searched the crowd for him. There, in the corner where she'd first spotted him all those months ago, arms folded across his chest and leaning against the wall, he was smiling at her. No cigarette this time though, she'd hounded him until he quit.

Making her way through the crowd, smiling and thanking everyone, giving hugs to some and wondering who the hell that person was and why were they here, she made her way to him. Most of the faces she knew well, some she hadn't seen since their small wedding on the beach Memorial Day weekend. Ian handled all the details. On the beach, in front of their home, in front of only a handful of friends and family, they pledged to be together. It was perfect.

She finally made her way to him and he swallowed her up into a hug, whispering, “Be nice. Leah insisted on this. And, since we’re all so damn proud of the youngest captain in department history, I let her run with it.”

Faye hugged him tight, overwhelmed but grateful, nonetheless. He stroked her back, giving her time to regroup and focus. He knew her so well, knew exactly what she needed. She sighed and relaxed against him.

One last squeeze and he pulled away, searching her eyes to be sure she was ready. “Come on, let’s get you a drink. Then, you can mingle, Captain.” Winking, he leaned close once again. “Oh, and by the way, nice outfit, Sugar. Don’t think I don’t remember. Perhaps a repeat performance is in order?” Wiggling his eyebrows, he palmed her ass.

She knew he was trying to get a rise out of her. “Oh you can bet on it, mister. I have my own surprise for you. Meet me in the alley. Let’s say one hour?”

Faye attempted to walk past him, wiggling her ass, but he grabbed her back for a long, hard kiss. “You’d better go mingle or I’ll throw you over my shoulder right fucking now.”

Damn him, she blushed. Always with the blushing with him. Before she could say another word, JoJo yelled over to them, holding up their drinks.

Sipping on her margarita, she made her way around the room. There were so many people cramped in the tiny neighborhood bar. Ian’s co-workers were there; she spotted them in the front, razzing each other.

Her thoughts turned to the events of the past few months. The trial was swift and brutal, brutal for Maliano and his cronies. The department was so impressed with her documentation and the airtight case she built, they'd practically begged her to take the promotion. She'd been terrified to accept and damn near said no, but with Ian's prodding and support, she accepted.

She and Ian were dividing their time between the beach house and their new apartment in the city. They'd each walked away from their dumps and moved into a two bedroom loft with a great view of the city. It wasn't the beach, but it was close to work and it was theirs, together. They were slowly decorating it with an easy combination of both their tastes, sometimes with a bit of loud compromising, but, they were making it work. He definitely was much more domestic than she was; which always made her grin and shake her head.

Finally, after much cajoling, she was able to get him to go back to work. But, he refused to go undercover now, if ever again. Reverend agreed, putting him to work as an instructor, and, so far, the recruits hated him. Reverend was never happier.

Leah approached her. "Hey, Captain Pip."

"Do you want to ruin the night by making me shoot your ass?"

Leah threw her head back and roared in laughter. "No, sir!"

Faye playfully pushed her. "JoJo would kill me if we got blood all over the place." Hugging her friend, she thanked her yet again.

Faye spotted Sonny and his wife, Anna. "Why hello, Detective." Sonny smiled wide. "I still can't believe it, thanks Capt..."

She held up her hand to stop him. "Seriously, why do you people insist on testing my trigger finger. Faye Ka-er-McManus." She laughed at her own gaff, not quite used to the new surname.

"Yeah, well, you earned it, Cap," Sonny smirked.

"I'm damn proud to have you on my team. We've got a shit ton of rebuilding to do, especially the department's reputation. Please, do me a favor and keep working with Zi. I got the okay to let him take the test soon." Turning to Anna, she smiled. "How is that gorgeous son of yours?" With the mention of their son, Anna lit up. Whipping out her phone, she began flipping through some recent pictures. "He's so adorable."

Anna nudged Faye. "When can we expect to see you flashing pictures?"

Faye nearly choked on her drink. Composing herself with effort, she smiled a genuine, big ass grin. "Let's just say I'm not getting anywhere near the water you've been drinking. At least, not yet."

She was so pleased to see everyone; especially her parents and brothers. They were huddled in the corner with Zi and his parents. Her parents were thrilled to have Christian home on leave, though he looked haunted. She and Sam had tried to corner him and talk to him, but he was his usual cagey self. It was enough that the three of them were together again. By the smell of things, she bet Momma supplied the food for this shindig. It meant the world to her that they came. Her family had been skeptical when she announced she was getting married, the first question from her oldest brother was if she was pregnant. With an effective fuck off and some playful banter, he backed off. Her father was the most skeptical but, she hadn't let him steamroll her.

And Ian, well, her family fell in love with him on sight. Especially after he'd stood up to her father when he tried to dictate when and where the wedding would take place. Ian had more fun planning the wedding with her mother than she had at the gun range with her father. How funny things played out, but, again, she couldn't be happier.

She looked up at the clock and realized she'd missed her one hour deadline. Pushing through the crowd, she headed out the back exit. Her head whipped around, searching. Not seeing him, she was about to turn around and head back in when he stepped out of the shadows. By the look on his face he'd seen the newly restored and face-lifted Broom Hilda, and he was in shock.

He walked to her with such a look of determination, she sighed audibly. Digging the keys out of her front pocket, she tossed them to him. In a flash he grabbed them, and for some silly reason, that action reminded her of a frog's tongue zipping out to grab a buzzing fly. He opened his palm and growled, "Fuck me, Sugar. You never stop surprising the hell out of me." He rolled the keychain in his hand and cocked an eyebrow at her.

She shrugged at his expression. She'd had an exact copy of her key chain made for him; she knew he'd get a kick out of it. Bridging the distance between them, she grabbed his hand and pulled him to the truck.

He let go of her and walked the perimeter, scrubbing a hand down his face, then through his long hair. "How in the hell did you find her?"

"Let's just say I drove Dilly to the edges of sanity until he located her. He and Leah barely had a moment's peace until he found ol' Hilda here." She patted the hood and shrugged again. "Then I coerced Tiny to put her in traction and get her some physical therapy. I hear that's some good shit, though personally I wouldn't know."

Tiny was a mechanic she'd busted a few years ago for running a chop shop. Since he too was a neighborhood kid, she was able to get him to roll over on his big boss and consequently, he owed her big time.

Ian threw his head back, laughing, shaking his head. "No wonder Dilly was in a piss poor mood. I had to deal with his whining, you know that? Fuck! And poor Tiny."

Faye laughed as she watched Ian hop in the truck and crank the engine, he was like a kid with a brand new toy. "Oh man, she sounds fucking sweet."

Sauntering over to the front of the truck, hands on the hood, Faye bent over so he had a clear view right down her top. Quickly, Ian cut the engine and exited the truck, pointing at her. "Don't. Fucking. Move." Then, coming up behind her, grinding his growing erection into her ass, he roughly tugged her hair back, hyperextending her neck. "You're playing with fire, Sugar," he growled in her ear.

Faye pressed back against him, grinding her ass against the bulge that she wanted inside her, now. "Yeah, yeah, like I haven't heard that before. Haven't you realized yet, I like getting burned?"

He whipped her around, placing his hand on her neck. "You want to get burned? I just got some new candles I'm sure will be to your liking, Captain McManus. We'll also be utilizing your handcuffs later, to help with the candle wax demonstration. However, unless we want to miss the rest of your party, we'd better head back inside.

Tapping her chin, she tried to be nonchalant, but her body quivered, instantly wet at the prospects of 'later.' Clearing her throat she played at being cool. "Promises, promises. But you're right, Leah will kill me. Never mind the looks on my family's faces."

She grimaced and Ian laughed. “Hell, who’re you kidding? Leah’d be right out here with Dilly, pushing us out of the way. Oh god, yeah, let’s not get your dad riled up, though.”

“Shit, you’re right. I can’t believe my parents are still going at it.” Faye groaned and rolled her eyes. “Okay, enough of the parent sex visual. I may never have sex again. Let’s go, you can show me your appreciation later.” Blinking up at him, she waited for him to release her. When he didn’t, she cocked her eyebrow.

He grew serious. “I’m trying to find the words for you. Trying to figure out how to convey just how much this,” he waved his arm over Broom Hilda, “means to me. How much you mean to me. I love you so god damn much, Faye. Sometimes, I still can’t believe you’re real.”

She wrapped her arms around his neck and used them to boost herself up, wrapping her legs around his waist. Her hands framed his face as he held onto her ass, securing her to his body. By the dim streetlight in front of his beloved truck, in the very alley that started the journey for them, the sparks still burned bright. “You just did. I love you too, Ian.” Then, leaning in and kissing him, she showed him, reminded him they were each other’s home, ports in every storm, anchored together, always.

He began to walk to the back door, back to their friends and family. Pulling away, she slid down his body, turning to head back inside.

SMACK!

Griff growled as he squeezed a handful of her ass cheek tightly in his hand. “Your ass is mine.”

She jumped a bit, rubbing her ass and grinning over her shoulder at him, dark lust reflected in her eyes. Smiling, she winked. “Always.”

***

Leaning against the door of a car he'd boosted, Carl's eyes scanned the outside of Stammers with narrowed eyes. He took one last drag of his smoke, flicked it at a passing car, and slid into the driver's seat. As he adjusted the mirror, he couldn't help the self satisfied smile that played across his face. "Can't wait to see the look on that bitch's face when she hears about this. Game on." Without putting the blinker on Carl pulled into traffic, cutting off another driver, disappearing into the late fall night.

THE END, BITCHES

A Taste of *Shadow Games*, the next chapter in *Partners in Crime*

April 29th

Carl circled his prey. She wasn't much more than a quivering, whimpering heap slumped over in the chair, but at one point she'd been his prey. He snatched a handful of her hair, yanking her head back. Both of her eyes were swollen shut, her face was purple and equally swollen, neither of those details stopped Carl from running his tongue from her chin to forehead, "Sweet to the bitter end."

The prey whimpered some nonsense that Carl didn't care to hear and he drew his hand back cracking her across the face yet again. When he drew his hand back a second time, his attention was diverted by the swirling blue and red lights of the impending arrival of a squad of angry and trigger happy law enforcement.

"Too bad our time's been cut short, little dove. You can really take a hit. Speaking of cutting..." He'd reached behind his back and withdrew a long bladed knife and without much more preamble, sheathed the blade into her abdomen. With a whispered growl, "Hope you live long enough to tell the bitch it was me. If not, I'm sure she'll get the message." Carl dropped the knife and jogged out of the room, unhurried.

BANG!

BANG!

BANG!

CRASH!

The heavy metallic door crashed inward landing on the floor with a reverberating CLANG! Half dozen men came storming in each yelling things like: Freeze! Police! BCI!

Guns pointed up, down, every which way and more yelling of: CLEAR! CLEAR! CLEAR!

Ian ran up to the body slumped over in the chair, covered in blood and bruises, "Shit! Shit! Get the EMTs in here, NOW!"

Quickly, he undid her bindings and lowered her to the floor. Her long hair was caked with so much blood the color was mottled. She couldn't open her eyes, but her lips were moving, trying to say something.

Ian leaned down, placing his ear close to her mouth, but he couldn't make out what she was trying to say, "Okay, baby girl, okay. Just, lay still. You'll be okay. We've got the ambulance with us." His hand moved over her body, landing on the abdominal wound inflicted by the knife. When he pulled his hand into the light he saw it was covered in black blood. "Jesus Christ! Oh Jesus! Okay! GOD DAMN IT! GET THOSE EMTS HERE NOW!"

The woman's body went rigid in a series of death spasms and then she went still. Her body went limp in Ian's arms and all he could do was sit and rock her. He pulled her body close and whispered apologies and promises to fix the fucker who'd done this to her.

A commotion at the door had Ian looking up; Brick was trying to hold someone back, a female someone. Shit, Ian thought. He gave the woman's still warm forehead a kiss and laid her down, gently. He hopped up and ran to the door grabbing hold of his wife's arms, "Faye, what are you doing here?"

Faye blinked up at him, shaking her head, "Faye. You said Faye, not Sugar. You call me Sugar all the time. Ian you only call me Faye when it's bad. Ian…"

"You don't want to go in there. Let's go and let the medics take care of her. I'll explain…"

"Fuck you!" Faye stepped back and then ran around him and skidded on her knees to the fallen woman. "Oh, nonononono." She picked up the woman's hand, putting it on her face, kissing the palm, moving so she could lift her head into her own lap, "Listen, you're going to be all right. You have to be." She whispered words and prayers as tears spilled down her cheeks landing on the woman's forehead.

Ian came up behind Faye, placing a gentle hand on her shoulder, "Faye, Sugar, we have to let them help her now. They're going to get her out of this place."

Faye looked up at him and nodded. She took his proffered hand and stood slowly, wrapping herself around the strong, protective arms of her husband, "She was my friend, Ian. She's dead. She's dead."

ACKNOWLEDGEMENTS

From Downey:

Thank you to every single author whose books I devoured, recommended, and sold (in my former career at Borders). But especially to Robyn Carr, Jill Shalvis and Kristan Higgins, to me these ladies are the trifecta of greatness in contemporary romance. And Kristan, thanks for inadvertently helping with my dedication.

A special thanks to Laura Moore for your friendship and kindness. Sharon Sala for telling me you're never too old to change careers. Mariah Stewart & Nancy Martin for pushing me to blog, which started this journey. Pamela Clare for your unending support, friendship and kindness. Teri Anne Browning you rock my socks off. Kristine Cayne your input and kindness are so appreciated. Maggie Barbieri your humor, friendship and support mean the world to me. Hayden Braeburn your example of juggling it all inspires me, xxoo. And to Cherry Adair for opening my eyes as well as a door and kicking my ass through it. I am truly lucky, these talented ladies all have touched me in so many ways.

Thanks also to…old friends who took me to book signings and fueled my love of books. The Elites…for your friendship support and all out awesomeness, love you ladies! And to Shane, for allowing me to write during nap time. To all those who encouraged me to do this…Sonia, Kamila, Terri, Lee, Kat and all the other RP ladies…xxoo. To Cindy, youtube. To my former customers turned friends…Regina, Diane, Lynne and Suzanne…BIG LOVE. To my incredibly talented writing partner, Alison Greene…YOU ROCK.

AND to our publisher…thanks for this incredible opportunity. Also a shout out to all of our FB peeps…your support has been very much appreciated. To the Downey clan and my Uncle Pat & Aunt Sue…family is everything.

Last but certainly not least…

Tyler, Allison, Nicholas, Christopher and Ryan, you are my heart. Each one of you amazes me every day. I'm blessed and honored to be your mom, love you to the moon and back. And finally to my other half…the best person I know. I love you more than I can possibly ever convey. Thank you for getting me, and loving me for me. Always & Forever John!

From Greene:

Goodness, my list will not be as long or as well known as Mrs. Downey's. Like her, thank you to all the authors out there, your words and worlds kept me company and sane during some pretty interesting times in my life. And to those authors I have yet to experience, it's all about anticipation… oooh, it's so good.

To The Pack: Lois, Nika, Helen, Trill…you girls are the ones who opened this can of worms. Be afraid…be very afraid. Oh…MOIST!

To Prin and Tal: Thank you for being so damn demonstrative and pushy. You are really amazing and I am honored to call you friends. (FYI: If you're reading this, check out the twins…Princess so and Talon ps, you won't be disappointed.)

To my most awesome writing partner, Maureen Downey. You frackin' rock. Without you, I would be lost in the world of romance language without an interpreter. Can't wait to see where our next adventure leads us. Twak Lathers.

To our publisher, Heather, I feel like I owe you a lap dance – not from me, god no! But from some hot dude who can shake it until he makes it. HA! Thanks for taking a chance on a couple of unknowns and for putting up with some crank yankin'. You're pretty awesome.

For all the FB peeps out there, some are on Maureen's list…Kamila and Gabrielle. Chrissy Szarek, another author you should check out, by the way. I'm sure there's many more that I have forgotten to mention. Please don't take umbrage, I'm blonde, what can I say?

To my kids, Cassie and Dallas. The two of you have kept my life interesting and have made for some great story telling. To steal a phrase from Maureen, love you to the moon and back.

And finally, To my husband, thank you for putting up with long phone calls, endless hours of editing, and random conversations about writing that make your eyes glaze over and your mind wander to ice fishing, hunting, and 4-wheeling. You're pretty damn amazing.

About the Authors

WE...yes you read right, we are two separate individuals who met in a writing group on Facebook. In this group we dabbled in writing and hit it off, each liking the other's strengths and complimenting the other's weaknesses. When the opportunity was presented to Downey to submit to a publisher, she approached Greene to join her in the journey. Both with hectic lives, they took turns writing, swapping ideas and chapters, thus creating their first book, Partners in Crime. Here is a little something about the Dynamic Duo.

Downey: Otherwise known as Maureen, lives in Drexel Hill, Pennsylvania. She is your typical suburban soccer mom, well okay, there is nothing typical about her AND her kids play EVERYTHING but soccer. Downey, as she is known in this duo, has 5 kids ranging from 13 to 19. And, to answer the question swirling in your minds, YES, she is crazy. She has been married for over 21 years to her best friend and love of her life. She LOVES to read, her appetite is voracious for all things books. Her job at a local bookstore was by far one of the best experiences and fed her addiction to the written word. Going to book signings and having them at the store were her rock star moments; she is a total fangirl for authors. When that job disappeared she felt bereft, and, after much floundering, she stumbled upon the underbelly of FB and fell in love with writing.

Creating stories and weaving tall tales helped ease the indecision that plagued her. The feedback and support for her writing blew her away and prompted her to open Word and create. Loving how Greene weaved a story, Downey decided they should become the Dynamic Duo. With the support of her family, she has embarked on a totally unexpected new path. When she is not carting kids all over, she is managing her kingdom; consisting of the books she reads, blogs she follows and writes (Bitch Can Write A Book), and submerging herself in her make believe worlds of sexy trouble. Some days she feels invincible, other days...well they should hide. Never in a million years did she ever think THIS was a possibility; as they say when one door closes another opens. In her case, truer words were never spoken.

Greene: Otherwise known as Alison to family and friends, Honey Bunny to her husband since the dawn of time – or so it seems, mom to her 2 children, and momma to her one grandson, lives in a small area of Western New York known primarily as the birthplace of Gabby Hayes. Alison has always loved reading, a voracious reader even from a young age when all she had was her princess portable record player, and the Little Golden Books read along books and records (45's...anybody out there old enough to remember what a 45 is?).

Alison was always seen with a book in her hands, not always age appropriate-thank you, Jackie Collins-but always entertaining. While writing was always a hobby, she's always harbored a secret dream to one day be published. How to do that when she's as twitchy as a long-tailed cat in a room full of rocking chairs? Find herself a writing partner. Enter Maureen Downey and history was made. The earth shook, thunder struck, countries crumbled, and Downey Greene was born.